CAROLINA CRIMES

CAROLINA CRIMES

NINETEEN TALES OF LUST, LOVE, AND LONGING

KAREN PULLEN, EDITOR

Introduction by Margaret Maron

WILDSIDE PRESS

CONTENTS

FOREWORD

Write a crime story about sex.

When the Triangle chapter of Sisters in Crime decided to create our first short story anthology, that was the attention-grabbing guidance we gave to prospective authors—Sisters in Crime members who live in the Carolinas. Interpretation of the theme was left up to the author, though we supplied examples:

> ...reproduction; lust and desire; genetic engineering; online dating; animal breeding; infertility; STDs; prostitution; obsession; gender dysmorphia; erectile dysfunction; romance; endocrine disorders; virginity; marriage and weddings; pornography; attracting the opposite sex (clothes, shoes, appearance); jealousy; chromosomes; plastic surgery; secondary sex characteristics; gynecology.

And the Carolinas' Sisters—and a few Brothers—came through, submitting wonderful, original, never-before-published stories around this most adult of themes. A blind judging selected the finalists, and we were so pleased to learn that for almost half the authors, it would be their first published stories.

Carolina Crimes was a Triangle SinC group project. I'm grateful to Britni Patterson, who efficiently coordinated submissions; Tamara Ward for compiling scores and comments; Ruth Moose for editorial guidance; Judith Stanton for copy-editing; Sheila Boneham and Toni Goodyear for proofing; Toni for querying publishers. The anthology committee—Sheila, Toni, and Sarah Shaber—provided valuable oversight. Margaret Maron, a past president of SinC, generously volunteered to write an introduction. *Carolina Crimes* could not have been produced without their significant contributions of time and expertise.

The greatest thanks are due to the authors for writing their stories. They've invited you, the reader, into their characters' lives at a moment when passion overrules morality, common sense, and the law. Who among us hasn't—in our imaginations—stepped close to that line? These nineteen tales of lust, love, and longing will give you chills, make you chuckle, and strike a resonant chord in your heart.

—K. P.

INTRODUCTION

Sisters in Crime was formally organized when Sandra Scoppettone invited a group of interested women to her Soho loft back in 1987. Approximately thirty women crime writers attended to vent about the inequalities we had experienced in trying to get a fair share of the advances, the reviews and the promotion routinely given to our male counterparts but stingily doled out to us. As the organization grew, we banded together to pool travel expenses, slept on the couches of Sisters who ran bookstores, and shared tips and promotional strategies. Today, we number around 3600 members in forty-eight chapters around the world. SinC in the Triangle is one of those forty-eight and this anthology showcases the emerging talents to be found in North and South Carolina.

In keeping with the theme of lust, love, and longing, these stories range from Marjorie Ann Mitchell's high-tech future of simulated sex play to Sarah Shaber's look back to sugar rationing during World War II. To illustrate the changing face of the state, Britni Patterson's story is set among Raleigh's Korean-American community, while Karen Pullen gives us a gently humorous take on some local "working girls."

The stories illustrate facets of sexuality often kept hidden and some even cross into taboo territory. The longing for love is universal. Equally universal are the evanescence of passion and the cruelty of lust. Love can liberate, love can suffocate, and sometimes love can even lead to murder.

Enjoy!

—Margaret Maron
January, 2014

THE BAD SON

by Britni Patterson

It had been a bad night. Not only had I blown my cover to the person I'd been tailing for a week, but then I lost her immediately afterwards.

I was having my usual breakfast of Mini-Wheats, trying to decide whether to quit the case or hope for the best, when the morning news reporter's deliberately regretful-yet-professional tones caught my ear. The top story of the morning was the brutal homicide of a Jane Doe who had been beaten to a pulp in front of the entrance to Umstead State Park off Harrison Avenue. The police were requesting help identifying her. I gave their sketch a look out of habit and dropped my cereal bowl. My target, Min-jun Kim, had been murdered.

Three hours later I was still sitting across from Homicide Detective Abram Shouft, a giant man of mixed Cherokee and German heritage with an impressive nicotine addiction and a lousy temper. His tiny office was dangerously full of files, empty to-go cups from Dunkin' Donuts, and two hundred and fifty pounds of nicely-distributed muscle crammed into a suit. Most men look good in a suit, but Shouft would have been better displayed wearing nothing but a loincloth and the blood of his enemies. His face is a little too savage in its lines to wear civilization well. The visitor's chair in his office was one object too many. I'm only 5'4", but my knees were starting to ache from pressing against the desk.

Shouft is never happy to see me in a professional capacity. In his opinion, good private detectives should join the police force, the bad ones should be shot, and neither kind should ever be involved in his cases. I'm one of the best, so he'd like to resent me on principle. But when I have to deal with the police, I go through Shouft, because at least he doesn't give a shit that I'm female, Korean-American, and have a worse temper than he does. There's also the fact that he'd be perfectly happy to see me in a personal capacity, if our professional ethics and instincts for self-preservation could be surgically removed.

"Transgender?" Shouft asked for the third time. "So what do you say, he or she?"

"She. I don't know what was still in her pants, but from six inches she passed."

"OK. One more time," he said.

I groaned. He ignored me. "So you were hired to follow the deceased, by a woman claiming to be the mother of the victim, because the victim had left home on bad terms and the mother wanted to be sure the vic was all right?"

"I verified her identity before I took the job."

Shouft shifted in his chair. "By her, you mean the mother, right?"

"Yeah. Mrs. Kim." Somewhere in her late fifties, built small and sturdy, with gray hair wound tightly in a bun. Small pudgy hands clenched tightly on her purse, trouble lines carved between her eyes and doll-size mouth pinched shut. Wearing black because her husband had died. Holding a check from the insurance company to prove she could pay me.

"And her son…daughter. Whatever. You followed her for a week, and then decided to approach her last night. Shitty surveillance tactic, Parks."

"I thought there was a chance for reconciliation."

"You stuck your nose where it didn't belong."

I didn't answer. It wasn't a question, and I half-agreed with him.

"According to this—" he tapped my statement with yellow fingertips "—last night, you approached Min-jun Kim at the club where she bartends. You didn't tell her who hired you. You started talking about mother issues. Kim got agitated, swapped your tab with another bartender, and left work early." He tapped the pages again. "That's the last anyone saw her until the park ranger found her body."

"Point of clarification, I didn't know she'd left until the new bartender came over thirty minutes later." I was being nitpicky, because I didn't enjoy Shouft rubbing my screw-up in my face.

"Shitty surveillance work." Shouft said again, savoring each word with all the righteous vindication of a Baptist watching a Catholic church burn down on bingo night.

"Blow it out your ass. I didn't have to come down here and give you a statement or my notes."

"You know, Parks, I can count on one hand how many times you've cooperated with this department. I don't like presents, even ones with big shiny bows."

"I'll remember that at Christmas. Can I go?"

"Tell me why you're feeling so charitable all of a sudden."

I thought about it. The real reason was I felt like if I hadn't slipped up, Minnie wouldn't be dead. I would have seen whoever attacked her. Maybe I could have helped. She'd seemed like a nice enough person, and she'd made one of the best margaritas I'd ever had. If my notes and pictures from the week I'd spent hunting Minnie down could help the police, they were welcome to them. But I couldn't blame Shouft for being suspicious that I had an ulterior motive. I'm not above seeing if I can get the police department to do my work for me, and he knows it.

"Call it good citizenship. Can I go?"

Shouft grunted and scratched his nose. He read my statement again. Finally he said, "We'll call if we have more questions."

I sighed and stood with extreme care. "Try not to make me regret my generous impulses." I managed to get out without knocking over the files stacked behind the door.

I spent the next few days working on other cases. I never sent Mrs. Kim a bill, figuring that the loss of her only child before the reconciliation she wanted was a high enough price. Especially since I'd lost sight of Minnie long enough for her to get killed.

A week after Min-jun's death, Shouft called. "Can you come down to the station?" Shouft never bothers with extra words like "Hi" or "How are you?"

"You know, these amazing inventions called telephones allow for conversations without costing me four dollars in city parking fees and thirty minutes of my time."

"Just get your ass down here, Parks." He hung up.

When I got to the station, I was directed down to the hall outside the viewing rooms. I found Shouft coming out of one.

"Come look at this guy. Tell me if you've ever seen him," he said tersely.

I looked through the one-way glass into the room where a scrawny young man slumped, tracing a shaky fingernail on the metal table. He looked like Shaggy from the Scooby Doo cartoons, if Shaggy had been Korean and wearing a Grateful Dead t-shirt. He had a mop-like hair-cut and a scraggly beard. His clothes were wrinkled, and his eyes had crow's-feet in the corners—a tell-tale sign of the heavy weed smoker in someone under thirty.

"Familiar maybe, but I'm not sure where. I might have seen him at a bar or somewhere in passing. You understand I don't know every Korean in town, right?"

Shouft pulled a small notebook out of his pocket and flipped it open. "Says his name is Jun-seo Lee. He signed in as John Lee."

"That's nicely Americanized. Still not ringing a bell."

Shouft made a growly noise in his throat. "He says he killed Min-jun. Says he was in love with her."

I gave Jun-seo a long look, before saying, "I didn't see anyone stalking Min-jun but me. And Min-jun's boyfriend is a white boy. Gerald something."

"We know. The best part is that Lee's got an alibi for the time of the murder and doesn't even know it."

"So he's crazy. I'm not a psychologist."

"Not crazy enough. He says he shot the vic, before beating her to a pulp with a tree branch."

"Again, so?"

"So we never advertised the vic was shot. That was our little secret. You saw the news. Would you have known cause of death was gunshot?"

I frowned. "No." My first thought had been that Minnie's parents had been abusing the love-stick. Traditional Korean culture is heavy on corrective beatings to properly raise children. I was fourteen before I discovered other kids didn't get welts for B's in Pre-Algebra.

"He even got the bullet caliber and proximate location of the bullet wound right. And the tree branch is bang on too."

"The alibi is that good?"

"He was dead in the back of an ambulance. Heroin newbie overdose. The medics got him back, but docs kept him on ice in a medical coma for twenty-four hours. Standard procedure. He checked out seven hours after Kim was killed. No way he did it."

"So he knows who did and talked to them?"

"Wow, Parks. Come up with that theory all by yourself?"

"Don't be a dick. You want to know if I'd ever seen anyone with this guy."

"That's right. And think fast. Our boy in there called the news before he turned himself in. We've got a roomful of reporters upstairs demanding to know if he's been arrested while they're writing the story on their phones."

"Have you told him he has an alibi?"

Shouft nodded. "That's the hinky part. He insists we're mistaken, he killed Minnie. It's the only time he got mad, because we called him a liar."

"But you're keeping him on ice so he doesn't end up on the news blabbing details about the murder, or dead in a ditch from a 'remorseful suicide.'" I made air-quotes with my fingers.

Shouft made that growly noise again.

"No lawyer?" I asked.

"One showed up, but he refused to see her."

"Determined to be guilty, huh?"

"Yep. I'll walk you back upstairs." Shouft already had a cigarette between his lips, and his lighter in one hand. The new no-smoking-in-official-buildings policy was killing him.

I made Shouft validate my parking before letting him go light up. I sat in my car for a few minutes. It wasn't my business anymore, but I found myself heading out to the cheap student housing near NC State where Min-jun and her boyfriend Gerald Beaumont lived.

Gerald had been lucky so far. No news vans clogged the parking lot of the apartment complex. I sat on the front stoop for two hours until I saw Gerald trudging up the street from the bus stop. He had curly brown hair over a face and frame built out of angles. He wasn't handsome, but his face could be interesting with its lantern jaw and upturned nose. Every day I'd been watching, Minnie had met him at the bus stop and walked back to the apartment with him. He walked like he'd forgotten how to walk home alone so I went to meet him halfway up the driveway.

"Hey, Gerald," I said. He stopped and stared at me through swollen, red eyes, as if unable to summon enough energy to care about a stranger approaching him.

"Hi…uh… Do I know you?" he asked.

"We haven't met, if that's what you mean. I knew Minnie. I'm so sorry for your loss." He flinched and started walking again. I fell into step next to him.

"She didn't come home, but I thought maybe she had to close," he muttered. "I fell asleep. I woke up freaking out because she wasn't home. You know how I knew she wasn't home? First thing she does when she comes home after working, is she sets up the coffeemaker. She says I can't make coffee—Said. Said it was like mud, so she would set it up, and I always woke up to the smell of coffee. There wasn't any coffee smell when I woke up."

"I understand," I said. "My mother died when I was eighteen. She'd had a massive heart attack in the middle of the night. She always watched the seven a.m. news, so silence in the morning woke me up." It was an old memory and didn't hurt too much anymore, but I will never forget that lead-weight panic and disorientation while my subconscious screamed at me to wake up because something was terribly wrong.

Gerald shook his head. "I don't understand how anyone could hurt Minnie. She was nice to everyone. Said you couldn't judge people because you didn't know how much crap they were trying to rise above. She was seriously Confucian."

"It's a Korean thing." I said. "I suppose you knew—"

"I didn't care," he said flatly. "Minnie was an amazing human being, no matter what…what plumbing she started with. We were…you ever just feel better with someone? You know they're the person who makes you right. That's what Minnie was." He stopped at his door, key in hand.

"Even now, you know, I think I'm going to walk in, and she's going to yell, 'Got you, fucker!' and…and laugh." He choked on the last words, his face contorting with the struggle to hold back the tears.

I waited until he regained control before saying, "I have a question, if you don't mind. About a guy named Jun-seo Lee? I was wondering if he and Minnie knew each other."

Gerald frowned. "Who?"

"He might have introduced himself as John or Johnny Lee. Scrawny Korean dude, shaggy hair, bad weed habit."

Gerald sat down on the step. I knew he was only talking with me to delay going into a more-than-empty apartment. "Oh, him. He's a friend of Minnie's from way back. More like an adopted idiot brother, really. He comes over for food or money, or just to sleep, and she lets him, sometimes spots him a twenty if tips are good. His dad has some kind of terminal cancer. Johnny takes care of him so he doesn't have a job or anything. He shows up when his dad gets checked into Wake Med for treatments. Most of the time he just sleeps until the hospital calls for pick-up. Minnie kept trying to get him involved in something besides being a nurse, and he kept saying he couldn't leave his dad. Guy had no life."

"Do you know why he might confess to killing her?"

"Why he…what?! No. I…I don't know why he would do that." Gerald looked genuinely confused. "The guy was baked most of the time. Maybe he finally blew a fuse, but he couldn't have hurt Minnie. Minnie would have kicked his ass. You know, that's the weirdest thing about… what happened."

"What?"

"The way she was…hurt. Like hand-to-hand, up close? Minnie was second-degree black in Tae-Kwon Do. By international ranking, not some strip mall dojo. And she was ranked expert in some weird kick-boxing style on top of that. She won tons of competitions growing up. Her dad was Special Forces and taught her like, eighty ways to kill people with her bare hands. I never worried about her getting hurt. Never."

I paused. "So if you had to make a guess as to what happened…"

"I'd figure you'd have to shoot her first, or she'd feed you your own arm. But then why bother with the beating? It's just…it was so unnecessary." He rubbed his forehead with his thumb and index finger. "I can't imagine anyone hating her so much to…to do that. Everyone liked her."

I frowned. I hadn't seen any signs of Minnie's martial arts training while I was watching her. It wouldn't have been something a stranger would expect. "Thanks for talking to me about her. Have you had dinner yet? I've got a car and I'll pay. It's the least I can do."

Gerald stared at me blankly, as if the concept of getting food seemed as incomprehensible as string theory. "I… No, thanks. I don't want to go anywhere."

I talked him into letting me order him a pizza, and I left.

On the way home, I couldn't stop thinking about Jun-seo. It didn't make sense that he'd suddenly jumped from marijuana to heroin and decided to confess to a murder he couldn't have committed. Either would leave his father without a caregiver. On a hunch, I started calling funeral homes until I found what I was looking for.

"Yes, I'm afraid the funeral was yesterday. The wake was held early and the service was expedited. The son had an unbreakable commitment, but insisted on standing as chief mourner."

"Do you mind if I ask if all the services are…taken care of? I know the family wasn't well off, and I'd like to contribute, anonymously of course, if they need help."

"Paid in full, but I believe the family asked for donations to a certain charity in lieu of flowers. I don't have the details in front of me, but they're on our website, under the announcements section. I'm sorry I can't be more helpful at the moment."

"No problem, I'll check there. Thanks for your help." I hung up and leaned back in my chair, propping my feet up on the half-open bottom drawer of my desk.

Jun-seo's father had died the day before Minnie's murder, probably shortly before Jun-seo had overdosed. Before he'd confessed to killing Minnie, he'd made arrangements for his father's funeral and burial, and stood as *sangju,* or chief mourner. Paid in full. Too quickly for a life insurance check. And Jun-seo didn't have a job. So they were living off what, disability? Social Security? If Minnie was spotting him tips, they didn't have family money. So where did the money for the funeral come from?

That answer came to me quickly. I called Shouft and got his voicemail.

"Hey. Jun-seo paid for his father's funeral yesterday morning, in full. Find out who paid him to confess, and you'll find your murderer."

I sat at my desk for a while, thinking. Then I got my car keys. I couldn't shake the thought that Minnie's murder was caused by love, not hate. If I was right, then her death was my fault.

I knocked at the door that was still hung with a black wreath and the traditional funeral notice for Ms. Kim's husband. A few minutes later,

Mrs. Kim opened it. She looked even smaller and older than before, her hair still up in its tight bun, dressed in a housecoat and slippers.

"Mrs. Kim? I came to talk to you. About Min-jun, and Jun-seo Lee."

"Jun-seo? He is a good boy. A good son. My son is dead. What can be said?"

"You wanted me to find Min-jun so he could stand as the *sangju* for your husband, didn't you?" Korean culture dictates that the eldest male son is responsible for officiating at the death of a parent, in the role of the *sangju*. The *sangju* takes the blame for allowing their parent to die, so the spirit will not wander lost and angry. To have a funeral with no *sangju* is unthinkable.

"So? What does it matter now, why I wanted you to find my son?" she asked, turning to go back in the house.

"Min-jun refused, didn't she, when you met her after work that night. From my reports, you knew where to wait. You asked her to come home, so your husband could be properly buried."

Mrs. Kim's mouth worked. "I knew they fought, but they were so close before…before the trouble. I never thought Min-jun would refuse to bury his father. It is wrong to hate your father so much. I did not raise him that way."

"Your husband was ex-Special Forces. I'm sure he had several weapons around the house. Did you take one to protect yourself, so late at night? And when Min-jun refused and was going to leave, did you pull the gun on her? Tell her that she needed to listen? Needed to come home and do her duty?"

"Stop saying *she*. I had a son! That's what Min-jun said. Said he could not stand as *sangju*, even if he wanted to, because he was no longer a man. My husband and I have no brothers, no other male relatives. It was Min-jun's duty to bury us properly." Mrs. Kim's voice was sharp and painful, the authoritarian tone far too reminiscent of my own mother's.

"Is that why you beat him after you shot him? To correct his behavior?" I could feel the old anger and resentment flaring up. Even after all these years, I still wasn't sure whether I'd been raised strictly or abused. I'd never been hit without knowing exactly why I was being punished. Even so, I'd been hit well past the American definition of abuse.

"No! If I must bury my son, I did not wish him to be seen as…with breasts and puffed lips. I did not mean to shoot him. It was an accident."

Guns go bang, I thought. "You must tell the police the truth. They already know Jun-seo couldn't have done it. He was in an ambulance when Min-jun died."

Mrs. Kim wrinkled her face into an expression of disgust. "Shameful boy! He should have told me that before I gave him the money."

"He wanted to bury his father. He had no money to do so. He came to ask you for a loan, based on his childhood friendship with Min-jun. Instead, you gave him a job."

She was shaking her head. "Disgraceful. He should have told me. Perhaps he was not a good boy after all."

"Mrs. Kim…" I started, and then stopped. Because I was staring now at the little pistol she'd pulled out of the pocket of her housecoat.

"You are a bad girl. This is a house of mourning." She squinted as the barrel waved slightly in the air.

"The police will be here soon." I took a couple steps back. Rule of thumb: if there's a pistol pointing at you, run. They're inaccurate past fifteen feet in amateur hands. Problem was, I was only five feet away.

"They're already here." I heard a deep bass voice rumble behind me, around the cigarette I knew was in his mouth.

"Put the gun down, Mrs. Kim."

Mrs. Kim lowered her arm when she saw Detective Shouft, standing out of the line of fire pointing his gun straight at her head. *Obedient to male authority,* I couldn't help thinking, though with relief instead of my usual irritation.

An hour later, after Mrs. Kim had been read her rights and arrested, and the neighborhood was no longer lit by lights and sirens, Shouft came over to where I was leaning against the fence. He lit another cigarette from the end of the last one.

"Parks."

"Shouft."

"Feeling suicidal?"

"Not really."

"I would have called you, told you she paid for Johnny's father's funeral."

"No, you wouldn't. Active investigation."

He didn't answer, blowing out a thin stream of smoke.

"Shitty detective work, Parks. You guessed."

"Beat you here by ten minutes." He made the growly noise that reminded me of a disgruntled bear. We stood in silence for another few minutes before he spoke again.

"Dinner?" His tone of voice was far too casual. I could feel my pulse quickening with the prospect of a familiar bad decision, the kind you don't start regretting until you can't get your underwear down from the ceiling fan.

"Only if you're paying."

"Breakfast?"

"Only if you're cooking."

ABOUT THE AUTHOR

Britni Patterson has been a mystery fiction fan since 1986 when she first read *Nemesis* by Agatha Christie. A native Texan who landed in North Carolina through a series of poor decisions that somehow worked out for the best, she's happily married with a daughter, a son, and a permanent belief in serendipity. She loves to write about strong female protagonists with sharp senses of humor and subtle love interests.

THE GAME

by Marjorie Ann Mitchell

Sam Breske stared in confusion across his boss's large mahogany desk, hoping that today would be the day the old man finally grew a sense of humor, and what he'd just heard was a failed attempt at a joke.

Martin Harrison, owner of Harrison SimTech and creator of VIC—Virtual Image Clone—looked back at him dispassionately, not a twinge of amusement on his face. "In order to do what's necessary to stay on top, there's bound to be collateral damage," he said, leaning back in his black leather executive chair and tenting his fingers. Behind him, a window displayed the view from the top floor of the six-story building—swaying pine and sweet gum trees, a cloudless blue sky. Their office buildings in Research Triangle Park in North Carolina were understated, especially given RTP's boost in prestige since SimTech claimed it as its headquarters. It was here that Martin ruled—a Caesar guarding his empire.

"That collateral damage you're talking about is my team. The same people who helped you build this company." Sam rose from his seat, incredulous.

Martin sighed. "There's no room for sentiment in business, Sam. It's not financially feasible to continue your project."

"Just like that? VIC is the highest grossing gaming system in history. How's it possible that enhancements wouldn't make money?"

Martin leaned forward, pointing at Sam accusingly. "You know as well as I, we're fighting to stay ahead of the competition. Tough decisions have to be made."

"That's ridiculous," Sam said, his arm slicing the air in dismissal. "You're asking me to fire the best assets this company has. How do you expect SimTech to grow without software engineers?"

"That's the other thing I wanted to speak to you about. You've been an integral part of the company, Sam, creating the HMC when the gaming commission threatened to shut us down over some unfortunate incidents."

Even though everything Martin was saying was true, Sam could tell he was being disingenuous. "By unfortunate incidents, of course, you mean the deaths caused by VIC's realism. You know damn well I didn't create the HMC all by myself."

After two gamers had died, Sam had managed the project team that created a Health Monitoring Component (HMC) that could detect a gamer experiencing an unusually high amount of distress. When the HMC triggered, it shut down the video game and sent a signal to emergency services in the gamer's area. The HMC had saved the company, their careers, and several lives.

Irritated, Martin continued, "Yes, yes, but the point is, I know how invested you are in this company and in VIC. That's why I plan to keep you on in a position I created specifically for you. There's a group of green engineers, fresh out of college, arriving next week. You'll be the Lead Training Specialist in charge of getting them up to speed. Then, perhaps we can revisit whether your project can go forward."

Sam ran his hand through his thick black hair. Had he heard right? "You expect me to train my team's younger, cheaper replacements."

Martin's smile was a cold reflexive twitch. "I expect you to do what's right for the company. I'll leave it up to you how to inform your team, but make sure they're gone by the time the new batch arrives. That'll be all, Sam."

"Fuck you, Martin." Sam stormed out of Martin's office, ricocheting from disbelief to anger to panic. He hadn't noticed Bryce Harrison standing in the hallway and he barreled into her. "Oh, sorry, I didn't see you," he said, embarrassed. The boss's wife. How much had she heard?

"Hey, Sam, no problem. Your mind must've been a thousand miles away. What's going—?"

Sam didn't wait for her to finish. He needed to find his team. He kept walking toward the stairwell. He'd worked with Bryce on the HMC project and been impressed by her creativity and cool intelligence. But once married, she'd become a full-time executive's wife. A waste of talent, Sam thought, but typical of Martin's ego to want his wife's full-time support all to himself.

As he trudged down the flight of stairs to his team's floor, his shoes felt like lead boots. He stepped out of the stairwell and surveyed the cubicle farm where his team huddled over their computers, intent and focused on work he'd told them was valuable. His stomach lurched and he covered his mouth until the feeling subsided. No. Martin was wrong, and Sam wouldn't be the one to tell them. He turned back to the stairway, heading toward the executive floor. He would resign, make Martin do his own dirty work.

He approached Martin's slightly open door and reached for the doorknob. At the sound of raised voices, he froze. Glancing around to make sure no one was in the hall, he leaned against the wall to listen.

He heard Bryce first.

"How much blood has to be on your hands for you to wake up?"

"There's no blood on my hands. The deaths caused by VIC before the HMC was added were unforeseeable. There haven't been any since."

"The HMC saves people while they're in the game, but what about when they're not? I've seen the statistics, Martin. Domestic violence and assaults have risen, specifically among VIC gamers."

"I can't be held responsible for the actions of gamers in their private lives. The game doesn't make people violent."

"You wouldn't say that if you'd heard the stories at the women's center. You have the power to change things. Why won't you listen to reason?"

"I understand your need to have hobbies, but if your charitable work upsets you, you should find something less stressful."

"It isn't a hobby. People's lives are being ruined. If you'd open your eyes to what's happening outside of SimTech, you'd understand."

"Between that coward, Sam, and you, I've had all I can take for one day. Go home. We'll discuss this later."

"You bet we will."

Sam pulled back from the door and slipped down the hall towards the stairs. He had to give Bryce credit. She had balls, to confront Martin like that.

* * * *

Sam scraped his meal of leftover spaghetti down the garbage disposal and dropped his plate into the sink. It made an awful clanking noise but didn't break. He slammed the faucet on and ran water into the dish to let it soak, then jerked it off. But his kitchen appliances and dishes were no substitute for the person he was boiling angry at.

Earlier in the day, he'd feigned sickness and left work. He still hadn't told his team, and he didn't plan to. Restless, he walked into his living room.

His furnishings were modest. Nothing embarrassing, but simple in style. The hardwood floor was cool against his bare feet. He walked down the hallway leading to the bedrooms and turned into the guest room he'd converted to a game room.

Stepping across its threshold was like entering a different dimension. Whereas the rest of his apartment was humble, he'd spared no expense here. The walls were covered with limited edition memorabilia from old science fiction movies, collected over the years with care so that each one represented a different period within the genre. The futuristic bar was custom-made from his own design and included a glass surface with interactive LED lighting. The sound system and entertainment screen were top of the line. In the center of the room was VIC's simulation chair.

Sam poured a glass of bourbon. He sipped, letting the whiskey burn down his throat to warm his belly. VIC had changed the way the world played video games. By simply uploading a photograph, the gamer could create a virtual image clone of himself or herself to play with, or a synthetic image clone of someone else to play against. Instead of the cartoonish characters players could choose from in other video games, VIC was so realistic that players felt they were *in* the movie. Yet it was better than a movie. It was as if they'd traveled through different dimensions of their own making. No fantasy was off limits.

It was time for a fantasy of his own. Setting down his drink, Sam slid his body into the VIC simulation chair. After hours upon hours of play, the chair's soft leather had contoured to the shape of his body. He closed his eyes, enjoying the feeling as his body relaxed into it. He clipped the cross-chest harness into place and wiggled his bare feet into the footgear attached to the chair, working his toes into the flexible foot glove that would read his movements and reflexes. Next, he slid both forearms into the gloves attached to the armrests. The gloves contracted comfortably around his arms. His fingers tapped the controls inside the glove, and the helmet and display settled around his head, blocking the sights and sounds of reality.

After the VIC intro, Sam set up his game scenario. He always played in Group Play mode as a default. The anticipation that an unexpected player might enter the game made it more interesting. After clicking several options, he went to his personal files and selected a picture of Martin from the company website. VIC searched its database, loaded the stored character, then prompted, "MR. HARRISON IS CURRENTLY IN PLAY. WOULD YOU LIKE TO JOIN?"

He selected *Yes*. He was more than ready to challenge the bastard. Maybe the defeat of Martin in virtual battle would salvage his bruised ego.

The VIC Sam found himself in the living room of a large pretentious mansion, one he could imagine Martin living in. His gorge rose when he found Martin—the VIC Martin—standing in front of an ornate fireplace. How he hated the man. Before Martin could react, Sam strode across the room and punched him in the face. Man, that felt good.

Martin staggered back, nearly falling. "You son of a bitch. Who do you think you are?"

"It's a game," Sam glared at him, making his hands into fists so tight his knuckles turned white. "Let's have some fun."

Martin grabbed a cast-iron fireplace poker from its rack and swung it at Sam. Sam ducked low and drove an elbow into Martin's kidney. Martin doubled over in pain, his grip on the poker loosened, and Sam yanked it out of his hands. Clenching his side, Martin looked up at Sam, his eyes wide. Sam stood over him, tightened his grip around the handle of the poker, and brought the heavy tool down across his boss's shoulders. Martin went down on his hands and knees, crying out in agony.

"This is for everyone you've stepped on to get to the top, you greedy bastard," Sam growled as he brought the poker down on Martin's body again and again. He swung until he could no longer catch his breath, then hunched forward with his hands on his knees, sucking in air, tears running down his face as he looked at the crumpled body. Embarrassed that his emotions had overtaken him, he wiped his face with his arm. It's just a game, he thought, though a sense of power surged through him and he allowed himself to feel a brief satisfaction.

In VIC, he was in complete control, but tomorrow he would have to do Martin's bidding.

* * * *

The next morning, Sam arrived at work later than usual, delaying the inevitable for as long as possible. He paused outside the lobby and squared his shoulders, taking one long, slow breath. Primed, he strode through the entryway and called out "Good morning" to the receptionist. She shook her head and gestured toward the lobby's waiting area.

Two men rose from the couch and walked toward him. Both were fiftyish, both dressed in slacks, white button-down shirts, and sport coats.

The taller man spoke. "Sam Breske? I'm Detective Rob Cresslar of the Raleigh PD and this is Josh Moore of the SBI's Computer Crimes Unit. May we have a word with you, somewhere private?" They flashed their badges, their faces serious. Too serious. Was his team playing a joke on him, and at the worst possible time?

Sam led them to a small conference room on the lobby floor. "What's this about?"

"Martin Harrison died last night in his home. Apparent heart attack," Cresslar said.

Remembering how triumphant he'd felt standing over the VIC Martin's body, Sam felt shameful, almost guilty. "Oh my God, that's awful."

"Mr. Harrison's death occurred while he was playing VIC," said Moore. "Seems the simulation was too realistic for him. Something your software was supposed to detect, right? Shut the game down and signal for help? Thing is, emergency services never received a distress call from Harrison's address."

Sam shook his head. "That doesn't make sense. We've never had reports of issues with the HMC."

"We had his game unit checked out," said Moore. "It was the current version with no signs of tampering. We also found he was in Group Play mode with you when he died. Want to tell us about that?"

Alarmed, Sam started to protest but stopped himself. He glanced from one detective to the other, searching their faces. "I don't think I should answer any more questions without my lawyer."

Cresslar raised both hands as if to protest. "Relax, you're not under arrest. Martin had a bad heart and his HMC seemed to have a glitch. How the glitch happened is the question no one seems to be able to answer. We thought it might have been hacked, but you built a firewall around the HMC to prevent that, didn't you? You're free to go unless there's something you want to tell us."

Sam shook his head no, hoping his calm expression didn't betray his conflicted feelings: guilt mixed with curiosity. Whatever happened to Martin's HMC?

* * * *

After his exchange with the police, Sam went back to work on his current project, carefully avoiding conversations with his team about Martin's death. Sam couldn't be sure where the project or his team's future lay, so he thought it was best to carry on until he heard differently.

The next day, Bryce summoned Sam to Martin's office. As Martin's heir, she had taken over the privately held company. He found her sitting behind the oversized desk, intently flipping through documents. He knocked politely on the open door.

She looked up from her papers and smiled. "Hi Sam, come on in."

"Sorry to hear about Martin."

She nodded. "Thank you. It was a shock."

"I wasn't expecting to see you in the office so soon."

"I'd rather be here. SimTech was Martin's baby. I want to take care of it for him."

He shifted from one foot to the other, nodding to show he understood. "I don't know what could've gone wrong with his HMC. Maybe if I take a look at it, I can find out."

Bryce fidgeted with the documents in front of her. "Listen, it was a glitch. It happens, even in the best software. Don't blame yourself. I tried to warn him about the violence in VIC, but he wouldn't listen."

Sam remembered their argument he'd overheard two days ago, the day Martin died. Ironic, that VIC was both Martin's greatest triumph and the cause of his death. "Is there anything I can do for you?"

"Yes. I'm still going to bring the green team on board and I need you to get them up to speed on your current project."

His heart sunk. She was no different from Martin. "Damn it, Bryce. My team's the best asset this company has. They're not replaceable by a bunch of twenty-year-olds."

"Hold on. I know Martin wanted to let your team go, but I think that's a mistake. I have a new assignment for your team I think you'll find much more challenging."

She wanted to save his team? "That's fantastic. What is it?"

"I want to replace the violence in VIC with simulated sex play. Your team will develop a full body skin suit to go along with it that'll increase the intensity of the action within the game." She grinned. "Can you imagine? Players can have simulated sex with anyone they choose. All they need is a photograph or a willing Group Play partner."

Sam's first instinct was to defend VIC, but given the circumstances of Martin's death, he thought better of it. Later they could discuss the viability of making both games available to the public. "Given the lucrative business of porn, it would sell, that's for sure."

The smile on Bryce's face spread wider. Sam found her cheerfulness the day after Martin's death odd, but her enthusiasm about the new project was catching, and he couldn't help but grin in return.

"Exactly what I was thinking. And I know you tested VIC's earlier releases with Reggie, but if you'd prefer a different partner, given the type of sim play we're talking here, I'd be glad to volunteer. We've worked well together in the past, don't you think?"

Sam felt heat rise to his cheeks. "We'd still have to worry about over-stimulation of the gamers."

Bryce burst into laughter. "Oh, right. But we'd still utilize the HMC, just in case."

At the mention of the HMC, his embarrassment waned. "About that—we need to figure out the bug in Martin's game. If there are more cases, it won't matter what we come up with next."

Her merry expression faded. "I don't think there will be more cases. It was just a one-time glitch. With preparing the newbies and getting your team started on the sim-sex game, you'll have no time to look into a singular problem."

How could she be so sure it would never occur again? Then it hit him. Bryce knew the HMC as well as he did. "Still, Martin's death should have been prevented by the software we both worked on. I can't have that hanging over my head without knowing what happened. Can you?"

Bryce's smile didn't quite reach her eyes. "Martin always said you were too honorable for your own good."

Sam kept his voice even. "I'm sure he didn't mean it as a compliment."

"No, he didn't." Her voice was neutral but her expression was cold.

"Then I'll research the bug myself, on my own time. The others can start prepping the new project. By the time we're ready to hit the ground running, I'm sure I'll have it all worked out. Let's make sure VIC is safe."

A chilly silence. Then Bryce said, "All right, Sam, if that's how you feel. When are you going to start?"

"Tonight."

Bryce leaned back in the black leather chair and made a tent with her fingers. Just like Martin used to do. Maybe it was a CEO thing.

* * * *

That night, Sam slid into his simulation chair and maneuvered into his equipment. With the head-mounted display in place, he set the scenario to return to his previous game, still in Group Play mode. Inside the game, he could enter Developer mode and review the processes that had been called earlier.

On his screen appeared the code for the mansion scene where Martin died. He quickly found where Martin had entered the game in Group Play. Sam reviewed the code line by line until he noticed calls to an unfamiliar procedure. *Sensate*. Martin's HMC had been hacked. "What the hell is *Sensate*?" he whispered, enlarging the phantom screen.

He focused so intently on searching VIC's code for the rogue procedure that he almost didn't hear the front door open. A new player had entered his game. Bryce. Sam wasn't surprised to see her. He had begun to suspect that she had altered the HMC code, and she'd known he was studying it.

"You found it," she said.

"Yeah, but what does it do?"

Bryce beamed. "*Sensate* will be fantastic in the new sim-sex game. I used medical theories behind the phenomenon of phantom limbs, where patients who'd lost limbs could still feel them, even years later. I've been able to recreate that effect through software. It fools the gamer's brain into not only visualizing the action, but feeling it."

Sam recoiled in horror. "You mean Martin felt everything that happened in our game last night?"

"I wanted to give him a taste of the pain that VIC had caused others. Teach him a lesson. I never meant for him to die."

"VIC doesn't cause pain, but your new coding does. And worse, it kills."

"Martin's death was—"

"Collateral damage?"

"I'd say an accident, maybe for the best. He would never have let us reduce the violence in VIC. Once we use the game to promote love instead of hate, crime rates will go down, and everyone wins in the long run."

"You're talking about lust, not love. You're substituting one base impulse for another."

"I wish you'd left this alone, Sam. I thought we were going to be great together, just like the old days." She drew a 9 mm pistol from her jacket and pointed it at Sam. "Before I entered your game, I inserted *Sensate* into it. I'm sorry it's come to this."

Bryce's hand shook as she squeezed the trigger and the bullet only grazed Sam's shoulder. As he felt its bite turn into a slow burn, he was amazed. How was it possible that *Sensate*-enhanced VIC could trick his brain so completely, so convincingly? The pain was real. Agonizing.

But he was in control, in Developer mode. Before Bryce could fire again, Sam shut the game down. His pain vanished. Astonishing.

He had enough to take to the police. But what could they charge her with? Being a fucking genius? And a madwoman, who'd converted virtual death into murder.

As the game faded, his head-mounted display turned dark and a single message appeared. "GAME OVER. WOULD YOU LIKE TO RESTART?"

Maybe tomorrow, after Bryce was arrested. He was eager to tinker with VIC. If *Sensate*'s brain probes or stimulants—whatever they were—created actual pain in a gamer's mind, what possibilities existed for pleasure!

Bryce *was* a genius. A realistic sim-sex game could take over the world. He smiled, realizing the irony. He'd have to test it with a different woman.

Computers weren't allowed in prison.

ABOUT THE AUTHOR

Marjorie Ann Mitchell is a freelance writer and business project manager for a personal computer company in North Carolina. She is a member of Sisters in Crime, Write On!, and The Raleigh Write to Publish writing groups. She graduated with a B.S. in Accounting from Appalachian State University in Boone, North Carolina. She has an interest in the science fiction and fantasy genres as well as essays that reflect social commentary.

WITCH HUNT

by Tamara Ward

The day after fire gutted The Pleasure Chest, the regulars at John's Pub & Grill stopped by the bar for a witch hunt, though if John asked them they'd deny it and say they came for a celebration. But he knew it was a witch hunt, even though his patrons downed drinks and spread smiles and slapped each other's backs like the time three years ago when the town's high school football team beat the boys from the big city.

Breaking a sweat as he filled glasses from behind the bar, John knew he ought to feel grateful for the boost in revenue; spring business typically dragged. Instead of allowing his customers' mood to buoy him, instead of soaking in the smell of draft beer and used dollar bills, he concentrated on maintaining his mask of benign indifference, on playing his role of aloof bartender. His jaw ached from clenching.

"So what do you think about the arson?" Nattie asked for the third time, still poking at him, trying to get the perfect opening quote for her article in the *South Wake Herald*, the local newspaper, which came out every Tuesday afternoon and consisted of exactly one section—usually eight pages, but on special occasions up to twelve. "What alerted you to the fire?" She pushed an incompliant curl behind her ear with a stubby finger. Everything about Nattie seemed stubby today—her double chin, her pale powdered nose, her muffin-top belly insufficiently contained by her skirt's elastic waistband. "It's my understanding the fire began at about 3:30 a.m.," she said. "Don't you think it's miraculous Darrel wasn't hurt?"

John stifled a groan. Nattie's questions mirrored those repeated by everyone in the pub—"When did the fire start?" "How did you notice it?" "Who do you think started it?" Even the town's one police detective dropped by John's Pub & Grill, asking John more of the same questions, before ordering a diet coke and hunkering in a back corner. The detective was getting an earful, liquor loosening tongues as the townsfolk mined each other for information to determine who set the fire while pretending to celebrate the demolition of The Pleasure Chest. No one knew anything helpful, or if they did they kept it quiet. But somehow, they all knew it was arson and they all knew John had been the one to call in the fire.

Even though John's customers claimed to disapprove of Darrel's carnal merchandise, quite a few had shopped there. But admitting their patronage would ignite their own social lives and livelihoods. The Pleasure Chest was like a Venus fly trap. In a town where so much depended on image, no one could afford to be caught inside Darrel's store, even as so many found it irresistible.

The Pleasure Chest had opened half a year ago, causing immediate uproar throughout the community, and not just because Darrel was the first man of color to open a business in the downtown strip. A sex shop in the historic downtown? How could the board of commissioners allow it to happen? And the store's merchandise—was it even legal to sell?

It was, and the commissioners scrambled to add language to zoning ordinances effectively banning any further such blights inside town borders. But Darrel's shop, grandfathered in, remained open despite the clamor.

"Did you see anything?" Nattie asked. Again.

"I'm charging you for every one of those you order." John jabbed his finger at the half drunk rum and coke, one of a steady stream she'd been gulping since she arrived. Nattie had been working the room, returning sporadically to John for more drinks and questions, but she'd finally settled herself at the bar and seemed to have turned her focus on John, her grand finale to the interviews, he supposed.

"Don't tell me you're sad Darrel's shop went up in flames," Nattie said.

"It's the third time you've asked me the same questions in as many hours," he said. And the first time she'd been in the pub since they'd broken off their relationship several months ago. John had given Natalie her nickname, for the way she constantly buzzed around people, not quite irritating enough for bug repellent, too springy to be swatted. But that was back when he hadn't wanted to squash her like the pest she was. Back when he'd known no better than to assume Nattie's loving was the best he'd get. Before he'd met Darrel.

"You want a different question?" Nattie asked. John shook his head, but she pressed on. "Because I'm not stopping until I have something to print."

"I'll give you something to print," said Miss CeeCee, pushing her saggy-skinned elbow against Nattie, two drinks over her usual order and no lipstick left to smudge the rims of her Bloody Marys. "You can quote me: the blight is burned to cinders! Peace downtown is restored."

Miss CeeCee was right, John supposed. With Darrel's shop gone, downtown would again be virtually indistinguishable from any other old small-town downtown in North Carolina, dotted with quiet brick storefronts selling the same quaint souvenirs and necessary wares, cars parallel parked on the gray, cracking pavement.

Miss CeeCee, head of the women's club and leader of historical preservation initiatives, had a past crammed full of contention, way back to her bra-burning days. She was always rallying against something. When Darrel's store opened, she organized a letter-writing campaign to the state legislators and newspaper. But John had seen her sneak into Darrel's store at least twice, furtively emerging with new bulges in her handbag.

"Do you think it can be salvaged?" Nattie asked Miss CeeCee. "The building, not the business."

"Why would anyone want to?" Miss CeeCee waved her age-spotted fingers so close to Nattie's face the reporter leaned back. "Didn't match the rest of the storefronts, and just look at it now."

John glanced out his big front window, across Main Street to the soot-stained cinderblocks of the squat building. A hole in the roof gaped as wide as the storefront's bay window—now shattered, revealing a blackened interior that used to be filled with intriguing merchandise. John, like Darrel and a few other downtown shop owners, lived in the same building as his business. Except John's living quarters were above his pub, and Darrel's, a room behind his store.

"We're finally free of that pustule!" Miss CeeCee said. "The eyesore building is now utterly impossible to save."

"With Christ, anything is possible," Pastor Clyde said, rearranging his lanky body on a stool on Nattie's other side. His gangly limbs elongated in the striped shirt and black slacks, Pastor Clyde reminded John of a heron—awkward curves and unexpected bends.

Pastor Clyde had entered the pub earlier with a "Hallelujah!" that echoed off the aged brick walls. His church was within view just up the street, the white steeple scraping the boundless blue sky. After The Pleasure Chest opened, Pastor Clyde frequented John's pub, scouting for souls drifting into temptation. He'd even organized picketers on Sunday afternoons to march in front of the store. A protest without teeth, since the downtown stores all closed on Sundays.

"Christ," Miss CeeCee said. "Christ wouldn't be interested in resurrecting that store. He'd have it burn in hell, along with its owner."

John shook his head, but only Nattie noticed the gesture. Her eyes sparked—she'd found what she sought, a weakness to probe.

"Any comments, John?" she asked, too sweetly.

John hadn't been the focus of Nattie's professional buzzing before, and he didn't like it now, but he knew any response would only fuel her interrogation. That was Nattie. If she smelled the slightest hint of scandal, she seized it and twisted. And when she published her article, she made sure the controversy mushroomed into such an uproar the entire town couldn't talk about anything else for another week, until the next edition.

Pastor Clyde clasped his hands and looked up, as if seeing beyond the plaster ceiling to heaven's gates. "I pray a wholesome store is built upon a solid rock in its place."

John knew Pastor Clyde's picketers. Most carried sins more damning than any they protested. But their sins—theft, physical abuse, substance addiction—were more easily hidden than Darrel's wares. What Pastor Clyde claimed to be wicked indulgences invented by the devil himself, Darrel displayed before all the town. But John didn't understand how sexual stimulants were immoral, especially if shared between husband and wife. The Bible didn't forbid handcuffs or edible lingerie.

"Do I hear an Amen?" Pastor Clyde asked.

"Amen," said Jennifer, swigging from her beer bottle. She climbed onto a bar stool next to Pastor Clyde, strands of her loose long brown hair swinging forward and sticking to moisture on the bar counter.

Jennifer owned Sweet Scoops, the ice cream store next door to The Pleasure Chest. For her, John knew, the timing of this fire was ideal. This time last spring customers had crowded Jennifer's shop, overflowing to the sidewalk benches outside. But families hadn't been visiting as much since Darrel's shop opened. Jennifer set her bottle down with force, her hair still caught on the countertop. "Maybe my customers will return, now they don't have to take their kids past a window with a light-up doo-hicky writhing around like a finger without a hand. Cheers." She grabbed her beer again and clinked it against Pastor Clyde's bottle of old-fashioned orange soda.

"Was your store damaged?" Nattie asked.

"Nope."

"That's a blessing," Pastor Clyde said. He looked at John. "I'll have one more, as it's a special day."

John popped open another orange soda and slid it across the countertop.

"Me, too," Nattie said. "And give me a quote. Tell me what you first saw when you looked out your window at the fire."

"Flames," John said, though he remembered something—someone—else, a silhouette moving in the shadows beside the building.

"The question is," Miss CeeCee said, "who had the balls to do it?" She looked around the pub. "They say an arsonist returns to the scene of the crime to admire his handiwork. I bet the arsonist is here among us."

John agreed with Miss CeeCee. The arsonist probably sat here in his pub, drinking and smiling and proclaiming satisfaction. No more blow-up dolls mocking the town, no more mannequins in lace tatters causing fender benders, no more "What's that, mommy?" from children as parents hurried past the window display. John felt a sudden, sharp pang above his ear—the beginnings of a migraine.

"Jo-ohn," Nattie said, singsong. "Hel-lo-oh."

John frowned. He wanted to tell Nattie to beat it, go somewhere else for her interviews. But he didn't want attention, not when the town wanted someone to blame. He didn't want to be the next target of their hatred, their hypocrisy. A good bartender listened, didn't talk. Never be the story; be the paper soaking up the ink. Once he and Nattie shared that. But it was also where they differed, as he swallowed secrets, and she spilled them.

"You're not answering my questions," Nattie said. "So far I've just asked the easy ones."

"I don't want to be quoted in the paper," John said.

"But you're a vital part of the story."

Vitality. The one ware Darrel offered that John could find nowhere else in this town.

John first met Darrel when he came in the pub for a drink. Olive-brown skin beneath bushy black eyebrows. Black eyes that had mesmerized John, captivated him, magnet-like, Darrel's presence awakening him like the electric charge he felt swimming in cold saltwater. John's other patrons pretended to be offended by Darrel's presence and deserted the pub. Darrel said he was sorry for spooking them, and John refused the apology. He gave Darrel a drink on the house, a first. From there a relationship had grown: a relationship overflowing with firsts, unfamiliar feelings, new experiences for John. Darrel had prompted him to do all sorts of things—wondrous things—he'd never done before, never knew could be done, with acceptance, without judgment.

They'd seen each other by an unspoken code. Darrel understood their relationship had to be clandestine. If the townspeople detested Darrel for his business, and ostracized him for his skin color, how much more would they damn him for his sexuality? And what would they do to John if they knew? Pastor Clyde's protests would expand and Miss CeeCee's prolific pen would scribble across the street.

"You don't think Darrel will reopen, do you?" Jennifer pushed her hair behind her back. "It looks like he lost everything in the fire."

"What do you think, John?" Nattie asked. "Will Darrel reopen?"

"How would I know?" John bit his tongue, instantly sorry for his outburst.

"You sure you want me to answer that?" Nattie let half of her upper lip curl into something that would have resembled a smile, if only the other half of her mouth matched it.

She knows. The thought struck John with such force he gripped his bar counter to steady himself. "You want to tell me why you think it's arson?"

Nattie glanced at the detective in the corner. "Someone told me off the record. A brick was thrown through the window. Inside the store were a couple shattered glass bottles. Molotov cocktails."

The front door clanged open, and Commissioner Buckers—up for reelection—entered like an actor on a stage, swinging an arm upward, embracing a captive audience.

"Evening, all! I've an important announcement." Buckers waited for the room to hush. "Regarding the building across the street, I've talked to the owner in Atlanta. It's still unofficial, but the town is in negotiations to buy the property. We're going to level the ruins and sell the land—for a profit—to the highest bidder." He paused for applause. "A round of drinks for everyone, on me!" Applause kicked up again as Buckers sauntered to the bar and ordered a scotch.

John disliked the commissioner's arrogance, but the distraction may have spared him from Nattie's questions. Maybe, after John had served drinks to everyone, Nattie would disappear and forget about crucifying him for his relationship with Darrel. John bustled into action, going from table to table, freshening beverages. By the time he reached the back of the room to refill the detective's diet coke, the commissioner had joined the detective.

"Arson is a serious crime," Commissioner Buckers was saying, "but a shop of that nature was a crime against family values and our citizens' quality of life."

The detective shifted in his seat.

Buckers slapped the detective's shoulder. "No one was hurt, and I'm sure Darrel has insurance. So Darrel gets reimbursed, the town gets a new property, and everyone is happy."

The detective didn't look happy.

"I understand you're not going to be able to put much effort into the investigation," Buckers said. "You'll be busy tying up loose ends with your eligibility for retirement coming up so soon—what is it, in a year and a half, two?"

"Four months," the detective said.

"That soon!" Buckers said. "Why, you're almost there. The town has an outstanding pension and healthcare program for retirees, don't you think?"

John set the detective's refill on the table and returned to the bar where, unfortunately, Nattie still perched.

"My police scanner lit up like stage lights at a rock concert," she said. "I sleep with it on so I don't miss anything. I got some great photographs of the smoke." An elated flush covered her face. John's stomach turned.

"It's a wonder Darrel wasn't burned with the store," Jennifer said.

"He wasn't there last night," Nattie said.

"How do you know?" Miss CeeCee asked.

"Where was he?" Pastor Clyde asked.

"John?" Nattie asked. "Surely you know."

And then Miss CeeCee's eyes widened. Did she finally understand what Nattie threatened to drop on John? "Do you know where Darrel was last night, John?"

John knew. Darrel had slept beside him, until they heard the crash of the store window and then the whomp as the fire caught hold. Darrel raced outside half-dressed and kicked open his door. Smoke gushed out; Darrel couldn't even crawl inside to save any merchandise. John dialed 911, knowing it was too late, knowing it was over.

"John?" Pastor Clyde said. "Where was Darrel last night? A man like that probably visited your pub, drunk himself silly, and let personal details slip."

John thought about what he could say without condemning himself. "I don't turn down a customer."

Nattie snorted. "I don't suppose he'd turn one down, either."

John clenched his teeth again, tried to swallow the anger back down. "I wasn't his customer."

"Then tell us." Nattie flipped a page on her notepad and poised her too-sharp pen above the virgin sheet. "What are you to him? What is Darrel to you?"

Partner sounded cold. Soul-mate, cliché. Darrel was straightforward and quirky. Quiet but full of life: Darrel was life! Utterly unlike Nattie who sucked life out of others then regurgitated a bastardized form of it for the town to devour in newsprint.

"So where was Darrel last night, John?" Nattie asked.

"I don't know," John lied.

"Come," Miss CeeCee said. "You admit he was your customer."

"I don't know," John repeated. His heart pounded. It was none of their business. "I don't really know Darrel," who then stepped into the pub, witnessing John's most shameful denial, rending John's heart in two.

Every conversation died; every head turned; every eye fixated on Darrel. His dress shirt was unbuttoned at the top, revealing tufts of coarse chest hair and smooth, tan skin. He held his lean, muscled body stiffer than usual, but still he reminded John of a superhero in plainclothes—his beauty and strength, his worth unrealized by most everyone in John's Pub & Grill. Darrel carried a tote bag, probably all he'd salvaged from the blaze. John had forgotten to turn on the pub's background music. In the silence, Darrel stood, with a proud tilt to his head as always, but his eyes held something—tears?

"I wanted to tell you all," he said, "I'm leaving. Unless anyone has something they'd like to say before I go." His gaze landed on John.

If John asked Darrel to stay, if he spoke the truth, his bar might be boycotted, even set afire. His reputation, his life, ruined. He'd lose his business, his investment, his livelihood. Customers, friends. Everything he knew and built his life around, almost. But if he didn't speak he'd be dead inside; Darrel would be lost to him forever. The joy—the energy and quickening—he'd experienced these past few months would be gone—a memory gathering dust. Fear trapped the words in his throat.

"We'll pray for you," Pastor Clyde said, finally, breaking the silence.

"Pray for *me*?" Darrel set his bag down, folded his arms, and studied their faces, one by one. John realized it wasn't tears he'd seen in Darrel's eyes. It was something fierce, indomitable. Darrel, like a destroying angel, possessed the power to shred their façades and reveal their secrets.

John knew what Darrel *could* say. Darrel could tell Miss CeeCee, now The Pleasure Chest was closed, how to order her special lubricant online. Could tell Nattie that new batteries for her personal gadget were sold at the watch counter. Could tell Commissioner Buckers if he tired of his current films, a certain website offered a good selection. Could tell Jennifer, who loved to read the kind of books they didn't carry in the library, where to find more.

Would Darrel reveal their relationship? John was the worst pretender of them all, Darrel's disciple in love, now too pragmatic—no, too cowardly—to admit the truth.

But when Darrel spoke, instead of anger and judgment, his quiet voice held disappointment: "If you want to pray, pray for yourselves."

And he left.

Pastor Clyde hummed "Victory in Jesus," until murmurs buried the solo.

"Darrel sure stared at you like you might have something to say," Nattie said to John.

John unfroze himself, wiped an invisible smudge from the counter. "He was staring at you."

Nattie's mouth popped open. John wanted to cram his rag down it.

"Why would Darrel stare at me?" Nattie asked, her voice elevated. "Why me when it's you he—"

"Nattie, I could have sworn," John said, following instinct, "I saw you outside his store last night."

"I was there for the story," Nattie said.

"Before then. Hiding in the darkness." John's vague recollections of what he'd glimpsed in the shadows outside Darrel's congealed into solid recognition. "You *made* the story."

Miss CeeCee and Pastor Clyde glanced at each other and then back at him and Nattie. Jennifer set down her empty bottle, nearly missing the counter.

"I will not be disgraced," Nattie said. She clutched her fist against her chest. "Darrel was polluting this town. If you're going to make accusations, make them against him. You knew him intimately. Do you deny it?"

John's ears burned. Somehow Nattie knew all about him and Darrel. But John knew this town. And he knew enough about Nattie. As much as the townsfolk liked to bemoan The Pleasure Chest, as loud as they'd howl about John and Darrel's relationship, they would recognize that an arsonist posed a much greater threat.

"Darrel deserved what he got," Nattie said.

No. But Nattie should get what she deserved. John put down the bar rag. "The detective," he said, "will be interested in what I saw last night."

"John. Nattie," Pastor Clyde said. "Cool down." He held his hands up as if in surrender. "Whoever set the fire committed a crime. But they also prevented further damage from that man's temptations into an eternity in hell. Surely you both understand." He looked at the detective, immersed in conversation with the commissioner. "I think, in this particular situation, we should agree he—or she—who is without sin should cast the first stone." He glanced at Miss CeeCee, who pursed her lips.

Nattie stared at John, as if daring him to speak. A minute passed, and the moment to condemn, too, and John felt those unspoken revelations settle like dark stones in the pit of his stomach. He'd made a covenant with Nattie stretching forward, an unvoiced pact—*if you ever tell, so will I.*

She chugged the rest of her drink. "I'll take my bill," she said, and left with the same wiggle to her gait John had observed from his upstairs window as the arsonist retreated into darkness and The Pleasure Chest exploded into flames.

So the witch hunt ended. Not with a burning at the stake, but with a drowning—Nattie in her rum and cokes, Miss CeeCee in her Bloody Marys, Pastor Clyde in his righteousness, and John in his silence.

ABOUT THE AUTHOR

Tamara Ward is a Barnes & Noble top ten bestseller and an Amazon top 100 bestselling mystery and romantic suspense author with storylines and characters that combine for fun, fast-paced, can't-put-it-down reads. Her published mystery novels include *Private Deception*, *Hidden Betrayal*, *Storm Surge*, and *Silver Flashing*. In her mysteries, you'll find characters who keep readers hooked, strong-willed sleuths, and a sprinkling of humor.

HEART SURGERY

by Toni Goodyear

Sara gave a grim chuckle as she slid the plastic vial into her carry-all. She knew that stealing Jake's Viagra was a ridiculously childish thing to do. Not to mention pointless. He was a doctor, for God's sake; there was plenty more where that came from.

Still, she supposed as she closed the nightstand drawer, it was kinder than castration…or something even more spectacular. That had been her first impulse, like that gal some years back who'd severed the family jewels and then chucked the offending member out a car window. Or the lady who'd made her point with super glue.

Other remedies had been proposed. A woman who described herself as SoVeryPissed made headlines when forty thousand women joined her discussion of the moral pros and cons of serving ground glass to unfaithful partners. A federal prosecutor barely kept a straight face as she explained to television reporters that no charges would be filed. She couldn't have people arrested for pondering general principles—and anyway, ground glass was so obviously unpalatable that it wasn't a serious threat unless you hid the shards in a piece of meat and served it to a man who, like a dog, swallowed his food whole.

Incidents like these, Sara decided, were milestones in female sexual history—tales that richly deserved to be, but, alas, almost certainly wouldn't be, included in the next scholarly treatise on human sexuality.

Jake's copy of *Certain*, the hip new sexual bible for the modern American male, stared up at her from the nightstand. Sunlight streaming through the bedroom window—the great bay window that overlooked the Pacific—set the voluptuous colors of the paperback cover art shimmering like baubles on a belly dancer. Two men and three women, quasi-Rubenesque figures in a western parody of the *Kama Sutra*, lay knotted together pretzel fashion, a blob of human plastique. A yellow sticky note marked page 188: "techniques for the three-orgasm encounter." For Jake, at fifty-nine, that was the gold at the end of the rainbow, the Maltese falcon of his sexual fantasies. His Land of Noir was a place of glory and conquest, a world devoid of things like high blood pressure, cold wives, and finicky heart valves.

Sara had been part of that fantasy for the past two years—two years in which she'd clung to the belief that Jake had outgrown his wife and now belonged to her. Today was their anniversary, the official celebration of that delusion; tonight the noir playing field was to be in motion, bathed in its signature smoky light. They had made the plans weeks ago. First, a romantic dinner at Charlie's, the ultra-discreet little bistro where the wine cellar was exquisite and the oysters and clams to die for. Joe, their favorite pianist, would play the perfect Sam to their Rick and Ilsa. Then a quick, private plane ride down the coast to the midnight jazz concert at Capito's, with tickets that had been so scandalously hard to come by. Afterwards they would wander back to their favorite small hotel carrying Capito's decadent *demi-monde zabaione*, a crème-de-menthe-infused whip of mascarpone and ganache that gave new meaning to the term foreplay.

Except none of that would happen now. Tonight Jake would not find her here waiting for him. Tonight he would wander alone through an empty, echoing landscape.

Her eyes went to the framed picture on the nightstand. She and Jake on a rented catamaran in the Caymans, the two of them radiating life, glowing in the sunlight, golden. She'd been his mistress not quite a year then. "I don't know how I ever managed without you," he'd said as they lay wrapped in silk sheets listening to the water gently lapping the bottom of the boat. "I need you to believe me, Sara. I'll be working toward the day we can be together."

She had shown him, then, her willingness to believe, though in reality she'd had no choice. She had been helplessly mad about Jake Douglas from the first moment they met.

She closed her eyes and rubbed her forehead. Her anniversary present would be their emancipation from bullshit. No more spurious out-of-town conferences or late-night rescues of fictional patients. No more pretending. She'd suspected for months that he was lying to her, from the stories of others—the blonde model, the theatrical redhead—that had come to her on the wind, rumors she'd fought hard not to acknowledge.

In the end, it was Jake's wife who'd delivered the *coup de grâce*.

Sara thought back to her chance encounter yesterday with a friend at a local coffee shop.

"I just ran into Jake," the woman had said quietly when they were seated with their cappuccinos. She caught Sara's glance and held it. "At Donner's. He was shopping."

"Oh?" Sara said, suddenly wary. Jake had told her he would be out of town all day at a medical confab. Somewhere down south. Not here, and certainly not at the town's leading jewelry emporium.

"It's not great news, Sara. Should I tell you?"

Sara hesitated a long moment, then gave a mute nod.

"Brenda was with him, trying on diamond necklaces. She said they were planning a trip to Tuscany to renew their vows after fifteen wonderful years of marriage, direct quote. They were holding hands. Hell, Brenda practically cooed while Jake stood there with a guilty grin on his face. It was nauseating."

She reached across the table and placed her hand over Sara's.

"I'm sorry, Sara. I'm sure Jake will say it's all just Brenda's deluded take on reality, that it means nothing. But I thought you needed to know."

Sara had sputtered into a napkin as a line of hot coffee snaked down her throat. It was so absurd—it had always been absurd. If it didn't hurt so much, she would have laughed out loud.

Surely Brenda knew her boast of marital bliss would reach Sara's ears. Did that mean Brenda knew about her and Jake? Sara was willing to bet the answer was yes. She'd returned her friend's consoling pat on the hand and managed a weary smile.

She hadn't bothered to raise a fuss when Jake called later that night, as predicted, to explain away the jewelry store incident.

"Brenda's crazy," he'd insisted. "She just can't believe the marriage is over, that's all it is, I promise you, Sara. She's pushing for a trip, nothing more. I wouldn't lie about a thing like this."

Sara had kept her tone expressionless. "It's okay, Jake, don't worry about it. Yes, of course, I believe you. Don't I always?"

She'd hung up with the word 'promise' hovering like a knife before her eyes.

Now she stood in the doorway of their bedroom and took a long last look around. She'd had enough; it was finished. The apartment, leased in his friend's name, had been Jake's idea, a safer alternative than her place or an in-town hotel. The bedroom's elegant color scheme of champagne and burnt umber had been her gift of love at their beginning. Now it was the perfect chromatic subtext to ruined glory. No more protestations of love, no desperate ecstasy between the sheets. Done.

Right, enough whining, she thought, as she slipped Jake's copy of *Sure* into her carry-all alongside the Viagra.

He'd have to do without his book, too.

* * * *

She threw her case into the cramped trunk and slid behind the wheel of her Austin Healey Sprite. The bright May afternoon was clear and cool, full of hope. She half expected to see the sun open an eye and wink, reminding her that all was illusion.

She pointed the car toward her shop, glad that traffic was light. What might she do to pamper herself, she wondered? Psychologically speaking, a trip to hone the spirits seemed in order. An African trek, perhaps. Or an architectural tour of the mountain provinces of China.

Except, she realized even as she considered it, she didn't need to leave town to hone her spirits. Her sense of well-being didn't need validation by Jake. She was a successful businesswoman; her spirits would be fine. *She* would be fine. Maybe a little assistance with forgiveness, or a class on how to forego retribution without remorse—those might be in order. Better yet, a few lessons in Italian *vendetta*, where the joy of planning revenge could be as filling as a plate of gnocchi. That thought raised a smile as she pulled into her parking space at the rear of the shop.

As always when she approached Sara's Cove, her soul rippled with pride. The upscale boutique for designer clothing had proved to be the perfect business for this moneyed city by the sea. Jake might be a famous surgeon, head of a renowned cardiac center, but she had Sara's Cove. She'd never had a child but, as her business grew, she'd come to understand the maternal urge to promote and protect one's creation like a madwoman.

She stopped in her office to check messages, then made her way down the long hallway to the showroom. Glass mosaic windows ran the full length, drenching the space in kaleidoscopic hues, bringing an otherwise lackluster passage to stunning, quivering life. It had taken her six months to get the mosaics right, six months of painstaking cutting and re-cutting, arranging and rearranging until each color-drenched fragment found its proper place in the whole. But the work had been worth it. Her passion for art glass fit perfectly with her passion for the boutique. Several display pieces already decorated the shop. Now she was ready to launch her new line of mosaic jewelry that would sell exclusively through the Sara's Cove brand. First, she would extend her reach to all of the U.S. Then she planned to take the enterprise global via the internet.

In the showroom, Mrs. Grayson, her silver-bunned associate of seven years, was showing an important customer—Julia Lawford, the mayor's wife—the proper way to wear the new teal cape just in from New York. Two well-dressed women in their thirties explored the elegantly spaced rows of new stock and accessories from Italy, France, and Brazil. Their faces were alight with eager determination.

At the far end, a customer perched on a white leather sofa studied a sage green sheath being modeled for her by one of the shop's young salesgirls. Sara thought the dress would look smashing on the woman, who sported a chic knot of rich auburn hair. From her dreamy smile, Sara fancied the woman thought so too.

The mayor's wife retreated to the changing room. Mrs. Grayson, momentarily free, headed for the accounts desk.

"Julia will be taking the cape, then?" Sara asked.

Mrs. Grayson smiled. "Of course. The mayor's annual reception is coming up."

The black-tie reception was the social event of the year. Sara would be wearing the latest one-shoulder silk chiffon from Gavonni.

She inclined her head toward the two women browsing the stacks. "Those two, do we know them?"

Mrs. Grayson pointed her chin in the opposite direction, toward the customer still studying the model. "They're all three together. Tourists from Vancouver. They heard about Sara's Cove and made a point of working us into their itinerary."

"Word is definitely getting around," Sara said, smiling.

It was not by accident. She'd worked very hard to establish Sara's Cove as a must-do shopping destination for visitors to California. She'd sacrificed life, time, and money over the past year to lobby for the head slot on the mayor's restructured Tourism Board, a powerful role that came with a grand budget and the political tools needed to jumpstart a big business. In that position, she could take her label—and her life—to an entirely new level. She would leave the Jake Douglases of this world behind like so many wisps of dandelion blown to the four winds.

She *would* get the appointment. She'd campaigned vigorously, contacting all the right people, making all the right promises. She was already a well-respected personality in the business community, one known for her marketing skill. And Jake, a major donor to the mayor's campaign, had called in a favor.

"The mayor owes me big time," he'd said as he nibbled her neck one passionate night. "I'll give him a call. Until he's ready to move on it, you'll need to keep canvassing for support publically, but, frankly, if I ask him to do it there's no way he can tell me no."

Sara had nudged him around so she could look in his eyes. "Why does he owe you?"

He grinned. "I can't say. You know how it is with politics."

Yes, she knew how it was—and she knew Jake could deliver this. "There must be something nice I can do for you in return," she'd whispered.

"Hmmm, yes…" he said. "Now let me see."

Two weeks later, he'd confirmed it was a done deal. She was glad now that he'd had to spend a big slice of his political capital on her, it was the goddamn least he could do. If she knew him at all, she knew the deal wouldn't change now that she was leaving. Jake was not a vindictive man, and there were rules between lovers. Take half the heart, leave the other, a minimum in civilized society. Jake would know he'd gotten off easy; he'd be satisfied with that. Besides, the board appointments would be made public at the mayor's reception on Saturday, so Sara expected to hear any day now. She itched to begin.

The bell over the front door tinkled, and Brenda Douglas stepped into the shop.

A handsome, well-stacked brunette a few years older than Sara, Jake's wife had an aristocratic face, high cheekbones and piercing green eyes. Her wardrobe reflected her story—money, breeding and taste, the perfect spouse for a man of ambition. Today she wore a doe-colored linen pantsuit of Italian design that she'd bought right here at Sara's.

Sara sucked in her breath and mustered a smile. "Hello, Brenda. Can I help you?"

Brenda's smile was a shade too broad, her tone a touch too gay. "Yes, you can, Sara. I'm looking for something very special today. I thought you might help me find a dress to go with this." She extracted a black velvet box from her purse and laid it on the counter. "Go ahead, please. Open it."

Sara hesitated, then slowly raised the lid. A string of pear-shaped emeralds alternated with flowers made of marquise-cut diamonds, each stone set in rosy gold. Sara caught her breath. The necklace must have cost Jake a bundle.

"My husband bought it for me yesterday," Brenda said. "Spectacular, isn't it? I immediately thought of you. I mean, since I'll need something simple but fabulous to go with it."

Sara shifted her gaze to Brenda's face. Brenda looked back at her with a studied half-smile. No question about it, Sara thought. Brenda knew.

"It's lovely," Sara said matter-of-factly. In truth, the casual indifference wasn't hard. The necklace was beautiful, yes, but finally that's all it was. Diamonds and emeralds elicited no pain; they were the last thing on earth she cared about. God knows, Brenda had paid for them tenfold.

Julia Lawford brought the teal cape to the counter. Her eyes widened when she spied the necklace. "My God, Brenda, is that yours?"

Brenda's sardonic smile was like the thin edge of an executioner's sword. "I've got a thoughtful husband."

"I'll say. May I?" Julia reached for the necklace and held it up. It shimmered like a summer leaf bathed in morning dew. She caught Brenda's eye and grinned. "Looks like things are going well at home. Have you done something particularly wonderful to deserve this, or is he simply your devoted slave?"

Brenda inclined her head. "It's been like a second honeymoon lately. Apparently he heard me when I said I needed to be more than just a shadow." Her gaze landed on Sara. "And that he owed me something meaningful of my own."

Julia grinned. "That's the downside of being married to an important man. You've got to carve out your own identity. Believe me, I know. Well, come next Saturday, a new beginning."

Sara looked from one woman to the other. "Saturday?"

"You need to keep this under your hat, Sara," Brenda said. She leaned forward conspiratorially. "I'm to be appointed head of the Tourism Board for the city. Isn't that a kick?"

Sara heard the words, then no others. Instead, her ears filled with a whooshing sound, as if a vacuum was sucking the life and energy out of her universe. She had no idea how much time passed before she could speak.

"Tourism…," was all she managed.

Brenda gave a half-laugh. "I know it sounds crazy. But the mayor felt that with my contacts and civic experience…and, of course, my husband's strong recommendation…I've known for weeks but I was sworn to silence. Very frustrating!"

"Brenda's perfect for the job," Julia said. "We're giving a private dinner for the appointees tonight, before the public announcements."

"Tonight," Sara said numbly.

"Last minute, I know," Brenda said. "I'm so sorry, Sara, but until I saw the necklace I thought I knew what I'd be wearing. Now I want to show it off." She turned to Julia. "You know Jake's tied up at the hospital until a little after eight?"

Julia nodded. "His secretary called. Dinner will be at eight-forty five. It'll be fine."

"Excellent." Brenda turned back to Sara. "Now we just need to find something to flatter this jewelry." She raised her arm as if holding a sword. "So lay on, MacDuff, and damned be she who first cries 'Hold, enough!'"

Within an hour, they found the right dress, a shimmering empire gown in soft taupe, with clean, elegant lines and the perfect rounded neckline to display the necklace.

The women from Vancouver had left happily with the modeled sheath, new belts and purses. At five-thirty, Sara said goodnight to Mrs. Grayson and the young model and snapped the front door latch behind them.

She walked to the leather couch and sat down stiffly, her hands gripping her knees to keep them from shaking as she forced herself to face Jake's betrayal. How and when did he plan to tell her he'd sold her future to his wife? She was sure his explanation would have been brilliant, just as she knew with steel certainty that it would have been a lie—an ultimatum from Brenda perhaps? Brenda who knew nothing about business but who knew about Sara and who would have it in for Sara's Cove from day one. Forgiveness? No, Sara thought, not this time. This time he had gone too far. This time he had taken the other half of her heart, the one all decent lovers left behind.

Her blood ran cold. Ultimately, infidelity wasn't about who was sleeping with whom. Infidelity was about the cold brutality of power. Infidelity was betrayal, and betrayal was annihilation. She remembered her high school history, learning about times when disembowelment was a punishment for treason. The idea had horrified her then. Now it seemed to perfectly fit the crime—that is, once you grasped the true nature of the offense.

She went into the dressing room and took her time, slinking into new underwear, and then the blue cocktail dress, a gossamer beauty that she'd set aside for herself from the new stock. New silver earrings, then silver shoes, delicate and strappy. She spent a long time before the mirror getting her hair and makeup just the way Jake liked them.

When she was done, Sara stared at herself—the confident, attractive, self-made woman. A cold calm settled over her as she reached for the phone and called Charlie's.

"I'd like to place an order to go, please. Five dozen of your premier mix of oysters and littlenecks, well iced, extra lemon and sauce, a large loaf of garlic French, and a double Roman salad." All would be ready in twenty minutes. Excellent.

She'd just hung up when the phone rang.

"Happy Anniversary, babe," Jake crooned. "Two years, can you believe it? I hope you know how much I love you."

"I love you too. And I'm really looking forward to tonight."

An awkward silence. Sara imagined she could actually hear him girding his loins.

"Um…Sara…sweetheart…I hate to tell you this but…something has come up. I've spent all day trying to get out of it, that's why I hadn't called yet, but it looks like I'm going to have to do it. I'm the one with the most experience with this kind of surgery."

"What are you saying, Jake?" She draped a multicolored Bernitti scarf around her neck and preened before the mirror as she listened, almost with admiration, to his lies.

"It's a difficult procedure, emergency basis, very tricky. I'm so sorry, Sara, I feel terrible, but I have to be at the hospital no later than eight fifteen. It can't be helped."

Yes, it would have to be a matter of life and death to cancel their anniversary plans and live to tell about it, Sara thought dryly. But that was Jake, always the right excuse for every occasion. She'd often wondered if there was a career in something like that.

"It's all right, Jake, you can exhale now," she said, forcing an even tone. "I mean, heart surgery is a trump card, isn't it—it pretty much leaves a girl with nothing to say."

She heard him let out his breath.

"You're simply the best, Sara. You're better than the best. How can I make this up to you?"

"Stay tuned, I'll let you know."

His tone went syrupy. "You just name it, sweetheart. Whatever you want. An anniversary present squared."

"We have until eight tonight anyway," she said. "I'll get some things from Charlie's, it'll be faster, and I'll make sure you get to your surgery on time. I'll meet you at the apartment."

"I really don't deserve you," Jake said, his voice rich with practiced intimacy.

"Can I get that in writing?"

He chuckled.

She hung up and methodically made her way to the back of the shop, shutting off certain lights and turning on others, setting night alarms. She went through her office and into her workroom, switching on the high intensity light over her workbench. Its strong incandescent glow drenched the stacked sheets of richly colored glass and the array of small, delicate tools.

Tonight she'd give Jake a dinner he loved, she thought as she reached for the ceramic canister in which she kept her glass sweepings, the unusable slivers and shards of her mosaic creations. Raw oysters and clams on the half shell—a Dionysian feast, as he liked to call it—slurped down whole by devotees in pursuit of the perfect aftertaste, where grains of pearl grit were just a part of the sea's great gift, a sign of authenticity, and a small price to pay for a true connoisseur.

A true connoisseur like Jake.

She tipped the canister and dumped the bits and pieces, the glass refuse of her art, into a Ziploc.

Then she slipped the bag into her purse, doused the workbench light, and went to fetch their dinner.

ABOUT THE AUTHOR

Toni Goodyear is a former journalist and freelance writer, winner of the North Carolina Press Association Award for feature writing. Other past careers include market research, public relations, ghostbusting (yes, really), managing data for clinical trials, and teaching university psychology. She holds a Ph.D. in Psychology from UNC Chapel Hill. Her short story, "Stuffed", appears in the Thanksgiving anthology *The Killer Wore Cranberry: Room for Thirds*. She has just completed her first cozy mystery, *Trouble Brewing in Tanawha Falls*, set in a craft brewery in Carolina's Blue Ridge Mountains.

ACCIDENT PRONE

by RF Wilson

Dappled shadows filled the parking lot of the Botanical Gardens. The late afternoon air was still warm, but a slight chill in the shade suggested that summer was coming to an end. More cars were leaving than arriving. Anthony looked in the rearview mirror, started the engine, and began to back slowly. Within seconds there was a gentle thump. In the mirror, he saw the other car at a right angle to his. He sat still for a moment, took a deep breath and got out.

The driver was a young woman, twenty-something he figured. Cute, blond hair pulled back in a ponytail. Alarm spread over her face.

"Oh," she gasped. "I'm sorry, I'm so sorry. I didn't see you. I looked behind me and didn't see—"

Anthony held up his hand like a traffic cop. "It's okay. I don't think we were going fast enough to do any serious damage." It looked like his bumper had slid a foot or so along hers. Some dust had been rearranged. A small scratch on her little Ford matched one on his Honda.

"Oh, God, my father will kill me."

"You can hardly see anything's happened."

"My father will see it. He will. He just got this car for me a month ago."

Anthony thought about how he'd react if his daughter had a fender bender in a parking lot, whether or not he'd even know about it. His face flushed with anger thinking about the years that had gone by without hearing from her. He wrested his attention back to the present.

"Birthday present?" he asked.

"Graduation. I got my master's degree this spring."

"Congratulations. Oh. I'm sorry. My name's Anthony Sturgess." He held out his hand.

She took it. "Lucy Bennett."

"Well, Lucy, I don't think this is worth calling the police or the insurance companies over, do you?"

She shrugged.

"Looks like we backed into each other. No damage to speak of. Nobody at fault. I'm okay with this if you are. Why don't we pull our cars back in and relax for a minute? You look pretty upset."

As if he'd given her permission to cry, her tears came freely. She was shaking. He gave her half a minute to calm down, then said, "Can I buy you a cup of coffee? There's that cafe just down the street."

She caught her breath and said with a slight chuckle, "You know, I'd really like a drink."

"Me, too. But you probably don't need to be drinking and driving right now."

"I've got some vodka at home."

It sounded like an invitation.

"I'd like to follow you," he said, "make sure you get home alright. You're still shaky."

"No, that's—"

"It's no trouble. Really."

She shrugged. "Okay, if you want."

Her apartment was a few blocks away in what he assumed was student housing with the misleadingly bucolic name of Magnolia Gardens on a wooden sign in disrepair. An end unit in a four-unit yellow brick building edged with untended shrubbery. He parked near her, got out and followed her to her door.

"You okay?" he asked. "I really think if you don't tell your father, he won't notice. But, I tell you what. I think those scratches will rub out. I've got some polish at home. What if I come over tomorrow morning and see what I can do?"

"You don't have to do that."

"I know. But I'd like to."

She opened her door. "You want to come in? Have some of that vodka?"

He stopped at the threshold and scanned inside. Fighting panic, he took a breath. It wasn't that the place was dirty, just disordered.

"You okay?" she said.

"Sure. I'm fine. Just got a little light-headed there."

While she was retrieving the vodka from the freezer, he fought the urge to gather up CD covers that had cascaded near a stereo system, pick up and fold clothes that had been tossed haphazardly around.

She returned with two rocks glasses, each with three fingers of clear liquid over ice. Vodka was not his drink of choice but it went down easily. She finished hers in a few gulps and went back to the kitchen, returning with the bottle.

"This is taking the edge off," she said.

He felt his own edginess slipping away. "You probably don't want to overdo it."

"Now you sound like my father."

He winced. "Sorry."

"That's okay. He's not a bad guy. Just a little overprotective." She wobbled some as she stood up. "I feel like crap. I'm going to take a shower."

"Okay, I'll go."

"Oh, I'll just be a minute. You can stay." She tottered some more but made it to the bathroom without incident, carrying what was left of her second drink.

While she was gone, he endured a growing uneasiness with the room's disarray. A phone in another room rang several times. According to his watch, she hadn't been gone more than ten minutes when she returned, hair dripping, dressed in a silky, kimono-like robe, smelling of soap. There was a time when he could have named the fragrance.

She poured herself another inch or so of booze and stood by the front window drying her hair. The late afternoon sunlight revealed she was wearing nothing under the flimsy garment.

"You had a phone call," he said.

She went into her bedroom, returning with a cell phone to her ear. "God, I wish he'd quit calling," she said, as she flipped the cover shut and threw the offending appliance into a drawer.

"I probably should go," he said.

"No, really. Stay. I can use the company."

"I believe you are, as they say, in your cups."

"'In your cups.' What does that mean?"

"It means you're drunk."

"Oh, not so much. Besides, I don't have to go anywhere." She leaned against him on the couch, holding a glass. "You don't have to go yet, do you? This has been such a crappy day."

He put an arm around her shoulder. "Hey, hey. We're gonna fix it. It's gonna be all right."

"It's not just the accident," she said. "I just broke up with my boyfriend. Two nights ago. I found out he'd been sleeping with an old girlfriend. The whole time we were going out."

He pressed his mouth against her wet, fragrant hair. She lifted her tear-stained face towards his. They kissed.

* * * *

Afterward, in her bedroom, she said she hoped he didn't think she was a slut. She'd never done anything like that, spontaneous sex with a stranger.

"If it makes you feel any better, I don't do this much either. Sex with a stranger," he said, but did not add, "young enough to be my daughter." He felt an ache in his chest, sadness replacing anger as he thought about the girl he hadn't seen in nearly twenty years. "Now I really ought to be going."

"Love 'em and leave 'em, huh? Or, is it, wham bam, thank you, ma'am?"

He laughed, embarrassed.

"It's okay," she said. "Really. I know this wasn't on your calendar for today. You've been really nice about...the whole thing."

"I'll come back tomorrow and rub that scratch out. It'll clean up. At least so your father won't notice it right away. If he does, you just say you don't know how it happened. You noticed it one day when you were leaving a parking lot."

"You don't have to come back."

"No, really. I'd like to."

She was slipping on the kimono when her phone rang. She looked at the caller ID and shook her head.

"It's him, my boyfriend, *ex*-boyfriend. Again. He hasn't quit harassing me since I told him we were over."

Anthony pulled on his shoes. "Do you feel safe?"

"You mean, do I think he'd actually hurt me? No, but I've seen him outside some of my classes. He'll be, you know, just standing there, leaning against a tree, looking at me." She shivered. "And there will be these calls where there's nobody on the other end. Creepy."

"He's stalking you. That's serious stuff."

She began to cry again.

"I guess I could stay a little bit longer."

* * * *

On Monday, Anthony kept to his workday routine, rising at 6:30 sharp. His pulse rate was 132 when he ended his workout at 7:00. After showering, his heart had slowed to sixty beats per minute. He dressed, ate a bowl of granola with blueberries and sliced banana, took his vitamins with orange juice, and was out of the door at 7:35, picking up the newspaper from the driveway on his way to the car. He pulled into spot #7 in the office parking lot at 7:52 and was hanging his suit coat on the rack at 7:54.

The headline on the front page of the Mountain Section read, WOM-AN FOUND DEAD IN CAMPUS AREA APARTMENT. Her name was Lucy Bennett. She was a graduate student, twenty-three years old. Anthony read the article closely for other details. According to the paper, the police didn't know the cause of death. He knew that may or may not have been true, that the police often withheld information in the course of an investigation.

When his phone rang, he felt intruded upon.

"Mrs. G. on two," the receptionist said.

He heard the slight chuckle in her voice. "Thank you, Karen," he sighed before picking up, prepared to talk to the woman known around the office as the client from hell. She had been bringing her taxes to the company for twenty years, and Anthony had been her accountant for the last five. "Yes, Mrs. G.," he said, closing his eyes. As expected, she launched into her litany of woes and complaints. He knew them by heart, most of them about her children stealing her money and altering records so no one could tell. Several times, he'd asked her, "If no one can tell, how do you know they're doing it?"

While she was droning on, his mind drifted to the idea of calling the police, although he didn't know what he could tell them. The girl's boyfriend, ex-boyfriend, had been harassing her with calls, but the police could tell that by looking at her cell phone. They might not know that the guy had also been stalking her.

"Mr. Sturgess?" Mrs. G. asked.

"Oh, yes, Mrs. G. You were saying?" While the woman continued her catalog of misery, he thought that if he did call the police, he'd have to describe his afternoon of drinking and sex with Lucy Bennett.

By the time he returned his attention to his client, he had decided against contacting the authorities. If they connected him to the dead girl, they would come to him.

At 4:55, he backed up the files on his computer. At 5:00, he stood and put on his suit coat. A traffic snarl on Merrimon Avenue slowed him down, and he didn't get back to the condo until 5:25, seven minutes off schedule.

Inside, he exchanged outside shoes for slippers. After a stop in the bathroom, he made his way to the bedroom where he hung up his jacket. He tossed the shirt into the laundry basket, hung up the trousers and put on his black warm-up suit. In the kitchen, he poured a generous shot of Scotch, added a splash of water and a twist of lemon, and shook his head, wondering how someone could prefer vodka. The chicken fettuc-cine dinner in the freezer looked good. He set the oven for 425°, took his drink into the living room, switched on the TV, and sank into his reclining chair.

This was his favorite time of day. Nothing to do but watch the news and sip his drink. In a few minutes the oven would be ready and he would put the meal in. The oven would signal that the chicken was done in time for *Wheel of Fortune*. That would be followed by *Jeopardy*, and then he would get on the computer, check email and the stock market until nine, when *Justified* came on. He'd be in bed by 10:10.

At 6:50, he took his dinner from the oven and removed the foil cover to let it cool. As he was preparing the TV tray, there was a knock at the door. It seemed to him that any time anyone came around for this or that, Girl Scout cookies or some damn cancer drive, he was just about to sit down to dinner. The knock was repeated, louder. He opened the door to a couple, a black man and a white woman.

"Anthony Sturgess?" The man flipped open an ID wallet.

"Yes, sir?"

"Detective Thomas, Asheville Police Department. This is Detective Matheson."

The man wore a crisp, white shirt under his neatly-pressed brown suit. The knot on his tie was taut. The woman's dowdy blue suit didn't completely hide her decent figure. Nice legs. She wasn't as meticulous as her partner—the blouse under the suit a little wrinkled, a spot on the skirt.

"How can I help you officers?" he asked. Best to be polite, though visitors would make a shambles of his evening.

"We'd like to ask you a few questions, sir," Detective Thomas said. "Do you mind if we come in?"

He did mind. He'd have to reheat his dinner if not throw it out, and he'd probably miss *Wheel*, but he didn't suppose he had much of a choice. He invited them in, asking them to change their shoes for slippers that were lined up near the door.

"They're disposables," he said. "You won't catch anything."

They took seats on the couch and declined his offer of coffee.

Anthony sat in the armchair across from them. "What's this all about?"

Detective Thomas looked in a small notebook he was carrying before asking, "Mr. Sturgess, do you own a blue 2007 Honda, license plate…"

As the policeman recited the plate number, Anthony knew it was a rhetorical question on their part.

"Yes, I do."

"Do you know this woman, sir?" Thomas said, leaning toward Anthony with a photograph of the girl. It wasn't a new shot, but there was no mistaking her.

"Yes. If it's who it looks like. I met her Saturday." He said it matter-of-factly although he could feel sweat gathering under his arms and at his neck. "We had a little scrape in the parking lot of the Botanical Gardens. Why?"

"Do you know the woman's name, sir?" Thomas asked.

"Lucy…Lucy…" He was surprised he couldn't remember her last name. "I'm sorry, that's all I can remember. Lucy something."

"Lucy Bennett. She was found dead in her Magnolia Gardens apartment yesterday morning," Thomas said. "And your car was outside her apartment Saturday afternoon."

"If you saw her Saturday, you may have been one of the last people to have seen her alive," Matheson said.

"You think I know something about her…death?" He hated that he couldn't control how fast his heart was beating.

"Right now we're collecting information. Like Detective Matheson said, we believe you may have been one of the last people to see her alive. What happened after this accident?"

Anthony bit his words. "Well, like I said, it was just a bump. Nothing that needed the police or anything. But she was pretty shook up." He took a deep breath, calming himself. "I offered to buy her a cup of coffee. She said she'd rather have a drink. So I followed her home to be sure she was okay and she invited me in."

There was another pause until Thomas said, "And then? After she invites you in. Did she have that drink?"

"She poured us each a vodka. All she had, she said. I'm a Scotch drinker, myself, but, when in Rome, you know?"

"And then what happened?"

"We talked some and I said I had to be going. As I was about to leave, her phone rang but she ignored it. That happened a couple of times and she'd just look at the caller ID. She said it was her boyfriend. Or rather, ex-boyfriend. She'd found out he'd been cheating on her, and she didn't want to talk to him. Said he'd been hounding her ever since she told him they were through and that he was following her around. She started crying again. I told her I'd come back Sunday to rub out the scratch."

"And that was it?" Matheson asked. "You had one drink with her and you talked for a while."

"We had another drink."

"And then?"

He'd thought about this. They hadn't said who had seen his car. If it was a nosy neighbor or a surveillance camera, they might know how long it had been there. And there were tests they could do on her and, after all, there was no crime in it.

"We had sex. Her idea."

There was a pause. Anthony's face was flushed, his hands sweaty.

"Mr. Sturgess, do you know how old Ms. Bennett was?" Matheson asked

"Early twenties, I supposed." He felt heat rising in his face.

"Twenty-three. And how old are you?"

Anthony looked at the detective, thought she could probably lose ten, fifteen pounds. "Forty-four. Yes. I know. I am old enough to be…to have been her father. It is unseemly. But I wanted to be sociable. She was very upset. I didn't want to say, 'Sorry, see you around.'"

"Yes. Very thoughtful of you, Mr. Sturgess," Matheson said. "Was the sex consensual?"

"You mean, did I rape her?" Anthony felt his heart beat faster, was afraid he might lose control. It never occurred to him this would be an issue.

The officers looked at him without expression.

"Yes, it was consensual. She actually initiated it. Or, at least made herself very available."

"She'd just broken up with her boyfriend. She'd found out he'd been fooling around on her?" Matheson said.

"That's right."

"So she had a little revenge sex with you."

"Could be," Anthony said, although he harbored the notion that there had been some mutual attraction.

The detectives asked about Anthony's defunct marriage, his work, what he did with his free time, until Thomas said, "OK. Just to be sure we have this right. You bumped into each other. You go back to her place. You have a couple of drinks. You have sex. That it?"

He knew how bad it sounded. "She obviously wanted to have sex. She was cute. I'm a red-blooded guy. Why not?"

"Okay, Mr. Sturgess. I think we get it. You took advantage of the situation."

"I went with the situation."

"Yes," Matheson said. "The situation."

"What time did you leave?" Thomas asked.

"Eight, eight-thirty, as best I recall."

"As best you recall," Matheson repeated like a Myna bird.

He thought that she really should have gotten that spot out of her skirt before she'd come to work.

"You said you were going to go back to her house on Sunday to rub out the scratch. Did you do that?"

Anthony wondered how this would be received. "No. I was afraid, you know, I didn't want to give her ideas."

"Ideas," Matheson said.

"You know, that there was anything other than…"

The officers let that hang in the air, until Matheson said, "Other than a one-night stand."

Anthony's face hardened. "Yes."

"Back to the boyfriend," Matheson said. "Did she say anything about him getting physical with her?"

"No. She said she didn't think he'd hurt her."

"Some women like that, though, especially during sex, men getting rough with them."

"I didn't get rough with her, if that's what you're getting at." His hardened face turned into a glare.

The detectives looked at each other. Thomas said, "I guess that's about it. You're not planning to leave town anytime soon, are you?"

"No."

"Good. While Lucy Bennett's death is still under investigation, let us know if you do. Plan to leave town, that is."

"So, I am a suspect."

"As we said, you may have been one of the last people to see her alive. We may want to talk with you later."

After the officers had gone, Anthony threw out the used slippers, ran the vacuum, tossed his dinner in the garbage. Although he believed food tasted better when cooked in the oven, he put a new meal in the microwave to save time. He'd already missed *Wheel* and most of *Jeopardy.*

* * * *

The next few weekends were cold and rainy. He got antsy sitting around. Two Scotches in the evening became three, sometimes four. He missed some of his regular TV shows, stayed on the computer longer. There were days he didn't arrive at the office until after eight—before most of his co-workers but out of character for him—and mistakes began appearing in his work. Finally, one Friday the forecaster said the next day would be clear and warm, a perfect fall day. He felt blood pulse in his veins in anticipation.

The next morning was sunny and breezy. With a bottle of water and an apple, he drove to a park outside Hendersonville. He backed into a space near the entrance at 9:51.

He checked his watch at 11:23. Nothing of interest had caught his eye. It was close to lunchtime and he was getting hungry. As he put the car in gear, a pretty blond woman in a little Chevy drove into the parking lot. She found a space about ten cars down the row, got out and walked past him. Early twenties, he guessed. Like Lucy. Hard to tell about her figure in the sweats she was wearing. Her hair was pulled back into a ponytail.

When she was out of sight, he started the Honda and moved so he was one car width away from the Chevy, on the opposite side of the lot. He pulled straight in. When he looked in the rear view mirror, he could not see her car but when he turned his head, there it was. The angle was just right.

He rolled down the windows and adjusted the seat back. It could be a long wait.

ABOUT THE AUTHOR

RF Wilson lives and writes in Asheville, North Carolina, using the backdrop of the Blue Ridge and Smoky Mountains and his thirty years' experience in the addictions field to inform his writing. His current novel, *Killer Weed*, is available on Amazon Kindle and will soon be available in paperback from Pisgah Press.

ICE CREAM ALLURE

by E. B. Davis

The August night I broke into Conner's Creamery, I had worked a full shift, said goodnight to my staff and closed the restaurant. At least some of my hours were alibied. I changed my black polyester shirt for the white uniform shirt I'd stolen in case passersby spotted me in the Creamery's large front windows. I wanted to look as if I belonged there, one of the store's chosen few, working long hours to ensure tasty pleasure for public consumption.

My wait-service shoes squished disappointment with every step I took on the hot concrete sidewalk. Designed for ambulatory work, the shoes epitomized my life situation. Managing a restaurant demanded long, late hours, ones I thought I'd left behind. Days of wearing suits and high heels, crafted by designers for sitting, were gone. I remembered the distinctive clicking sound of success my heels used to make as I strode. Now, I trudged on the sizzling sidewalk in clodhoppers.

In the changing and downsized newspaper industry, I'd been laid off from *The Charlotte Dispatch*, bringing me full circle to my humble beginnings. I had waitressed most of my life. During the day, I'd taken my journalism degree and then written for years as a member of the food section staff before attaining my dream job—restaurant critic. I'd worked so hard.

My family attended my college graduation, a momentous occasion since I was the sole college graduate. The name on my degree: Carlotta Giovanni. Dad and Uncle Warren spent time in the joint for their numerous B & E escapades, robbing from the rich to fund the family. Fortunately, they were free on graduation day.

Because of our sordid reputation, I'd written my column under the name Carlotta Jones. More fool me, I'd worked hard—too hard to have a ten-year setback. Anger flashed through my nerves like lightning. Powerless to change my circumstances, I'd planned tonight's B & E to satiate my pent-up frustration.

Conner's Creamery created the best ice cream in Charlotte. This past spring, I'd reported on the top three local ice cream stores. After devising a rating system and sampling ice cream from all the local vendors, I'd published the results in my column. Conner's bested the best with its silky texture, rich denseness, and flavor depth. Had it been available to buy at another store, I might have restrained my criminal proclivities.

Columbian Calypso induced images of my mother's kitchen where coffee perked on cold mornings, seducing me with reminiscences of security and home welcoming. The flavor held no bitterness of the liquid brew. One taste of Roasted Almond Fudge had sent shivers to my nether regions. A hint of cinnamon perhaps to tickle the erogenous zones? Deep Throat Chocolate's richness made me groan with pleasure, licking and swirling the flavor over my tongue while I closed my eyes to concentrate on its smoothness. Going to Conner's Creamery seemed like entering an orgasmatron from Woody Allen's *Sleeper*.

Ryan Conner. I'd never forget him. He'd called me for dates after my review, saying he'd spotted me when I was in his shop sampling flavors. Knowing how I reacted to his frozen concoctions, I wondered what he'd seen, wondered if I'd embarrassed myself. Because he wanted my review to be impartial, he had waited until my contest results were published before asking me out.

I appreciated his concern and ethics, but I had turned down the dates because I feared a future conflict of interest. What a fool! Had I known *The Charlotte Dispatch* planned on kicking me onto the tarmac, I would have gladly gone out with the dreamy Mr. Creamy, who I suspected knew all about teasing erogenous zones. Ice cream was his art, and his art was culinary seduction. If only I had accepted his dates.

Conner's Creamery had called to me all summer, drawing me to its front windows lit by cool LEDs highlighting luscious tubs of cold perfection, but I couldn't step inside the store. If dishy Ryan were there, he'd see me in my polyester uniform and squishy shoes. It was too much of a comedown. Would he feel like taking out an insignificant restaurant manager instead of a sophisticated and industry-powerful restaurant critic? I doubted it.

The memories of ice cream temptations and Mr. Creamy remained, living inside and plaguing me. The heat of the Charlotte summer had continued for weeks. Every day I longed for the cold, lusted for the taste, and wondered if Ryan would remember me. Would he scoff at my decline in the food industry? The ice cream and its creator filled my senses, intensifying and overriding all rational thought. Reduced to basic impulses, I was losing control.

Unrequited passion fueled me to find a solution. With my diminished status, Ryan would no longer desire me, and if I couldn't have Ryan, I'd abandon myself to his creation. It took a few days, but I formed a plan, watched the store on my days off, noting when his white-clad personnel came and went. One day I noticed a staff member roll a container full of soiled-white uniforms to a commercial laundry's truck parked behind the store. I stole a shirt from the container two days later. At home, I washed it to unblemished brightness.

Whenever Ryan appeared in my view of the store's windows, I'd quiver at his bulging arm muscles exposed by his white short-sleeved shirt. His arms worked the ice cream, digging with his scoop, tracking through its texture, and leaving waves of frozen cream as a wake. I licked my lips and imagined kissing him. Seeing him made me pant. It was time to stop watching.

* * * *

I tucked Dad's tools into the pocket of my skirt. He wouldn't miss them because the state of North Carolina once again provided his accommodations. My other equipment was folded neatly into a fanny pack wrapped around my waist.

The dim streetlight illuminated my walk through the steamy night, but as I neared the Creamery, I ducked into an alley and snuck to its backdoor. I picked the lock with ease using my hearing and tactile senses to release the mechanism. The mechanical and electronic skills my dad taught me helped, but sensory detail, my forte, contributed far more to successful lock picking.

In the backroom of the store, I opened my fanny pack and put on plastic gloves and a plastic cap, tucking my black curls inside its elastic border. Mr. Creamy would have no trouble with the Board of Health from this burglar. I would do no harm to this talented man's business, nor leave forensic evidence.

From the darkness, I peered through the doorway to the front of the store where the delicious frozen treats awaited me. Surrounded by the LEDs, they glowed in colors like a kaleidoscope. Armed with a handful of wooden taster spoons, I took step after squishy step into the front room. I lifted the plastic lids that covered four of the ice cream barrels and read their names; Butterscotch Dumpling, Caramel Caress, Dark Dutch and Pecan Pie. I would try them all. With Butterscotch Dumpling on my spoon, I opened my mouth, put the dollop on my tongue, and pressed it on the roof of my mouth, letting it melt before swallowing it. I tasted the buttery freshness and swooned. My knee bent and my calf lifted behind me as if I had been kissed by Mr. Creamy. Would he taste as good?

I tucked the spent spoon into my fanny pack, took another from the pack, and sampled Pecan Pie. The rich flavor of brown sugar and toasted pecans took me to a Thanksgiving Day during my childhood when my life was ripe with possibility. I swirled my tongue into its creamy melt and savored both taste and memory with closed eyes.

"I hoped you couldn't stay away—not in this heat," a low, vibrating voice said to me.

My eyes opened at the sound of Ryan's voice. I swallowed, closed my eyes again as my spirit sank—busted! Head lowered, I turned to face him. "I didn't mean any harm, I couldn't resist," I said, feeling his gaze bore into me.

"Why didn't you come—"

"I was ashamed," I said, mortified and caught with a sample in my mouth.

"I heard you'd gotten laid—"

"Don't say it. I lost my job in the cutbacks." How could I explain how diminished I felt?

"Carlotta Giovanni."

"You know?" A cold sweat broke on my brow. I thought my professional pseudonym had hidden my identity. I felt exposed.

"I made a point to find out everything about you. Are you going into your dad's profession?"

"No, this was an exception."

"You're more embarrassed about losing your job than B & E." It was a statement of truth but also a question.

"Yes." My voice was defiant. "Will you have me arrested?"

"That depends on you," Ryan said. He stepped closer and gazed into my eyes.

"I took precautions. You won't have to take responsibility for my weakness. I won't complicate your life. I haven't contaminated any product," I said to assure him, but my voice grew husky as he placed his hands on my shoulders, then traced my torso until his hands rested on my waist.

"I see you came prepared and succumbed to your desires. I've longed for you." His chest brushed mine, and he lifted my chin, forcing me to look him in the eyes. "When you wouldn't go out with me, I nearly lost my mind. I admit it. I'm damn glad you lost your job. Can we see each other now?" His lips were inches from mine. "You know the business," he hesitated, "inside and out."

And then he kissed me. My calf lifted again, and I swooned, melting into his arms. My body rumbled from my lips to my Creamy Crevice.

"The Pecan Pie tastes good on you. I want to taste more," he said.

"Can we try…Deep Throat?"

"Yes, a thousand times, yes."

I felt naked as I took two taster spoons from the packet, offering him one. Ryan lifted the tub of Deep Throat out of the freezer and descended to the floor taking me with him. Together we exposed ourselves to the rich succulent chocolate, savoring it on our comingled tongues and wallowing in our sensory pleasure. "Sometimes you have to surrender," he said. We sat on the floor satiating our desires, our passion melting ice cream and whisking creamy puddles of love.

The next morning we awoke early still lying in each other's arms on the floor. Stains of many varieties spotted our white uniforms. We faced each other unashamed of the evidence of our lust.

* * * *

The restaurant manager agreed to see me after I used my journalism pseudonym and reminded him of the rave review I'd written a few months ago. When I arrived at the restaurant toting an insulated Conner's Creamery sample kit, his bushy white eyebrows rose. I removed two pint-sized tubs of ice cream and placed them on his kitchen's counter. "What's all this?" he asked.

"Buying Conner's Creamery ice cream for your dessert menu and using them in your recipes will increase sales. Your dessert menu relies heavily on International flavors," I said.

"But that's what people want." He gestured with his hands denying my pitch.

"That's not all they want," I said with a seductive smile. "A regional favorite creates intimacy and balance, allowing patrons to choose depending on how they feel. Conner's ice cream, a hometown creation, provides sensuality." His eyebrows narrowed with skepticism.

"Let's try a sample because I can see you don't believe me."

The ice cream had softened enough during our discussion to be just the right consistency. I took out two sample spoons and gave one to him.

"First, notice how the ice cream resists the spoon," I added, "like a woman trying to resist seduction." I dug the wooden sample spoon into the tub, prompting him to do the same. The ice cream was hard enough to fight back. "But with just a gentle tug, it can be penetrated." I tilted my head and smiled, lifting the corners of my mouth. "Spooning like lovers do, and every dip like caressing a lover's back." I drew the spoon across the frozen delight, making it crest into a creamy curl. "But even though it's hard, its texture is smooth. So much like a man."

His eyes were trained on my face, and his mouth hung open. But then he closed his mouth around the spoon and tasted. "And the texture melts into a sensual soft cream." I slid the sample into my mouth. "Just like lovers respond to a warm touch. The taste is rich and full. It satisfies and satiates as favorite lovers do." I closed my eyes to the view of his surprised eyes and let the sample melt in my mouth before I swallowed.

"Ahhhh," I said. "This flavor we call Deep Throat. It's a jungle-rich chocolate flavor that singes with heat." I opened my eyes and smiled at the restaurant manager.

"What flavors do you recommend?" He gulped and slowed his breathing.

I named a few of our bestselling flavors and then recommended some that best blended into sauces, a groundbreaking tactic few chefs had tried.

He bought fifteen gallons.

I placed the tubs back into my sample kit and gave him my business card. "Let me know when you're running low or if you want to try our seasonal favorites."

"Thanks, I'll do that. Maybe we can sample more flavors." A hopeful look crossed his face. He read my card. "Oh, you're a family member. Carlotta Conner."

"Yes, my husband and I own Conner's Creamery. We take pride and pleasure in our work."

He smiled. "Yes, I can see that you certainly do."

"We know the effect of our ice cream, and I can assure you that when it's on your menu, romance will follow."

I headed for the door. My designer suit form-fitted my figure and my high heels clicked on the floor, their distinctive sound the ring of success. I'd call the order into Ryan from my air-conditioned car before driving to the next restaurant.

Our newest flavor, created on our honeymoon, would interest the manager. We called it Sexolicious.

ABOUT THE AUTHOR

E. B. Davis is a member of the Short Mystery Fiction Society, Sisters in Crime and its Guppy and Chesapeake subchapters. Her short stories have appeared in online magazines and in print, including the Shaker of Margarita anthologies. "Lucky In Death" appeared in *Chesapeake Crimes: This Job is Murder*, and "The Acidic Solution" was published in *He Had It Coming. Fishnets*, a Guppy anthology released by Wildside Press, included her short story, "The Runaway." The next Chesapeake Chapter anthology, *Chesapeake Crimes: Homicidal Holiday* will include her historical short story, "Compromised Circumstances."

BOOMERANG

by Bonnie Wisler

Harry Wellington III struggled out of his Range Rover into the hot sun, leaned on his cane, and wiped his brow. Putting out a cigarette under his foot, he steadied himself then headed into the Gentleman's Club. A strip club was not where most folks would think of going on a beautiful Sunday afternoon, but this Sunday was his birthday. And audition day. As one of the Club's most generous patrons, he often received invitations to watch private auditions. What better way to celebrate his special day?

Several young ladies in stilettos, tight shorts and low-cut tank tops were waiting inside the dimly lit club when he arrived. Two giggled and smoked in the corner, one texted, and the fourth, wearing jeans, her blonde hair in a ponytail, looked too young for a place like the Gentleman's Club. He didn't have high hopes for this group to have much stage presence.

But when the blonde—Lacy Jane, she said her name was—took the stage, he changed his mind. She stripped down to a thong bikini, shook out her hair, and executed suggestive pole acrobatics that Harry had only dreamed of watching.

"OK, ladies. You three can leave. You're hired," the manager said, pointing to Lacy.

"Thanks so much, boss!" she exclaimed. "And thank you, Mr.... what is your name, sir?"

"Harry Wellington. But honey, you can call me Uncle Harry," he said, taking in every luscious square inch of the half-naked Lacy. *Young, but certainly not naïve*, he thought. "Only my favorite girls call me Uncle Harry, and I have a feeling you will be one of my favorites." He pulled a wad of money out of his pocket and tucked a hundred-dollar bill in her thong. "Remember to keep that on, honey. I don't want you to be locked up for causing a riot."

"Well now," she said, glancing down at the money, "Ben Franklin is one of my heroes, and I do believe *you* will be one of my favorite customers." She gave him a long kiss, sending shock waves from head to toe, arousing long-sleeping parts. "One more thing, Uncle Harry. Do you know where a girl like me might be able to find a nice place to call home?"

Harry certainly did; opportunity was a good friend of his. It seemed that he and Lacy were made for each other.

* * * *

Luther Small was in love. Lacy Jane didn't belong here at the Gentleman's Club; she was too sweet and too pretty to be dancing for men for money. He knew she went behind the curtains with those men, but she did whatever it took to take care of her sick mama and he admired her for it. For months he'd been trying to get up the nerve to ask her out. If his buddies were around it would be different. But the work release program had made it difficult for him to run with the same crowd, cutting off his connections and his courage.

Sweat beaded and dripped from Luther's brow as he worked over the steaming stove in the Club's kitchen making hot sandwiches and wings. His heart lifted when the kitchen doors swung open and Lacy Jane sashayed in, wearing a short turquoise robe. Her blue eyes, accented by bright blue eye shadow and heavy eyeliner, excited him.

"Hey sugar—look what that gentleman from up north gave little ol' me for a lap dance. Wow, if I keep this up, I'll be able to call that nursing home in Charlotte and get Mama moved in real soon." She blew him a kiss, grabbed a handful of pretzel rods, and disappeared back into the smoke and noise of the strip club.

And if I got a job that paid real money, I could help you, he thought as he dropped a basket of wings into the fryer. "I love you, Lacy Jane," he said under his breath, wondering how she could stay so upbeat and happy while doing such demeaning work, but that's what made her so special.

The kitchen door swung open again. "Luther honey, would you drive me to the garage to pick up my car later?"

"Anything for you, Lacy Jane."

* * * *

The morning sunlight was always a shock after leaving the dimly lit bar. Luther was tired after a long night in the kitchen but eager to spend time with Lacy Jane. "How about we go to your place and I cook you some breakfast first?

"That sounds yummy. You smoke?"

"Depends what you're smoking," he said with a chuckle. His smile widened as she pulled a baggie of pot from her purse. He wanted to kiss her right there in the parking lot, but didn't have the nerve.

A quick stop at the grocery store gave him all the ingredients he needed for this to be his lucky day: bacon, eggs, bread, and rolling paper.

"Whoa—this is some place, Lacy!" Hardwood floors with a white fluffy rug in front of the fireplace, eat-in kitchen, and a lake view. His confidence faded. Maybe Lacy would laugh at him for even thinking he'd have a chance with her. But watching her role a joint, he felt better. He needed a hit bad.

"Isn't it great? Uncle Harry, you know Harry, the old guy with the cane that comes to the club all the time? The whole building is his, so he gives me a special deal." She lit the joint and took a long hit before handing it to Luther. "I'll stir up some bloodies while you make breakfast. This will be so much fun!"

A couple of hits were all Luther needed to feel comfortable and cocky. Stoned with Lacy in her apartment—he was in heaven. He took another hit and moved behind Lacy, kissing her silky shoulder, her neck, inhaling her sweet flowery scent as she leaned back against him.

He didn't even mind, leaving her room hours later, that the groceries were still in the bag on the counter.

* * * *

Harry pulled the Range Rover into his reserved spot at Lacy's apartment complex. Glancing in the rear-view mirror, he smoothed his silver hair, and popped a blue pill. What started out as one afternoon a month to "collect" from Lacy had quickly turned in to an almost-daily addiction. His step quickened as he approached Lacy's apartment and heard smooth, sultry jazz emanating from within. He raised his silver cane and gently tapped on her door.

"Hey, Uncle Harry," she purred, as she opened the door a few inches to reveal a shapely naked leg. "Want to play doctor today?"

His eyes consumed the sensual beauty before him, from her long legs to her low-cut, short candy-striped uniform. Lately, he felt like a schoolboy, consumed with thoughts of Lacy, day and night. In one step he was with her. His cane fell to the floor.

Their afternoon trysts were anything but routine, and Harry sighed heavily when he realized it was time for him to head home. "Here's a little something extra for that sick Mama you keep talking about. I'm still not sure if you're telling me the truth about her, but at my age, it doesn't matter. You're the best thing that ever happened to me, Lacy."

"Harry—you have to believe I love you—you're the best thing that ever happened to me too." Lacy rummaged through her purse and pulled out a DVD. "Here you go—I was thinking of you when I recorded this. But make sure you're alone when you watch it!"

Harry grinned down at his little vixen as he accepted the DVD. "If I didn't have a pre-nup that would land me in the poor house, I'd marry you today—you are the sweetest little southern belle I ever did meet." He pulled a fat money clip from his pocket, peeled off several hundreds, and slipped them into her pink bra.

* * * *

Monday. Luther's day off, and the day he and Lacy got together for his weekly fix of pot and sex with his darling. He found her in the lounge, touching up her lipstick. No one was looking when he took her arm, pulled her onto his lap to look into her crystal blue eyes. "Baby, what do you want for breakfast today? Pancakes? My special sausage?"

Lacy poked her lip out, so cute. "Oh, sweetie, I can't see you today. Harry is coming over. So sorry, you know I am."

Harry again...Luther couldn't disguise his disappointment. "You've been spending a lot of club time with that old man lately, and I'm getting jealous."

Lacy put her arms around him, her soft cheek against his throat. "Baby, you know I'm only playing up to old Harry for money to help Mama. It's you I really care about, but today's his birthday and I kind of promised."

"I thought *we* were an item and you were just using the old man to get money for your mama. Now you're spending more time with him than me. It's not making sense." He'd never cried in front of a woman, but he was about to lose it.

"No, Luther, don't be silly, it's not like that. Think about it. Harry's rich. Richer than you or I could ever hope to be. He owns half the city. He has no children. He doesn't have anyone else to spend his money on, so why shouldn't he help me and my mama? And he's harmless; he can't get it up any more. He says he'd marry me, Luther! We'd have it made then, wouldn't we?" Her big blue eyes gleamed. "Of course, there's the teeny weeny problem of the wife."

He was being stupid and selfish. This beautiful girl loved him, asked him to understand that she would do anything to help her mama. He wanted to help her in the worst way. The wife...the wife. Harry must not even *like* his wife, the way he dotes on Lacy. If Lacy *could* marry Harry...was that the answer? "Baby, I'll find a way," he said, regretting he'd shown her his jealous streak.

* * * *

Luther tugged on his baseball cap, pulling it low over his eyes. He slumped down in his parked car, waiting for the vintage blue Mercedes to park in front of Harry Wellington's large stone home. A steady rain provided the perfect cover for him. He felt hot and clammy, his clothes clung to his body. But he had to focus and wait for the blue Mercedes. That was his target. He was nervous, and his heart raced. He had to help Lacy Jane.

Getting rid of Mrs. Wellington would solve all their problems. It would open the door for Lacy Jane to marry Harry, get his money, take care of her mama, and still have plenty left over for the two of them. His sweet, pretty girl wouldn't have to work at the strip club any more, and the two of them would be set for life.

Guns and knives were not his style—too bloody, too violent. And he didn't want to go to any of his old drug buddies. Helping his pretty little princess was his job, his responsibility. And when Lacy Jane told him that Mrs. Wellington always parked her vintage Mercedes on the street because she couldn't back out of the driveway, he knew he could arrange an accident.

Headlights flashed in his rear-view mirror as a Mercedes, an older model, drove slowly past him and parked in front of the Wellingtons' house. Had to be the wife's car, that beautiful dark blue. Luther's heart raced and he swallowed hard. *A shame to damage that car, but the hell with that.* He started his engine, waiting for the driver's door to open. The windshield wipers smeared the glass, blurring his view. "C'mon, old lady, step out of the car...what are you waiting for?" Blood pounded in his head, his arms. He felt a surge of pride at his daring. Lacy Jane would be so proud of him. Finally, a large black umbrella emerged from the car, then a leg, and another. Adrenaline surged and he floored it.

"For Lacy Jane!" he yelled above squealing tires as his car raced toward the Mercedes, slammed into the body, and with a screech of metal, ripped the car door off its hinges. Something hit his windshield and bounced off. Glancing back he saw in the street—glistening in the rain, lit by the streetlamp—a silver-handled cane.

* * * *

Driving rain pelted down on Harry Wellington III, lying in the street next to his soon-to-be widow's blue Mercedes. As he took his last breath, his hand released its grip on a sodden envelope. A legal-sized envelope containing his ticket to a happier life with his sweet Lacy.

Divorce papers.

ABOUT THE AUTHOR

Bonnie Wisler is a member of Sisters in Crime and Romance Writers of America, and has participated in numerous writing groups. Her love of animals, nature, travel, and mystery is vividly reflected in her writing. Her first novel, *Count a Hundred Stars*, received five-star ratings from both *Foreward Clarion* and *Midwest Book Reviews*. Bonnie is retired from the federal government, works part-time for a major airline, and lives in Raleigh, North Carolina with her family.

CATCH YOU NEXT TIME

by Donna Campbell

Doreen set pork chops and butterbeans on the table and poured the tea. "Vern, come eat." A meat-and-three man, Vernon liked his big meal at noon.

She reached for the remote to mute the mid-day news until Vern could mumble grace, but a reporter caught her attention. The woman's blonde hair captivated her. Did she use Miss Clairol or L'Oreal?

The camera cut to a shot of a young girl about the age of Doreen's twins. Miss Yellow Hair's carefully pitched somberness cast a chill into the room. "Yesterday, ten-year-old Louise Hardwick of Pine Hollow vanished while retrieving her grandmother's mail. Grace Hardwick watched from the porch as her granddaughter walked toward the highway mailbox. She says she left her porch to answer the phone, but when she hung up, Louise had not returned. Linda Jenson is reporting from the scene."

Eyes riveted to the television, Doreen ignored the food shedding steam. Linda Jenson stood in the yard of a weathered dogtrot house. "Fear has gripped this rural community of Pine Hollow. One of their children has become the latest in a string of unsolved disappearances here in the Midlands. Little Louise was the apple of her grandmother's eye, a happy girl who loved horses and baton twirling. Her family asks for your help and prayers to return Louise safely to them." The camera focused on Mrs. Hardwick's devastated face as she begged for someone to bring her granddaughter home.

Four women and two little girls had vanished since spring. Louise made seven. Doreen thought of her twins, only a year younger than Louise. They were with Memaw, Vernon's mama, for the afternoon. Doreen knew they were safe with Memaw. No small woman, she could have worked the pro wrestling circuit. Thank goodness, the girls took after Doreen's side—blonde-haired and small-boned. She'd call after lunch and make sure they'd heard about Louise.

Vernon came to the table. She pointed at the television. "There's another one that's disappeared, a little girl over in Pine Hollow."

"Damn. That's what, maybe twenty miles as the crow flies?"

"About. Hush." A police sketch filled the screen—a man, about Vernon's age, maybe late thirties, with narrow eyes and high cheekbones like Elvis.

"Authorities ask that you call 911 if you see this man, believed to be driving a blue Ford pickup with a broken headlight on the right side. A neighbor saw this individual near the Hardwick home shortly before the child's disappearance."

She hit mute. "I don't want to hear any more."

"Best to know so you and the girls can protect yourself. Lock the screen doors and the deadbolts when I'm not here. I'll put the shotgun behind the coat rack. Just don't shoot anybody."

"It's an awful way to live, looking over your shoulder every minute."

"Ain't no use getting ill over it. Just use good sense. Where *are* the girls?"

"Over to your mama's. I got to get my hair cut and then go out to Kitchens Mill to Jeanine's. She's going to hem my new skirt. Memaw said she'd take the girls to Sears this afternoon and buy them something for back-to-school."

"That's good of her. Mama ain't going to let anybody near 'em. Hell, she scares me. You got any chow-chow to go with these butterbeans?"

"Sure. Let me get it."

Doreen pushed her dinner around with her fork. The picture of the man with the Elvis cheekbones had taken hold of her. She only ate because it was a sin not to.

Vernon gobbled his cobbler and retreated to his recliner for a nap. She cleared the table, but she could not clear her mind of the man, his narrow eyes, his ears too large for his head. He looked like the kind of man who would steal little girls. That poor grandmother.

Doreen called Memaw. The twins were fine. She'd heard the news. They'd take no chances.

Doreen dragged her worries with her into the shower. The man violated her peace of mind as he'd surely violated his victims. More than once she glanced nervously over her shoulder while she bathed.

She applied a little makeup. The laugh lines around her eyes seemed deeper than before. *Good thing I got Vernon. Gawd! What'll I look like at forty? Hell, just shoot me.* She'd had her share of suitors, not so long ago. She'd been hot stuff when she'd met Vernon.

She returned to the den where he still dozed. Before the twins arrived, the man in the chambray shirt had rocked some deep part of her. But their struggle to keep it all going—the fields, the fences, the pastures—had banked those fires. How long had it been since she and Vernon drove down a firebreak in the pine forest and made the truck rock and roll?

"Hon', where you working this afternoon, the hay field or the soybeans?" She wished he would throw in the towel and move them all to Greenville where the plants were hiring. Lately it had been a hardscrabble life. She liked to kick up her heels once in a while. She wouldn't mind being closer to the malls and the Walmart. Not much worth doing in the country.

"The hayfield. Just waiting 'til it cools off a bit. Junior's going to drive the truck." Hay had been good to them this year what with the horse farms spreading out from Aiken.

"I got to get these errands done, but if I get back in time, I'll drive while you boys load."

"That 'ud be good, sugar. Be safe. Keep your eye on what's behind you and lock your doors."

"Don't worry. No pervert would want me." Doreen half hoped he'd say something nice, like "I want you woman" or "Say what you will, but you're one fine looking hunk of womanhood"—anything but silence. Just a few years past thirty, she sometimes felt like sixty. Deflated, she pecked Vernon on his damp forehead and headed out.

Doreen locked the car doors, then relocked them, to be sure, before she pulled onto the road that wound between fields of wilted soy beans and cotton. She kept her eyes on the blacktop and the rearview mirror.

Geeze Louise! What would I do if I saw a blue Ford pickup? You'd think they could be more specific about that truck. Old? New? Half the state owns a damned Ford truck.

She'd never realized how empty the countryside was. Not a house to be seen until she got to Bebe's. It was lonesome here where the pine trees grew so dense they sucked in the daylight and made it disappear into black tunnels of straw and shadow.

She wished Vernon would get her one of those cell phones. She'd feel better driving around by her lonesome if she had one.

Doreen couldn't shake a feeling that passed over her—like someone had walked over her grave.

Oh God! Why in the world did I think that?

She made the sign of the cross, and then felt guilty about it. She was bedrock Baptist, but she'd seen folks on TV do it and found it comforting. It was the same as when her mother said, "Bread and butter!" if they were walking down the street and had to split on either side of a pole. Mama said it out of habit, and, Doreen suspected, superstition. Making the cross was like that—something she needed to do when the hair rose on the back of her neck, as it was doing now. By the time she reached the sign that read "Bebe's Bee Hive—Full Service Beauty Salon," her palms were drenched. She wiped them on an old tissue from her purse and parked the car.

Bebe had done her hair since her first highlights at fourteen. Doreen shoved open the swollen door on the cinder block building. It reeked of permanent wave solution and hair spray. "Hey, Bebe! I'm ready to get this hair cut! Make me beautiful, girl. Old age is chasing me and damned if it isn't winning." She plunked into the chair in front of the shampoo sink.

Bebe stood at the counter combing out what was left of Alma Poole's white hair. She laughed. "If you're expecting miracles you ought to go to church, but I'll do the best I can for you. You got time for me to touch up those roots?"

"I'm all yours long as you get me out of here before three. Getting my new skirt hemmed at Jeanine's. Vernon and me are going to his family reunion." Doreen picked up a magazine and flipped the pages.

"You know who that little girl is, don't ya', Bebe?" Alma said. Doreen looked up.

"Naw, Alma, who?"

"Elsie Powell's great-granddaughter, out at Little Springs. Wasn't her youngest daughter, Annie Alice, in school with you?"

Bebe held the comb over Mrs. Poole's thin crown of hair. "I don't think so. That girl was a few years behind me. Sorry to hear it."

Doreen put her magazine down and chimed in. "The noon report said they'd seen a blue Ford pickup not far from where she disappeared. Had a police sketch of some man, looked maybe late thirties or forty—dark hair, small eyes, kind of like the Hutto family around these parts. How come they can't tell us more about that truck? How many people you know drive a blue truck? They all look alike to me."

Mrs. Poole and Bebe agreed.

Bebe put her teasing comb down and looked at Doreen's reflection in the mirror. "My Janie swears someone followed her last night after her basketball practice. Said she thought it was a truck but wasn't sure cause of the rain. Every time she speeded up, whoever it was did too, and when she slowed down, same thing. Makes my hair stand up thinking about it."

Bebe rummaged in the drawer below the counter for a moment. She pulled out a silver pistol and laid it gently on the stained Formica. "Promise not to tell nobody. I'm not taking any chances, especially when J.W. isn't around." She carefully lifted the pistol for their inspection, then placed it back in the drawer, covering it with an old towel.

"Oh, crap!" Doreen gasped. "Bebe, you scared me to death with that thing. I just wish Vernon would get me a cell phone. I hate riding around in the middle of nowhere and can't even call someone for help."

"Well, don't fret it," chided Mrs. Poole. "No cell phone's going to help you out here. None of the cell towers are close. My girl Lonnie Sue's got one, but it don't work until she gets almost to Aiken. Save Vernon's money. Get yourself a baseball bat or a claw-foot hammer. Keep it under your seat where you can get it and put your faith in the Lord. That's what I do."

Doreen laughed. "I guess you're right."

The rattle and bump of a truck coming down the washboard road halted their conversation. Like triplets used to moving in unison, the three heads turned toward the door and waited, frozen. The intruder drove into the driveway and stopped. Doreen sensed Bebe reaching toward the drawer.

A truck door slammed shut. The three women sat as if suspended in time. No one breathed. When the shop door burst open Bebe slumped against the counter and breathlessly declared, "Holy crap, James William! You scared two years off my life. Don't you know every woman in the county is jumping out of her skin at the sound of a pickup truck, what with that pervert out there?" She gave her husband a withering look, joined by the others who glowered at him as fiercely as Bebe did.

Chastened, J.W. bowed his head. "Ladies, my apologies. I didn't think driving into my own driveway would scare you that way." He looked like a man carrying heavy news in his pocket. "You ought to be scared. I saw the deputy sheriff at the hardware store. They found that blue truck. It 'ud been ditched in a kudzu thicket at Miller's Pond. The sheriff's there taking prints. That little girl's clothes were stuffed back under the seat. No one knows what vehicle he's driving now. The deputy said they'd just gotten a stolen car report a few miles from the pond. He raced off like a cow with its tail on fire."

Doreen sighed a 'what can a body do about it anyway' sigh and checked her watch. Bebe was slow today. Doreen didn't want to be too late heading to Kitchens Mill. There wouldn't be time for her roots, no way. She felt guilty leaving Vernon with the haying. It was hard, hot work, but hay was their bread and butter. Maybe, if the haying was really good, they might manage a weekend trip to Branson, maybe fire up a little romance. They hadn't had much excitement since the twins were born. Most times they were too damn tired to feel excited.

Bebe misted Mrs. Poole with hairspray and walked her to the door. "You be careful, Alma. Call me when you get home. Make me feel better to know you're safe."

"I'll do that. Get yourself a hammer like I said."

Bebe turned to Doreen. "Let's get you shampooed. I got a new shampoo smells like oranges, brings out the blonde highlights."

The smell of citrus relaxed her but not enough to stop thinking about the man in the blue truck and the little girl who'd gone missing. Someone awful lurked in the kudzu shadows or waited out of sight where clay roads met blacktop. Just walking to the mailbox wasn't safe anymore.

Bebe sprayed Doreen's blonde bob and sent her on her way. Feeling rejuvenated, she drove toward Kitchens Mill, winding through the peach orchards. She'd get herself a bushel of Albertas if her friend Peggy's stand was open and make the girls a churn of ice cream on Saturday. She wanted really ripe peaches. That's what made a good churn.

Doreen turned into the little gravel lot at Peggy's and parked. She almost flung open her car door but hesitated, startled by the crunch of gravel. A battered green Chevy veered toward her, then braked to a hard stop, kicking up dust. Unnerved, she waited until the driver, a man, emerged from the Chevy and sauntered to the counter where Peggy stood. Doreen joined them. He doffed his Allis-Chalmers cap and wiped the sweat from his brow. She felt she ought to know him—he seemed so familiar. He looked like a country boy, a working man.

Doreen studied him. She wasn't thinking of the mid-day news, of the women and girls gone missing. She was caught up in the Southern game of "Who's your daddy and where do your people come from?" She ought to know his name and was embarrassed she couldn't call it.

She raised her hand in greeting. "Hey, Peggy. You sold enough peaches to get rich and leave that farmer of yours?" Peggy's husband was Doreen's second cousin once removed.

Peggy laughed. "Not yet. Just got to sell a thousand more bushel baskets and I can run off with the propane man to Dollywood. What's up with you, girl? Like your hair. Been out to Bebe's?"

"That I have. I'm heading out to Kitchens Mill." She cocked her head toward the man she thought she ought to know. "Afternoon. Hot enough, ain't it?" She was sure she must know his people. Doreen knew most of the folks in the county and who was related to whom. Vernon said she'd make a good Mormon. But she couldn't quite put the peg of this man with his cockeyed smile into its proper hole.

Impudently his eyes swept from her ankles to her bosom to her face. He gave her a leer no gentleman would ever give a lady. Doreen was insulted and unnerved. Worse, she felt a bit titillated. Good grief, was she *that* desperate to believe she hadn't lost her strut? She didn't need this crude man's attention. His rough hands made her think of grease pits and wrenches. She turned from his lewd gaze and toward Peggy, whose tight expression and raised eyebrows declared her disapproval.

"What can I help you with, mister?" Peggy's voice was all frost. Her arms tightly folded across her chest, her legs planted firmly apart, she made it clear that the man should transact his business and go. Doreen didn't doubt Peggy had a "guardian angel" like Bebe's hidden beneath the counter by the cash box.

The man took a step back. His eyes ogled Doreen's bosom and her face exploded scarlet when he said, "I'd like me some ripe peaches—two perfect ones. This is a peach stand, ain't it?"

Peggy didn't flinch. She plucked two unblemished Albertas from a basket, placed them in a small bag, and thrust them toward the man.

He took his time reaching for them. "How much I owe you?"

"Nothing, if all you want's them two. You better get 'em home before they get bruised." The man flashed a lecherous grin and strutted like a bantam rooster to his car.

Peggy and Doreen waited for the Chevy to pull away. The man leaned out the window and waved at them, a little four-fingered wave, like "La-de-da! Catch you next time," then accelerated slowly until the car disappeared around the bend.

"Well, I'll be," Doreen said. "Who in the world was that? He looked familiar—one of the Hutto clan maybe. They got some Indian blood. He's dark like them."

"Never saw him. Good riddance to bad baggage. What can I get for you?"

"I need a ripe peck. Gonna' make ice cream."

She wedged the peach basket into the back seat and turned the car toward Kitchens Mill. Once she lost sight of Peggy's, that lonesome feeling settled again into the front seat with her. She kept an eye on her rearview mirror and popped in a Shania Twain cassette to soothe her nerves. It was awful they were so poor they couldn't afford a car with a CD player.

Doreen checked her mirror as Shania sang "Feel like a woman!" A car behind her was coming on fast. She couldn't tell what color or what make, but it wasn't a pickup truck. Even though the sheriff had found that blue Ford, trucks still made her edgy. It's a shame they hadn't got the man. All those little girls and women. God knows what awful things he must have done to them.

When she reached the crossroads at Chapin's store, the car pulled within a few hundred feet of her. She turned left toward Jeanine's. A glance in the mirror confirmed she wasn't alone on the narrow road. The car had turned too. The sun threw a strong glare on her mirrors, so she couldn't be sure whether it was green or aqua blue.

Every time she looked, the car still tailed her, maybe two hundred feet or so behind. Nobody lived out here except Jeanine. The timber companies owned everything else. She wondered who it could be.

Doreen sped up a bit. So did the car. Anxiety plopped into the seat next to her. The turnoff onto the clay road leading to Jeanine's lane was just ahead. Her palms felt warm and moist. She turned onto the rutted clay and willed her mirror to be empty, but it wasn't. There was the car—green—she was sure of it. The man at Peggy's, his car was green. Maybe he lived out this way. She signaled her turn into Jeanine's long gravel drive that wound its way down the hill to the old farmstead. The driver—a man—doffed his cap and waved. She felt certain he was the man at the peach stand. She gripped the wheel a little tighter.

She hoped he'd go on down the road. As she jounced her way between stands of turkey oak and scrub pine hugging the lane, she saw in her mirror a flash of chrome, heard the sound of tires on gravel. The green car—coming up fast behind her, bursting around a bend, almost on her bumper. She recognized the man from the peach stand for sure. Anxiety grabbed the wheel and floored the accelerator. She took the last curve toward the house with horn blaring, again, and again. The car was right on her bumper until they lurched into Jeanine's dirt-packed yard where—Thank you, God!—where Jeanine was standing in her front door with an old double barrel pointed at the porch boards.

The man slammed his brakes, sending the Chevy skidding across the yard. He cut a tight circle around a pecan tree and headed out the way he'd come in, so fast the car fishtailed, spewing gravel. But somehow he managed a little wave of his hand—all four fingers waving one right after the other—like he was saying, "Gotta go! Catch you next time."

And, as if lightning had struck and illuminated all things, she understood why she felt she knew him—he was the man in the police sketch, the man in the blue Ford truck. She had no doubt he'd snatched that little girl. She rolled down her window and shouted, "For God's sake, Jeanine, call the sheriff! That's the man who kidnapped that little girl!"

The two women huddled with the shotgun in the locked house until the sheriff and a deputy arrived, sirens wailing. The sheriff dispatched the deputy to fetch Vernon and drive him back to Jeanine's. After draining Doreen of every detail she could remember, the sheriff had his deputy follow her and Vernon home.

Vern never let go of her hand. He wouldn't let her out of his sight. He'd never told Doreen that he loved her so much as he did in the hours after bringing her home. Vernon couldn't seem to say it enough. A lucky thing the twins stayed the night with Memaw.

* * * *

The sheriff called early the next morning. They'd caught the man—a drifter come up from Florida. He'd blown a tire and was riding on the rim when some deputies happened across him. They cornered him a few miles from Peggy's peach stand. Little Louise Hardwick's pink sneakers and blood-stained socks were in his knapsack. The sheriff hoped Doreen could ID the man.

Vernon drove her over to the county jail. The men in the lineup did not know who stood on the other side of the viewing window, but still, she was afraid she'd lose her breakfast when she saw him. "Number three. That's him. I'd know his eyes and those Elvis cheekbones anywhere." The truth, for sure. She suspected she'd see his face in her nightmares. Doreen and the sheriff watched as the men filed out. Number three paused and turned toward the mirrored wall. He grinned, and then lifted the fingers of his right hand—all four fingers waving one after the other—as if to say, "Gotta go! Catch you next time."

Doreen's knees trembled and her hands shook, but she stared right back and whispered, "Don't you just wish, you pervert—don't you just wish."

ABOUT THE AUTHOR

Donna Campbell is a member of the Greenville, South Carolina chapter of Sisters in Crime. Her stories and poems have been published in the South Carolina Writers' Workshop literary journals—*Catfish Stew* and *The Petigru Review*—since 2005. Pushcart Prize nominations have been given to two of her stories, "Under a Good Hat" in 2009 and "Shooting Stars" in 2013. She graduated with a degree in English from Clemson University and received her Master's in Education from Rutgers University. After many years of teaching English in New Jersey, she and her husband retired to South Carolina where she grew up.

THE FOURTH GIRL

by Karen Pullen

When the principal told me he wasn't going to renew my contract, I smiled numbly and slouched out of his office, saving my tears of humiliation for the walk home. Weeping, cussing, I almost didn't answer my cell phone.

"Reenie Martin?" Speaking in a crusty solemn voice, the man identified himself as a lawyer. "Your Aunt Peggy died. She's left you her entire estate—her house, her car, and liquid assets."

Life *is* fair! The universe *does* care! Visions of stock portfolios, a cottage surrounded by white picket fence, and a life far, far away from the New York City public school system danced through my head. I brushed away the tears of the recently-fired and shrieked with glee. Scooping up Mango, my orange tomcat, for a furry hug, I danced around my coffee/dining/desk table, bounced on the daybed that also served as my sofa, then rummaged through my tiny fridge for a beer, the closest I could get to bubbly.

OK, back up. I wasn't ecstatic about Aunt Peggy's death, but not saddened either, as our relationship consisted of a card exchange at Christmas. I lived in Brooklyn, she in North Carolina, and our paths hardly ever crossed. She was my father's much older half-sister. So this windfall, this unexpected bounty, wasn't accompanied by grief. Curiosity, mainly. What kind of life had she lived? What life would I be stepping into?

I was eager to leave New York. A, I couldn't afford to live here. B, nearly all my friends had married, moved to the suburbs, and produced two-point-one kids. C, my most recent romance had ended in a shouting match worthy of the Jerry Springer Show. (Did you know there's a Blackberry app that tells his wife his exact location—not his office on Broadway, where he's supposed to be working late, but a restaurant on West 43rd, where he's eating sushi with me? No? He didn't either.)

I'd come to the conclusion, based on personal experience, that any New York City man interested in me was either a cheater or a mouth-breather. But getting fired was the straw that broke this thirty-two-year-old's ties to the Big Apple. I shoved my clothes and books into a dozen boxes and called UPS for a pick-up. Said *adieu* to my studio apartment, a twelve-by-twelve space with one grimy window overlooking an alley of dumpsters. Slid Mango into his carrier, took the subway to Penn Station, and boarded a train for the twelve-hour trip to Raleigh, dreaming Martha Stewart fantasies of a real house. With a garden. Maybe even chickens. Martha has chickens. And goats. I could make cheese.

* * * *

"Why me?" I asked.

The crusty solemn voice belonged to a spare, white-haired man with a benign expression of lawyerly rectitude. "You were her only living relative, Reenie. She was once an English teacher, like you. She was adamant women should have financial independence."

I'd forgotten Aunt Peggy had been a teacher too. My concept of the size of her "estate" fizzled. "What can you tell me about her?" I could hardly wait to see my new house and let Mango out of his carrier, but this man had known my aunt for years, would know her friends, her life.

He tapped his lips then appeared to choose his words. "A very private person. You'll meet her friends; I'm sure they'll stop by. What are your plans for the house? Going to sell it?"

"I'm going to live in it."

He raised one graying eyebrow. "Indeed. Well then, welcome to Verwood." He handed me a set of keys. "Doors, garage, car. I transferred her bank account to your name. Sign here, please."

I scanned the form, a statement of my newly inherited assets. A house plus two acres at 601 Wiley Jones Road, a 2005 Toyota Camry, a bank account with a balance of $6,754.52. Not much. I'd have to get a teaching job. I shuddered.

* * * *

I wasn't used to driving, but there was so little traffic in Verwood that I felt no qualms about steering the Camry onto the highway and four miles later onto Wiley Jones Road. I passed three trailers before I saw 601's mailbox. A washboard driveway wound through vine-covered underbrush and towering pines.

And there was my house, one story with a crumbling front porch, neglected hollies growing up to a rusty tin roof, plywood covering a broken window. And out back, a tiny rough-board shed surrounded by a wire fence—a chicken coop!

I was beyond excited. My Martha instincts kicked in—this house could be *cute*. Mango meowed plaintively in the carrier. "Your ordeal is over. We're home, boy," I said, skipping up the steps.

Oh my. I'd landed in the 'seventies. Shag carpet so grimy you couldn't tell its original color. Flocked wallpaper. Avocado green sofa and chairs, the upholstery worn down to the foam. A dark room made darker by heavy brocade draperies at the windows. Mango began to explore, tentatively sniffing every square inch of that carpet. I counted seventeen candles burned down to wicks, and any number of dust-covered silk flower arrangements. But I couldn't stop smiling, so happy was I to have my own place. With a fireplace!

And a letter on the mantel, addressed to me:

Dear Reenie,

It gives me great pleasure to know you will be my beneficiary. I realized many years ago that teachers work very hard for little pay, even less status and no chance of advancement, so I am delighted you can benefit from my experience.

Twenty years ago I found another way to make money with little work and no stress, and I hereby bequeath it to you.

In addition to my cottage, you have inherited a home-based business that ticks along without much effort. It will generate enough income to pay your expenses if you live modestly. Five days a week, my girlfriends Connie, Fran, and Lilac arrive just before noon. Shortly thereafter, three clients appear at your door, one per girl, and each couple disappears into a bedroom. At the end of one hour, each client will hand you $50, tax-free, and depart, smiling. (They pay the girls separately.)

I hope you enjoy living in Verwood as much as I did. People are friendly but fortunately for me and now for you, they mind their own business. No one seems to care about my little lunchtime club, and that's the way my girls and their clients like it.

From this day forward, you'll be able to see a yellow school bus without shuddering.

Much love,
Aunt Peggy

My mouth dropped open: I had inherited a brothel.

My good-girl Methodist side was horrified, but Peggy's clever reminder of yellow-bus-dread hit home, making my pragmatic burned-out side think *What the hell! This could work.*

But what were the girls like?

* * * *

They showed up at 11:30 the next day, a Friday, and what astonished me was how ordinary they looked, like any forty-something women waiting on a Bronx subway platform. Lilac was a petite blonde with thick glasses, missing an incisor. Fran wore a long flowery dress that disguised her too-ample curves, while Connie, in purple skinny jeans, had lovely cheekbones and knock-knees. In no time we were chatting about their families, diets that didn't work, best store for shoes. And their clients.

"Each one's different," Fran said. "Some might say peculiar." She giggled, and her whole body rippled. "A regular schedule, the same ones each day of the week."

"We're picky," Lilac said. She was studying a Scrabble wordbook.

"What's today, Friday? My dentist. He likes to be scolded," Connie said. She'd changed into an eighties-style power suit, red lipstick, and heels. She took out a knitting project in blue yarn, "a sweater for a Siamese, to match its eyes." She told me she knitted clothing for pets and sold it on Etsy. She was saving to send her son to college.

Lilac looked up. "'Siamese,' that's an easy bingo." She explained that she played competitive Scrabble, and bingo meant a word that used all seven tiles. "My client today is the fire chief. We usually play a game after our feather frolic."

Feather frolic? My mind boggled.

Fran squeezed herself into a naughty nurse uniform "for the professor" and offered me a homemade toffee. Hard at first, the sticky candy melted in my mouth, leaving a hint of chocolate mint. "I sell them at the farmer's market," she said. "If there's any left!" She laughed, severely testing her costume's seams.

As they waited for their clients, they gossiped. Connie bragged that her son made the honor roll, and Fran said she ought to be proud, he was one fine boy. Lilac told a story about her dog humping the plumber who was replacing her garbage disposal. Connie knitted, Lilac studied word lists, and Fran nibbled, until *clonk clonk* went the doorknocker. I ducked into the kitchen, to watch from behind the door.

The first client was Fran's professor, a jockey-sized man with a goatee. He hung his tweed jacket in the hall closet and began to limp, whimpering with each step. *What a faker*, I thought.

Fran tugged up her red thigh-high stockings, tucked a stethoscope into her cleavage, stroked his cheek. "How're you doing, sweetheart?"

"I feel terrible, from head to toe, just terrible."

"Let's check you out. Exam room one." Fran sashayed down the hall to the bedrooms, beckoning him with a crooked finger to follow.

Clonk clonk, and the front door opened again. The dentist was a paunchy man with thick white hair, smelling of Old Spice. He planted himself in front of Connie, who didn't even glance up from her knitting but said, "Go to your room. You have been a very bad boy." Looking hang-dog guilty, he slinked down the hall. Connie slid a marker onto the needle and put her knitting away. She took a ruler from the closet and followed him, smacking the ruler against her palm and growling for him to hurry.

Lilac pushed aside the heavy brocade draperies, looked out the window. "Chief is always last." She poked inside a tote bag. "We could use some new feathers. Chief took a few home last week."

OMG. I closed the door. I'd seen enough. I spread a drop cloth over the kitchen floor. I'd decided to paint the kitchen's burnt orange walls and ceiling a creamy ivory. As I spackled and taped, I worried. Last night's heavy rain had proved too much for the rusted roof, and I'd dashed around putting pots under a half-dozen leaks. Clearly I needed a new roof. As far as beautification went, I'd whacked the hollies into submission. But my Martha-vision included paint, landscaping, better furniture, repairing windows, replacing heavy draperies with white sheers, grading the quarter-mile driveway, and a lot of fencing (for the goats I didn't yet have). Obviously I needed more income. I'd ask the girls what I should do.

* * * *

"Don't raise your prices," Lilac said. "Once Peggy went up twenty bucks and we lost a bunch of guys."

"What about taking on a few more clients?" I asked.

Connie frowned. "You mean two in one day?" They exchanged looks. "That's like cheating."

"Yeah. Each client has his day, no sharing," Fran said. "Like a date."

Whatever. "Alrighty then," I said, "we need a fourth girl." I studied the three women. Connie's face was getting that crepey look. *She's experienced, surely that's desirable?* Fran's belly bulged; you could see her red thong where her zipper had come unstitched. *Oh dear.* And Lilac—squinting at her word book—she should replace that missing tooth. *Not a good look.*

"It shouldn't be hard to find one," Lilac said. "The economy and all."

"I don't know where to look," I said.

Connie said, "Try Walmart. Or Target."

I imagined wandering around discount stores for hours, the horrified expressions of sales clerks and customers as they realized the job I was offering. "I don't think so," I said.

"I could check out the lady farmers at the market," Fran said. "They could use the cash, but they're a bit weathered, if you know what I mean."

Lilac looked up from a list of words containing Z. "What about Splits and Tits?"

"What's that?" I asked.

"Strip club. Girls gyrating around poles. Neon lighting kept dark so customers can't see cellulite and varicose veins."

"Lilac, you're a genius. Sounds perfect."

I made up business cards with an image of hundred-dollar bills raining down. *Part-time work, easy money!* I drove to Splits' parking lot and as the dancers arrived for work, I handed out my card. "Call me," I say, waggling my thumb and pinky. "Guaranteed income, homey surroundings."

* * * *

By the following Friday I had my fourth girl.

A redhead with a cockney accent, Ginger wobbled slightly on five-inch leopard-skin heels. She wore a black leather teddy decorated with fishnet and straps and nailhead trim. She sauntered into my living room and looked around. "Place seen better days, innit?"

Lilac's eyes widened, but she offered a friendly "Hi." Fran held out her box of toffee, and Connie said, "It's great to have a new face here."

Impressed they were so welcoming, I told them my plan. "I'll introduce Ginger to your clients, and ask them to spread the word."

"Why not let her take our place today?" Connie asked. "We talked about it, and we three could use a day off." Fran and Lilac nodded.

"Will your clients object? They're awfully fond of you," I said. "Used to a certain, uh, routine."

Connie shrugged. "Tell them we'll be back next Friday." She gathered up her knitting. Lilac said she'd find an online Scrabble game. Fran wrestled off the naughty nurse costume and pulled on stretchy waist jeans and a tee shirt. They left, seeming pleased to have free time.

* * * *

One by one, the regular clients arrived. I ushered the professor into the bedroom where Ginger waited, dressed in the naughty nurse costume taken in with safety pins. She wriggled seductively as she beckoned him to lie down. "Let's take a look at you, dearie," she said, twirling the stethoscope.

The professor frowned. "Uh, you're a skinny little thing, aren't you? Except for those basketballs on your chest."

I closed the door. Surely Ginger could work through his crankiness. She'd assured me she knew how to make a man happy.

Five minutes later, he stormed into the living room, shoving his money at me. "It better be Fran next week, right?" He stomped out.

I knocked on the closed bedroom door. "You OK?"

"Hell, yeah. Daft old sod."

When the dentist arrived, Ginger had changed into a tweed suit with big shoulder pads. She ordered him to sit on a stool in a corner, facing the wall. She started scolding him, as Connie would have, and I left, thinking *This one will be OK.* But soon, too soon, from the bedroom the dentist yelled, "That's not right! You're doing it all wrong!" He left, weeping, refusing to pay.

I sighed. Transitions are rough.

Ginger came out, dressed in her leather teddy. She rolled her eyes. "What a perv. OK, bag of feathers?" She tucked the Scrabble board under one arm, gathered a bouquet of feathers, and waited by the window for the chief, who was late as usual. "Firefighters are buffed, aren't they? Hang around the station doing pressups? I'm ready for a real man." A moment of silence, then, "What's this? Looks like a social worker."

I put down my paint roller and glanced out the window at a woman with short dark hair, big sunglasses and a navy pantsuit, admiring my bed of annuals. She clacked the doorknocker.

"Is Lilac here?" the woman asked, when I opened the door.

Lilac hadn't mentioned that the fire chief was a woman.

"Bugger all." Ginger dropped the bouquet of feathers and the Scrabble board. "I don't roll that way. What kind of place is this? Where's a normal man?"

I had to think a moment. "Define 'normal.'" I sent the chief away, whispering that Lilac would be back next week.

What a huge mistake I'd made. "Ginger," I said gently, "it's not working. My clients are used to my girls. They don't want anyone else."

Ginger hissed, "You're making big lolly here off twats and lezzies, and I want five thousand dollars to keep my piehole shut. Or else I tell the coppers."

"What?" I needed that money for a roof, siding repair, furniture, a fence. "Give me a week, honey. I'll see what I can do." I gave Ginger a little push out the door, gratified to see her lose her balance and nearly fall off her fuck-me shoes.

* * * *

The following Friday, noontime, the girls waited for their regulars. Connie was knitting doggie booties out of gray heathery yarn, a complicated pattern with double-pointed needles. Fran offered me a piece of toffee topped with chocolate and almonds. *So* so good, but quite a jaw workout to dissolve it. Lilac was absorbed in a word list, muttering what sounded like *drachms, klatsch, scarphs, schmalz, schnaps, sclaffs, scratch.*

I told them Ginger would be along soon. "She wants severance pay to keep our little business a secret. So I'm off to the bank, to withdraw funds. When she shows up, ask her to wait."

The girls exchanged looks. "Don't worry, Reenie," Connie said. "We'll manage."

* * * *

A half hour later, back from the bank, I parked the Camry in the garage and entered my house through the laundry room. I passed the bedrooms, briefly listening at each door. I heard Connie barking orders, Fran's directive to "Say 'Ah,' baby..." and the chief's feather-induced giggles. All was back to normal, or near-normal, except for Ginger's threat. I was thankful the girls forgave my mistake, relieved the clients came back. Now I only had to negotiate a more modest payment to Ginger.

But Ginger wasn't waiting impatiently for her blackmail money.

She lay face-down on the living room floor, her stiletto-clad feet splayed wide in a scatter of toffee candies and Scrabble tiles. She clutched to her neck a tangle of gray heathery yarn and double-pointed knitting needles. One of the needles had punctured her throat, and blood oozed from the wound into the shag carpet. My heart ratcheted into overdrive as I knelt and searched for a pulse. None. Ginger was surely dead, the body still so warm that Mango had wedged himself against her hip.

I pounded on the bedroom doors. "Get out here! Now!" As soon as the girls and their clients emerged, I questioned them. "What the hell happened?"

Fran clasped the professor to her bosom. "We didn't hear anything," she said.

"Me either." Lilac looked frightened, and the chief patted her back.

All six denied hearing or seeing Ginger. "She must have come in while we were in the bedrooms," Connie said. "Was it a break-in? Anything missing?"

My mind reeled as the girls, the clients, and I stared at each other in shock and mistrust. A burglary gone wrong? Had one of the girls killed her out of spite? Or to save me from blackmail? Or maybe one of the clients killed her, in the mistaken belief that Ginger was going to replace his favorite. Irrational motives, bizarre means. Alibis all around—or were they?

I called the police.

* * * *

"Looks suspicious, all right," said the detective, solidly-built in a snugly-fitting tailored uniform, a sight that normally activated my flirt gene, but today I was angry at the official attention and very very worried. First and foremost, what happened to Ginger, in my house? Was this death going to destroy my brand-new business, drive my girls onto welfare rolls, disgrace my clients?

A forensic team booted us out. The three girls, their Friday clients, and I went to the police station to be interviewed separately, but we all had alibis and the clients were solid citizens. The detective brushed off the issue of three couples in my bedrooms.

"I'm investigating a death, not misdemeanors," he said. "Everyone knew your aunt ran a lunchtime social club. No harm done."

Whew. One less thing to worry about, and I mentally smacked my forehead—Ginger's threat to tell the police had been empty.

After a few hours, they allowed us to return. Connie was annoyed because they'd confiscated her needles and yarn. Since they'd also gathered up the Scrabble tiles, Lilac would have to buy a new set. Fran shrugged; she could always make another batch of toffee. We gave each other hugs, and they departed, leaving me alone in a house with a blood-stained shag carpet.

I checked the locks on my doors and windows. It would be a long time before I could forget the picture of Ginger's still body, posed as though she'd collapsed without a struggle, a size 4 double-pointed knitting needle piercing her throat. I'll admit it—I was afraid. To distract myself from my fears, I began to spray the flocked wallpaper with water and peel it off the wall. Mango watched me work, the tip of his tail twitching. *What did you see, Mango?*

* * * *

"It wasn't murder," the detective declared, a statement I had trouble believing until he explained. "Forensics worked this case over good. Ginger's fingerprints covered Connie's on that needle, meaning no one else held it. And the ME found a big wad of toffee lodged in her throat, and cat hair on the toes of her shoes. So here's a likely scenario. She was annoyed with you all, right?"

I nodded. "I'd promised her employment, but it didn't work out."

He nodded and smiled, a crooked smile showing white teeth, a nice contrast to his warm brown eyes. "She knocked the Scrabble tiles to the floor and stuffed three toffees in her mouth. Those toffees don't dissolve easily; they turned into a sticky mass, making it difficult to swallow. She grabbed the knitting project, intending to pull it apart, but as she began to choke, she clutched her throat, tripped over the cat in those ridiculous shoes, slipped on the tiles, and fell onto one of the needles. She stabbed herself. Case closed."

Sweet words. *Case closed.* I thought they only said that on TV.

* * * *

We were all *so* grateful to the detective, whose name was Jack. Fran gave him a tin of assorted toffee, Connie knitted a stylish black sweater for his bulldog, and Lilac—well, she offered a feather frolic that he gracefully declined, claiming an allergy.

One night, I cooked him dinner, and he was so appreciative that he came back the next morning with tools. Together we ripped up the blood-stained carpeting. A filthy job made tolerable by the way his shoulders moved under his tee shirt.

I offered Jack a beer. "We're a sight," I said. Visible grime coated his face and arms.

He tipped the can for a swallow, then another. "A shower would be nice."

"Use mine, if you like," I said, glad that I'd put out clean towels that morning.

"Ladies first," Jack said. "Or, might I join you? You know, for lunch?"

And just like that, I realized that the fourth girl had been here all along.

ABOUT THE AUTHOR

Karen Pullen left a perfectly good engineering job to make her fortune - er, maybe not - as a B&B innkeeper and fiction writer. Her stories have appeared in *Ellery Queen Mystery Magazine*, *Spinetingler*, *Sixfold*, *bosque (the magazine)*, *Every Day Fiction*, and anthologies. Her debut mystery novel, *Cold Feet*, was published by Five Star Cengage in January 2013. She has an MFA in Popular Fiction from Stonecoast at the University of Southern Maine, and lives in Pittsboro, North Carolina where she occasionally teaches in Central Carolina Community College's creative writing program. Visit www.karenpullen.com for updates and her blog.

THE WHITE VAN

by Joanie Conwell

The late afternoon sun stung my eyes as I drove west on I-40, past Greensboro, past Winston-Salem, into the foothills of the Blue Ridge Mountains. I didn't know where I'd end up, running like I tended to when things got bad. Mama used to say, "The blues is heritable," and she was right.

The sun sank low in the sky, rivers of darkness swallowing gold-green hills with no remorse. With the changing light, visions rose like a mist from the highway. Daddy home from war, gripping my small arm as I poured him tea from a china pot. A whisper from the back seat, *save me, sugar.* Daddy, in his dress blues, hanging slack-jawed from the woodshed rafters out back on the farm. Black shoes polished, clean laces tied in bows, buttons shined.

For a while they thought I'd turn out fine, children resilient as they are. It's true, I'd done well in school, won a scholarship, left the farm. I traded wire-framed glasses for contact lenses and started wearing make-up. Not too much, just a sweep of mascara here, a dab of tawny liquid there, to mask the brokenness. I dated. Polite boys said I was pretty, gave me roses on Valentine's Day, and for my birthday, gold-plated necklaces with gemstones or tiny pearls.

Lately, though, I'd taken to avoiding people, like I did right after. I was lonesome by nature. As Mama used to say when I passed through the kitchen after school, "like a train whistle through a graveyard." Being around folks was worse than being alone. Enough years had gone by that the ones who knew about Daddy, about family matters, I could tell they judged me hard. "Get some help, honey," they'd say.

I considered the word help, rolling it over with my tongue, wondering what it might entail. The word tasted bitter. Daddy, he'd seen the doctor, taken pills and such…

Swollen clouds hid the first stars, and the sweet-astringent smell of loblolly pines cut the damp of night. My eyelids grew heavy. I pulled into a Waffle House parking lot next to a beat-up white van with a faded *semper fi* bumper sticker. I napped for a few minutes in the car until fragments of memory lured me to nightmare and I woke in a sweat.

Inside the restaurant, I huddled real small in the booth, shivering. I ordered an egg sandwich with hash browns regular and orange juice. Out the window, a rainstorm brewed. When the food came, I couldn't stomach the grease or acid. Soon I was back behind the wheel in the steamy heat, hair and shirt clinging to my damp skin until the air conditioner kicked in.

As night fell and the highway stretched out a black ribbon of tar, a leaden heaviness wrapped itself around me. There was Daddy again, like in my nightmares. Alive, but not alive. Stiff, wooden in the mechanical dream coffin that opened and shut, tilting vertical on moving gears. Daddy stepping out of the box with a vacant gaze, orange extension cord taut round his neck. Leathery skin and a flat voice so unlike the gentle one he used in life.

Save me, sugar.

The median vanished, and I felt a familiar urge, to careen the car into the next oncoming eighteen-wheeler.

Save me, sugar.

Jesus, shut *up* already.

A light flashed to my left. Lightning, or maybe a police cruiser hiding in a thicket of pines. Then it happened again—flashing to my left, too close, jarring me from my self-sorry thoughts.

I swerved the car right and hit something hard with a metallic clunk. The car began to waver. A flat. As I slowed, a white van pulled alongside. Its cab light was on and the driver peered at me through his open window. He looked like a scruffy surfer, early twenties, wind fluttering the blond hair that fell over one eye. Nice looking, in a dirty sort of way. Could he see me? It seemed that he could. He wanted me to see him, that was for sure. Sure as the vine twines 'round the stump, as Mama would say.

When I glanced at him, he blew me a kiss.

"I love you," he mouthed. He grinned, teeth gleaming.

A normal girl might have been disgusted, even scared. I fixed my gaze straight ahead at the yellow line, a spastic squiggle with each wobble of the car. I had to keep tugging the wheel to the left to avoid skidding off the road. I slowed to let him pass, but he slowed his van to match my speed. He edged closer. If I let go of the wheel, I could have reached out of my window and into his. He was going to push me off the highway and I would crash the car. I tapped on the brake to slow even more. A few minutes ago, I had wanted to die. Now, picturing a stranger's hands squeezing my throat shut at the side of the road after a crash, I was wide awake.

I didn't look again.

At last, he passed me, the semper fi bumper sticker caught for a moment in my headlights, and the van kept going until its rear lights vanished. Clunking along, now accompanied by a chorus of scraping metal, I willed the car to stay under my control. It was real dark now, dark all around. Faint thunder drummed in the distance.

Save me, Daddy whispered.

I gripped the wheel harder. Keep going, I told myself.

In the middle of nowhere—finally—came the smell of diesel and blinding fluorescent lights. A new gas station with twelve automated pumps and an open mini-mart.

I parked, then walked around my car to look at the tire. Not only was it flat and shredded, but the wheel had warped in on itself. I went inside to ask for help.

Two men leaned against the counter at the front of the store. They wore ski masks and one pointed a pistol at a gray-haired man beside the cash register. He too had a revolver, aimed squarely at the second robber, who didn't appear to have a weapon. I'd walked into a standoff.

The gray-haired man said, "I ain't handin' out shit. You losers get out of my store afore we all die."

Too many guns. And I was too close. The gunman grabbed me and jammed the black metal into the side of my neck. It felt like he would kill me by pressing so hard into that artery—what was it called? Cartoid? Carotid? I looked at the colorful row of cigarette packs displayed behind the owner. Camel was yellow. Kool was blue. Marlboro was red. Newport was green.

"Drop the gun or she dies." He trembled as he shouted, the gun grinding into my neck.

Daddy, he'd kept his guns locked up.

The storeowner stared at me, eyes wide like Road Runner on the Looney Tunes reruns Daddy and I used to watch. Whenever Road Runner pulled a fast one on Wile E. Coyote, honking, "Beep, Beep," Daddy would raise his beer can and say, "Semper fi, motherfuckers." It was the only time I heard him swear.

The owner placed his gun on the countertop and stepped back, hands raised. The gunman shoved me aside and grabbed the owner's weapon. "Give me all the money."

When the owner didn't move, the gunman fired, a deafening crack that slammed the owner back against the cigarette case, clutching his right side. The gunman leapt over the counter and kicked him to the floor, out of the way. He opened the cash register and shoveled money into a plastic garbage bag. I tried to slink away, but the barrel of the gun found me. "Do you want to die?"

I didn't panic. I didn't care if he killed me. I mean, I cared but it was like watching myself in a movie, more alive than life. After weeks of barely having energy to wash my hair or brush my teeth, my heart raced, my ears rang, and my neck throbbed where the steel had pressed it real hard.

"Dude, hurry up," the second robber hissed, backing toward the exit.

The gunman dumped the last of the money into the plastic bag and waved the pistol at me. "You're coming with us."

I didn't want to go with them. I had that much will left.

"Let me go. I haven't seen your face," I stammered. "I don't know what you look like. I can't identify you." I scanned the store for an escape route.

That's when the man in the white van showed up. He must have U-turned on the highway and stopped when he saw my car at the only gas station for miles. He wore ripped jeans, a t-shirt, flip-flops. He held a rifle. He strode in, aimed, and shot the two robbers point-blank, the gunman first then the poor kid diving for the door, like he'd done it a dozen times. His eyes shone. I'd seen that look before. He blew me a kiss.

"Remember me?" He slung the rifle over his shoulder, grinning that crazy grin, floppy blond hair falling over one eye. "I'm Chase."

I had never been fond of violence. But there in the mini mart, when Chase shot those men, the crack inside me tore open.

On the floor behind the counter, the storeowner groaned. "I'm bleeding here."

Chase threw me a cell phone. "Call 911," he said. Moving quickly, he picked up the blood-spattered bag of money and collected the weapons while I reported hearing gunshots near a gas station. He grabbed food off the shelves and a twenty-four pack of water. The wounded storeowner cussed. Nearby the two robbers lay in pools of blood on the linoleum floor. I hung up without answering the dispatcher's questions. When I gave Chase back the phone, he smashed it against the wall.

I could have walked right out the door. I didn't think he would stop me. I had a flat tire, needed a new wheel, yes, but the police were on their way. They would have gotten me home safe. I could have gone to bed and dreamed of extension cords.

I didn't leave. I watched him, this kiss-blowing vigilante with electric eyes, as he collected the money, weapons, food and drinks. I watched him like a child who stands in the middle of a field in a thunderstorm to watch the lightning strike. Finally, when he had loaded everything, he gripped my arm, dragged me through the rain to the white van and shoved me in the back as distant sirens pierced the night.

He drove for hours. It was hot in the back of the van and the thin carpeting on the floor itched me. I slept a dreamless sleep, lulled by the heat, rain on the roof, and the vibrating hum beneath me. As dawn broke, Chase parked and flung open the rear door and squinted at me pensively. The sun was out and the ground looked dry. Up close in the daylight, Chase's tanned face, although youthful, was rough and battered. He gave me some water and a granola bar, let me out to pee.

He looked away while I squatted behind a tree to relieve myself. The air was thinner here. We were in the mountains, by a roadside patch of Queen Anne's lace. He pulled a handful of flowers from the hard dirt, stems and all. He knelt down on the asphalt, removed my glasses and looked into my eyes. He was unshaven and smelled of alcohol and sweat and lonesomeness that matched my own, repelling me and making me long for him to touch me.

"I can take you to a bus station in the next town," he said. "If I let you go, you'll never see me again." Gently, he touched my face. He swept my hair with the bouquet. "Or, come with me. We'll be on the run and you'll have to do everything I say. It's no kind of life. You might get hurt." His fingers grazed my lips so lightly, they almost didn't touch. "Choose now."

I slipped my hand into his. My smooth fingertips met his calloused skin. His palm pressed mine. He dropped the flowers.

"You know I love you, right?" he said softly.

I brushed a lock of golden hair away from those light eyes and saw tears. "You said that."

"I'll show you."

I took his other hand and pulled him into the back of the van.

His fingers found my face, my skin. I closed my eyes. Hot tears wet my cheek and dampened my hair. His lips burned mine. He tasted of whisky.

The voices in my head, the visions that swirled around me and hovered like mist—they dissolved.

Finally. I could forget.

ABOUT THE AUTHOR

Joanie Conwell lives in Cary, North Carolina.

HAPPY PILLS

by Linda Johnson

Rose fluffed the silk flower in her hair, then rapped on the door. "Herbert? You in there?" No answer. Rapped again. Still no answer. Probably taking a nap with his hearing aid out, deaf to the world. She'd try again later. He was worth the wait.

She maneuvered her walker around the corner to Jack's apartment. Azalea Abbey, an independent living facility (*not* to be confused with assisted living, thank you very much!) was laid out in a square: apartments on both sides, views of the center courtyard for the fortunate, views of the parking lots for the rest.

Rose was one of the fortunate ones—not that she cared about the flowers, gazebo or reflecting pool. Rose used her binoculars to spy on her fellow residents. Sometimes she'd get lucky and spot someone parading around naked: men with their bony arms and legs, sunken chests, and sexy little pot bellies. She tried to catch them first thing in the morning, their flags flying high—at least, the ones on Cialis. The droopy ones had not yet discovered the miracle of modern medicine.

She even watched the naked women—compared her body to theirs. Rose took great pride in maintaining her figure—even though it meant skipping the dessert tray. She'd been blessed with ample boobs, a small waist, and a round rump. Although the sands had shifted a bit, she still boasted an hourglass figure.

All she had to do was add a little sashay to her hips, and the geezers' mouths dropped open. Sometimes the bolder ones grabbed her ass, then pretended they'd had a senior moment. Most of the time, she'd let them get away with it, unless one of the ladies was around, especially a wife. She didn't want any trouble; married ladies ruled the roost.

Barely wheezing, Rose made it to Jack's door and knocked.

"Who's there?"

"Rose. You up for a visit?"

Jack opened the door. "All I need is my magic pill and twenty minutes, babycakes." He held the door for her, patted her bottom as she walked by.

"Perfect. Give me a little time to freshen up." She followed him to his bathroom, watched him take his Viagra, then shooed him out. When the door closed, she turned on the faucet full blast and checked out his meds. Score! He'd just gotten his oxy scrip filled. A hundred pills, he'd never notice the missing ones. She counted out ten and put them in her purse. She went through his other bottles—nothing worth taking other than Valium and he only had three left. Hopefully, she'd snag his next refill.

Now that the business end of things was taken care of, it was time for a little afternoon delight. She sat on the toilet and took off her tennis shoes and socks. Hard to look sexy in white orthopedic knee socks. Next she wiggled out of her pink polyester slacks—thank God for elastic waistbands. She left on her new panties, red silk with black lace. She liked to keep things spicy.

She kept on her top, a stretchy low-cut turquoise number that hugged her curves. Her bra matched her panties and Jack was pretty nimble with hooks. Some of the geezers with arthritis struggled forever.

She checked her face in the mirror. Time for the beauty parlor: her lavender rinse was fading and she needed her eyebrows waxed. She drew on a nice set each morning (a high arch to look wide-awake and youthful), but a few stray hairs ruined the effect. Her Elizabeth Taylor violet eyes were as bright as ever, her nose small and perky, no sign of a double chin. A little lip gloss and she was good to go.

She opened the bathroom door, ready to strut her stuff, but stopped when she heard the snores. Based on the tent pole under the bed sheet, the magic pill had worked. All she had to do was wake him up. "Hey, sailor. Ready to rumble?"

Jack's eyes flew open. For a moment, he looked dazed, then he let out a wolf whistle. "Holy moly, Rose. You could give a guy a heart attack."

"That's okay, honey. I know CPR."

* * * *

When she finished up with Jack, she headed back to Herbert's. More pills added to her stash, another romp in the sack.

Herbert's hand stroked her thigh. "That was amazing, honey. Was it good for you?" His warm brown eyes held her gaze.

"Lovely," Rose said. Such a charmer. No wonder single gals lined up with casseroles.

He put his arms around her, and she snuggled against him, enjoying the cuddle. The other geezers would turn over, fast asleep before she hopped out of bed.

She twirled his chest hair around her finger. She loved a nice carpet, didn't get why the young guys waxed. She'd almost nodded off when he kissed her forehead.

"How about some tea and scones?" he asked. "I baked them this morning."

"Why not? We worked off the calories."

"Right. I'll add whipped cream. Unless you have another idea for the whipped cream?" He wiggled his eyebrows.

"Maybe next time." Rose laughed. Herbert always made her laugh.

While Herbert fixed their snack, Rose sat at the dining room table and surveyed his apartment. No Rooms to Go decor for him. He had a burgundy leather sofa that was as plush as a pillow, handsome wood furniture polished to a soft glow, and a collection of artwork he'd told her he acquired while traveling the world. Having tea and scones in his apartment was what she imagined high tea at the Ritz Carlton would be like.

As they ate, they chatted about current events, clashed over politics. He was a staunch Republican, she a die-hard Democrat, but they teased more than argued. Rose glanced at her watch, surprised. Almost four. The hours with Herbert rushed by. "It's getting late. Better get home."

He kissed her hand. "See you at dinner."

She made it back to her apartment in time for a nap before dinner, exhausted. Two men a day was her limit.

* * * *

Rose was on her way to the dining room when a motorized chair side-swiped her walker. She barely stayed upright. "Estelle! You did that on purpose." Estelle was Azalea Abbey's resident witch and seemed to love to make Rose's life miserable.

"You were hogging the hallway." Estelle turned around to glare at her with pursed lips and nailed a potted plant. Dirt and leaves flew everywhere, but she didn't slow down.

"Damn hit-and-run driver." Rose's voice shook with anger.

Estelle gave her the finger and sped off.

A door opened and Rose's best friend poked her head out. Martha had cropped gray hair, enormous tortoiseshell glasses, and half the wrinkles of most women her age. "I thought I heard you. What's going on out here?"

"That nutcase Estelle. First she tried to run me down, then she crashed into a plant."

"You should report her to management. A few more incidents, and they'll pull her license. She'll have to go into assisted living if she can't use her cart."

"It can't happen soon enough."

"You just don't like the competition."

"What competition? That scrawny little body and that red wig. Like anyone thinks it's her real hair, especially when half the time it's on crooked."

"The men like her, though."

"Only because she takes out her dentures when she gives them a blow job. Not my fault I have all my teeth," Rose said, feeling her stomach growl. It was time for dinner. After her busy day, she could eat a horse.

They walked to the dining area and surveyed the room—forest green carpeting, salmon colored walls, white tablecloths. The clink of silver echoed through the cavernous space. Oh dear. Jack and Herbert sat at their usual table by the window, with Estelle between them. When Rose and Martha approached, Estelle made a point of rubbing Jack's shoulder. "Sorry, there's only one chair left. No room for you two. And I know how inseparable you are. If we didn't know better, we'd think you were lesbos."

Jack winked. "I can vouch for Rose. How about you, Herbert?"

Herbert raised his hands. "A gentleman never discusses his love life."

"Oh, really?" Estelle laughed. "You boys gossip more than us ladies."

"Lady?" Rose snorted. "There's nothing lady-like about you, Estelle. Your only friends are men, not a single lady."

Jack chuckled and patted Rose's arm. "Now, now. No cat fights."

At least Herbert had the decency to blush. He was the one who'd told Rose about Estelle's dentures, although he'd insisted it was just hearsay, that he'd not taken advantage of Estelle's special talents.

"Let's sit over there," Martha said, nudging Rose's walker and pointing to a table with four women. "You know I'd rather sit with the girls," she added, when the men were out of earshot. "I can't stand the way Jack chews with his mouth open. And I hate having to yell so Herbert can hear."

"Oh, they're not so bad. They have their moments."

"I know all about their moments." Martha raised her eyebrows. "Not personally, of course."

"Of course not, holy Sister Martha. How many years has it been?"

"Twenty-two. Ever since my darling husband passed."

"My God, you're a virgin. Doesn't the vault seal up after all those years?"

"It would, if not for my joy toys."

"That's right. You have your joy toys and I have my boy toys. Sometimes I think you're better off. A lot less drama anyway."

"Who are you kidding? What would you do without your love triangles? You, Estelle, and every single man here."

"A few married ones, too, you know."

"You're asking for trouble with the queen bees. If one of them finds out, they'll swarm all over you."

"I'm very discreet. Besides, what do they expect if they put on chastity belts? I swear these old geezers have more testosterone now than when they were teenagers. At least the ones on happy pills."

They arrived at the girls' table just in time to be overheard. "What about happy pills?" Claudia asked. "I'm out of Prozac. Two wasn't doing the job, so I switched to three. Now I'm out and my doctor won't up my dosage."

"Why not?" Rose asked. "You might get too happy? Start singing in the shower?"

"Who knows? It's all about the rules. He's such a hard ass." Claudia's eyes filled with tears.

Rose sat next to her and patted her hand. "Don't worry, honey. I'll help you out." She dug around her purse, found the right bottle, and poured a handful into Claudia's open palm.

"Thanks, Rose. I don't have my wallet with me, but you know I'm good for it."

"Swing by my apartment after dinner. Just not after seven. That's when *Sex and the City* starts. I love watching those pretty young things."

"How do you always manage to have extra pills, Rose?" Miriam asked.

The table went silent. Five pairs of eyes bored into Rose's. Only Martha knew about the pill-pilfering. "I have a generous doctor. She thinks us seniors should have all the pill-induced happiness science can provide. I don't take half of what she prescribes."

"She taking new patients?" Claudia asked.

"No. She's full up. But I'll ask her nurse to put you on her waiting list."

Four arms went up, with a chorus of *me, too*.

"Sure thing." Rose said, with no intention of following through. "So what's for dinner tonight?" She wanted to change the subject. She knew it was tilapia, rice, and green beans. Like everyone else, she pored over the menu each week.

"Overcooked fish, and not enough sauce to save it."

"The rice is sticky again."

"Cook never gets it right."

"Beans are cold."

"Waxy, too."

"Came out of a can. You can taste the aluminum."

Rose relaxed. Subject changed. No one cared about her pill stash when there was food to complain about.

Benjamin appeared at her side, placed a glass of milk with the precision of a waiter at a four-star restaurant. "Good evening, Mrs. P. May I bring you a salad?"

"A Caesar, please."

"Coming right up, Mrs. P."

Dinner was plated and served by waiters, but residents went to the salad bar for their greens. Rose's walker made it tricky to manage a salad plate, plus she liked the extra attention from the wait staff.

She watched Benjamin walk to the salad bar. The buns on that young man. Tighter than her late husband's fist when she'd ask for a bump in her grocery allowance. Allowance was Joe's word for it. She was *allowed* to buy food. She was glad he'd died young, even if it meant the money ran out. Only because she was never *allowed* to work outside the home. He didn't want anyone to think he couldn't support his wife. There should have been plenty of money, but Joe liked to gamble, so it all went down the drain, except for a nest egg she'd managed to squirrel away. Just enough to buy into Azalea Abbey, but nothing to live on but a Social Security check. She couldn't afford the monthly dues without her side business.

Benjamin returned with her Caesar. The front view in those tight black pants was even better than the rear. What she wouldn't give for a love session with him. He could probably go all afternoon without medicinal help.

"Thanks, Benjamin. You're a sweetheart." She gave him her flirtiest smile.

"Anything for you, Mrs. P."

If only that were true.

* * * *

The meeting room held six rows of tables, three across, room for two at each table. Thirty-six seats, and they were always filled. Bingo was the most popular activity at Azalea Abbey. The activity director called out a number and Rose bit her lip, concentrating on her two bingo cards. Surely she had G-17 somewhere, but figures swam in front of her eyes. Was it time for cataract surgery?

"Bingo," Estelle yelled, and fist-pumped the air.

"Cheater," Rose said. "You wouldn't win all the time if you didn't sneak the cards home to memorize them."

Estelle's eyes narrowed. "Sore loser."

"It's against the rules."

Estelle glared at her. "I'm not the only one breaking rules around here."

As if on cue, the meeting room door opened and a policeman burst through. His squinty eyes raked the room. "Rose Peabody?"

"That's her right there." Estelle pointed her bony finger.

The cop marched over to Rose. "You'll have to come with me, ma'am. We have some questions for you down at the station."

"What? What's this about?" Rose saw her shock reflected on the faces around her.

Estelle jumped from her seat. "I ratted you out, Rose. And a couple of the wives backed me up. We told the cops all about your drug dealing. I hope you rot in jail."

Rose stood, her legs shaking. Her Bingo cards and markers spilled onto the floor and she felt humiliated. The officer took her arm with a vise grip and led her to the door.

Martha jumped to her feet. "Don't worry, Rose. I'll get you some help."

* * * *

The interrogation room felt like a coffin. The officer questioned her gently. His bluster had been for show. Rose didn't deny Estelle's accusations and she could tell the cop felt bad when the D.A. charged her.

"Sorry, ma'am, but we have no choice. It's against the law to sell drugs." He told Rose she'd have her bail hearing that afternoon. "If you can arrange for bail, you won't have to spend the night in jail."

Even though the officer felt sorry for her, the judge apparently didn't. He set bail at a hundred grand; Rose needed to find ten thousand. Despondent, she curled up on the lumpy bed in her cell. Where would Martha get that much money? Finally, a guard unlocked her cell and told her she had made bail. When she stepped through the locked doors, she was stunned. Instead of Martha, Herbert rushed over, his face etched with worry.

"I heard what happened. Got here as fast as I could," he said, winded like he'd just run a marathon. He put his hands on Rose's shoulders." I'm crazy about you, honey. Can't live without you."

"Herbert, even if I'm free now, they're still going to throw me in jail after my trial."

"Not going to happen. We'll make a break for it. Go to Vegas and get hitched."

"We can't get married. I'll lose my Social Security."

"Doesn't matter. I'm loaded." He dropped to his knees, put his hand over his heart. "Will you marry me?"

"What if they come after me?"

"They'll never take us alive, Bonnie."

For a moment, Rose panicked. Had he forgotten her name? Early stage Alzheimer's? Then it hit her. "Of course, I'll marry you, Clyde. Let's blow this popsicle stand."

ABOUT THE AUTHOR

Linda Johnson is originally from Chicago where her first career was in advertising. When the cold and gray got to be too much, she and her husband packed up their dogs and horses and relocated to warm and sunny North Carolina. After working for several years as the owner and manager of a hunter/jumper equestrian facility, she decided to trade riding for writing. Linda writes suspense novels and short stories and particularly enjoys creating smart, psychopathic villains. She is a member of Sisters in Crime, Mystery Writers of America, and the North Carolina Writers Network. She has published two novels and several short stories as e-books. Find her online at LindaJohnson.us

MAMA'S BOY

by Ruth Moose

Mama never liked any of the girls I brought home but she liked Dina the least so I married her. Only time in my life I stood up to Mama.

Disaster from day one.

Mama wore white to our wedding. Then, while we were on our honeymoon to Myrtle Beach, she rearranged our whole apartment, spoons to slumber cushions. "I know what Herbie likes," she told Dina who stood there with her mouth open. The minute Mama left, Dina put everything back the way she wanted it. I never said a word. After all, she WAS my Mama and she meant well.

Dina had wanted to go to Niagara Falls for our honeymoon but Mama's heart was acting up and I didn't want to be too far away.

"Wasn't acting up too much to move all our furniture around," Dina said.

Once a week Mama let herself in and cleaned our apartment. "You can't be too careful with Herbie's allergies," she said, and I told Dina how she was helping us save money, not hiring somebody.

"Snoop," said Dina. "She's a snoop."

Two or three times a week Mama brought over casseroles, stayed to eat. "It's hard to cook a real meal when you work full time. And Herbie has to watch his diet."

When Dina complained to me, I said, "Think of all the money we're saving on groceries."

Holidays were trials. Whose house do we eat at, and what time? Do we open gifts Christmas Eve or Christmas Day? Both, I finally decreed. You can't have too many gift-opening occasions. Even though Mama said Christmas really wasn't Christmas unless there were children around.

That was another bone she picked with Dina. "Career my eye, children come first. I'm not getting any younger and who knows how much longer my heart will hold out."

I wasn't surprised when Dina, for our fifth wedding anniversary, presented me with plane tickets to New York, a weekend's hotel and meals at Niagara Falls. A second honeymoon. "Finally," Dina said.

Even Mama was pleased. "Your daddy and I went to Niagara for our honeymoon. Bring me back a picture just like this one." She leafed through her photo album, handed me a yellowed Polaroid of herself, pretty and slender, straddling a railing overlooking the falls. "I was brave in those days."

Mama even loaned Dina her biggest, sturdiest, bright red umbrella. (Mama collects umbrellas like some people china teacups. She's got over a dozen stuffed in her hall stand.) She told us we had to see the butterfly pavilion at Niagara and the flower clock and Dina could use this red umbrella to keep off the mist. But be sure to bring it back.

Peace, I thought, the two women in my life finally making up.

At Niagara Falls we drank champagne in our hotel room, then ate dinner overlooking the Falls, lovingly, leisurely.

As the sun was setting, we walked along the path beside the Falls, Dina with her umbrella under the mist, me with my camera.

"Take my picture," Dina said.

"Hey," I said, as she climbed up and straddled the fence, "is that safe?"

"I'm fine." She smiled and lifted the red umbrella over her head.

I aimed the camera, a great shot of my beautiful bride. Dina's pretty face framed by golden wisps of hair, red background, fast, falling water, sunset colors.

Lights came on for the Falls, a sudden gust of wind blew past and over Dina went.

I rushed to the fence but she went down in a swirl of color, then disappeared.

They found the umbrella but not Dina. Not ever.

Mama tried to console me. "Herbie, she was never right for you. Nobody loves you like your Mama. Nobody."

I remember that every time I see Mama's hall stand full of umbrellas, her sturdy red one like the tallest arrow in a quiver.

ABOUT THE AUTHOR

Ruth Moose taught creative writing at the University of North Carolina-Chapel Hill for fifteen years. She has published three collections of short stories and six collections of poetry. Individual stories and poems were published in *Atlantic*, *Yankee*, *The Nation*, *Christian Science Monitor* and other places. Moose won the 2013 Malice Domestic competition for her novel, *Doing it at the Dixie Dew*, published by St. Martin's Press in 2014. She is on the web at ruthmoose.com.

POUND OF FLESH

by Sarah Shaber

"Miss Louise," Dellaphine whispered, wiping her strong brown hands on a dishtowel, "a policeman's here to see you."

"What? Why?" I asked. I couldn't imagine.

"When I got to the Western Market this morning to do the grocery shopping, there was a big crowd in front of the store. Like in one of those crime newsreels, there were flashbulbs popping, cops everywhere, and one of them black police wagons backed up to the rear door."

I felt a sick sensation in my stomach. I pulled off my gloves and hat and tossed them with my pocketbook on the tapestry chair in the entry hall.

"The policeman's waiting in the lounge," Dellaphine said. "With Miss Phoebe and Miss Ada."

My stomach churned in earnest. I thought I knew what this was about. Though you'd think the D.C. police would have better things to do than run down a couple of pounds of sugar bought without a ration coupon. Best face up to it.

* * * *

Phoebe, my landlady, never forgot her manners, no matter who her visitor was. Wearing a threadbare Fortuny caftan, she presided over her Limoges coffee set, pouring for the police officer perched on her davenport. Ada, her platinum hair in crimps and curlers tucked under a scarf, curled up in an armchair.

The policeman rose when he saw me.

"Officer Bennett," Phoebe said, "this is Mrs. Louise Pearlie, one of my boarders."

"Ma'am," Bennett said, touching his forehead.

"Good to meet you," I said, smoothing my skirt under me as I took a seat next to Phoebe.

Bennett sat back down, rather stiffly. He was an older man, with plenty of gray streaking his hair, but his age wasn't unusual these days. The young men were all in the military.

Ada and Phoebe both looked so worried that I felt quite nervous. It was just a pound of sugar. So difficult to drink coffee without it, especially if the coffee was mostly chicory. I had never been able to get used to chicory, no matter how much milk I added.

"Mrs. Pearlie," he said, pulling a notebook and pencil from his pocket. "I need to ask you some questions."

"Officer, I think I know what this is about. I admit I bought a pound of sugar without a ration coupon at the Western Market last night. I'm sorry, I know I shouldn't have, and of course I will pay the fine."

"What time did you buy the sugar, ma'am?" Bennett asked.

"About nine-fifteen, after the store closed."

"Was there anyone else in the store? Did you see anyone enter after you left? Anybody suspicious loitering outside in the street?"

"No," I said. "I don't understand. What's going on?"

"Dear," Phoebe began.

"Please, Mrs. Holcombe," Bennett said gently, "let me finish. Mrs. Pearlie, do you know of anyone besides yourself who purchased black market goods from the owner of Western Market, Mr. Elmer Metz?"

I tried not to glance at Ada.

"I've already told him, Louise," Ada said. "I've bought three pounds over the last year. That's all."

"No one other than Ada," I said to the policeman.

The words "black market" had such nasty ring. Surely Metz would be in trouble, not Ada and me. Selling black market goods was a much more serious offense than buying an occasional bag of sugar.

"I'd like you to think again, Mrs. Pearlie," Bennett said. "This is important. Did you see anything suspicious, anything, when you were at the Market? Or after you left?"

I thought back. The café next door to the market had been closed and dark. Of course the windows upstairs, where the café owner, her son, and her boarders lived, were still lit. The filling station on the corner was closed and the nearby movie theatre marquee was dark.

"No," I said. "I didn't see anything unusual."

"Then," Bennett said, turning another page of his notebook, "it looks like you were the last person to see Mr. Metz alive."

"Excuse me?" I wasn't sure that I had heard him correctly. I thought he was investigating black market racketeering. "What do you mean?"

Officer Bennett looked up from scribbling in his notebook. "Mrs. Pearlie, Mr. Metz was murdered last night. His colored boy found him when he came to work this morning."

"Louise, he was stabbed with a butcher knife," Ada said, leaning forward in her chair. "Can you imagine? It was buried right in his chest. Isn't that awful?"

"Oh no," I said, swallowing a gasp of shock, "That's terrible!"

"Poor man," Phoebe said. "More coffee?" she asked the police officer.

"No thank you, ma'am. And please, Miss Herman," Bennett said to Ada, "let me finish here. You can gossip after I've left."

"Of course," Ada said, subsiding into her seat.

"Mrs. Pearlie, it's early days in our investigation yet, but we've gone over the last twenty-four hours of Mr. Metz's life pretty thoroughly. Our doc figures Metz died before midnight. Mrs. Jane Jones, who owns the café next door, was doing paperwork at her desk upstairs when she saw you enter the back door of the Western Market after it closed, right about when you said you did. She saw you leave around fifteen minutes later. She worked for two more hours at her desk and saw no one else go inside, and didn't see Mr. Metz leave. She thought nothing of that. He often stayed late or slept on a cot in the storeroom."

"Someone else must have come later," I said.

"Not that she saw, ma'am. Now, the filling station owner, Mr. Pete Cousins, went into the market by the back door, before you. About eight. Several people leaving the café noticed him."

"Really, officer," Phoebe said, "this is uncalled for. Surely someone could have slipped into the store after Louise left. That Jones woman couldn't have been looking out her window the entire time she was working at her desk."

Bennett ignored her. "When Mr. Metz's stock boy—" and here he consulted his notes "—Sid White, arrived at seven-thirty this morning, he found Metz dead."

"How terrible," I said. "But you can't think I had anything to do with this."

Bennett closed his notebook and stuffed it into his pocket. He looked at me with light blue, inquiring eyes. He didn't seem to be accusing me of anything, but he struck me as a man who wouldn't stop asking questions until he got answers.

"Mrs. Pearlie, do you have anything to add to what we've discussed?"

"No," I said. "I don't. I hardly knew the man. I mean, I just bought a couple of pounds of sugar from him."

"I need to collect your fingerprints now. To compare to the ones on the butcher knife. There were several sets."

Both Phoebe and Ada protested.

"Not right here in my lounge," Phoebe said.

"It's all right," I said to them. "I don't mind. I never touched that knife, so this will clear me."

"But you're not a suspect, surely." Phoebe said.

"We need to identify every fingerprint we can on that knife handle," Officer Bennett said. "And you're right, of course. If your fingerprints aren't on the knife, that clears you."

"See?" I said to Phoebe and Ada. "It's okay."

A small black leather case sat at Bennett's feet. He lifted it onto the coffee table. Open, it revealed a tidy collection of bottles, brushes, rollers, and fingerprint cards. Ada and Phoebe couldn't help but lean forward to watch. Bennett rolled my fingers in ink and pressed each finger onto a card, then handed me a cloth to wipe my hands.

I didn't tell Bennett that I'd had my fingerprints taken when I swore my loyalty oath early in 1942. I preferred that he know as little about me as possible.

"If you think of anything else, please come around to the station," Bennett said.

"Certainly," I said.

Phoebe showed Officer Bennett to the door.

I wanted a martini in the worst way.

* * * *

I loved Dellaphine's fried chicken, which was a good thing, since we had it for dinner twice a week. I could live happily with less beef to eat, as long as I could get chicken and plenty of potatoes and vegetables from our Victory garden. Most Americans, like Henry, our male boarder, who sat scowling at his dinner plate across from me, missed fresh beef badly. Tongue and oxtail weren't good substitutes for steak.

It was just the three of us at dinner—me, Phoebe and Henry. Ada had gone to her gig at the Willard Hotel, where she played clarinet in the house band. Joe, our other male boarder, was in New York City on business.

"You know, Louise," Henry said, spearing a crispy chicken drumstick from the platter, "you're probably the main suspect, being the last person who saw Metz alive."

"Don't be ridiculous, Henry," Phoebe said. "I'm sure the police don't suspect Louise of anything at all. Someone must have gone to the market after Louise left and killed Mr. Metz. The police just want to know if she saw anyone."

It was so stupid of me to have bought that sugar. Because I wasn't just any government girl. I worked for the Office of Strategic Services, America's spy agency, in the Registry, where all the OSS documents were filed. I had Top Secret Clearance, and I didn't want to lose it. Which I might if my name hit the newspapers associated in any way with a murder. I hoped Officer Bennett could solve this case quickly and keep my name out of it.

After dinner Phoebe and Henry went upstairs to their rooms, so I wandered back into the kitchen looking for company. And maybe some gossip.

Dellaphine was drying the last of the dishes. Her daughter, Madeleine, still dressed in the neat blue suit she'd worn to work at the Social Security Administration, sat at the kitchen table reading the evening newspaper. Madeleine was the first colored girl I knew personally who wasn't somebody's maid or cook. I admired her.

"Want the funnies?" she asked, sliding them across the table to me when I sat down.

"Sure," I said, flipping through the section looking for Brenda Starr, girl reporter.

Dellaphine joined us with a tall glass of iced tea adorned with a sprig of mint from our garden. "Miss Phoebe said you were the last person to see Mr. Metz alive," she said. "Except the murderer," she added hastily.

"Looks like it," I said. "The police don't seem to think I'm a suspect, though." I tried to laugh, but the sound emerged as a halfhearted squeak.

"I heard that that butcher knife was real deep into his chest," Dellaphine said. "A woman couldn't have done it."

Madeleine looked up from her newspaper. "You don't need to worry, Miss Louise. They'll arrest the colored boy, they always do."

"Madeline," her mother said. "I didn't raise you to talk like that."

"Please, Momma, you know Sid was working off his mother's debt," Madeleine said. "For practically no pay. He hated that man. Why look for the real killer when there's a Negro with a motive so handy?"

Officer Bennett didn't seem to me to be the kind of person who'd arrest just anybody to solve a crime, but I didn't like coming between Dellaphine and Madeleine when they argued, so I kept my opinion to myself.

"What debt did Sid's mother owe Mr. Metz?" I asked instead.

"He gave credit for groceries during the Depression," Dellaphine said. "Lots of folks would have gone hungry otherwise. They weren't all colored, neither."

Madeline rolled her eyes. "All those poor folks are paying him back with interest now. And then some. When the police find his book, I bet you a Hershey's bar that his murderer is listed right there."

"His book?" I asked.

"He kept a ledger with the names of everyone who owed him," Dellaphine said.

I wondered if that book contained the names of people who bought black market sugar. My name. Ada's.

When I got upstairs, I mixed myself a martini from the pint of Gordon's gin and bottle of vermouth I kept in my dresser drawer hidden under my panties and slips.

* * * *

Saturday morning after the breakfast rush, I pushed through the café's swinging doors and found Mrs. Jones sitting alone at a booth drinking a cup of coffee and scribbling in a notebook. I slid onto the bench across from her. As soon as she saw me, she flushed bright red. She patted her face with her hands, worn from years in the café kitchen, to cool off her cheeks, and then tucked her dyed auburn hair behind her ears.

"I'm sorry," she said. "Don't be angry."

"I'm not," I said. "You had to tell the truth."

She dropped her pencil onto the opened notebook and rubbed her temples. "We're out of coffee. Would you like some tea? Cocoa?"

"No thanks. Have you heard anything more from the police?"

She shook her head. "Not yet. It's all so terrible. Mr. Metz was a good man. After my husband died I didn't know how I'd survive. And I had a son to support. Without the credit for groceries he gave me, I couldn't have kept the café going. For years he wouldn't let me pay anything, just wanted to eat his meals here for free. Now I could pay him in full, but he wouldn't let me. Just said he wanted his meals here every day like always. He sat right at this booth." She patted the bench beside her. "Three times a day."

"I hear not everyone thought so well of him," I said.

She shrugged. "It's hard to like a man you owe money to."

When she reached for her coffee cup I noticed the gold circle on her left ring finger. "When did you get married?" I asked.

She smiled happily. "Just last weekend," she said. "Do you know Tom? Tom Murray? He rented one of my rooms on the third floor. He works for the bus company. We've been keeping company for almost a year, and, well, we're so happy now. And he's good to my son, treats him like he was his own."

"Congratulations," I said. "So I guess you go by Jane Murray now?"

"I still answer to Jane Jones. That's how the customers know me."

* * * *

On my way back to the boarding house, I passed the rear of the Western Market. The back door was ajar. Curiosity got the better of me and I slipped inside.

"Come to see the blood?"

I started at the voice, my hand over my heart. "You frightened me."

"Didn't intend to," the colored boy said. He was about sixteen years old, I guessed, clad in loose denim trousers and a pressed white oxford shirt with ragged cuffs. He wielded a mop with a thick rag head.

"You're the fourth sightseer that's snuck in here today. Sorry, there's no blood, I done washed it away already. Officer Bennett said I could."

"You're Sid."

"Yes, ma'am."

I noticed a dented tin bucket at his feet. The water in the bucket was a rusty brown. I felt my heart clutch.

"Yes, I cleaned up his blood. Hard to believe, isn't it? Every night of the last two years I've prayed to Jesus to be released from this job, and now I'm free, and here I am cleaning up the place." He shook his head and set to mopping the floor again. "It just seemed wrong to leave things such a mess. But after I leave tonight I ain't coming back."

I sat on a crate of cabbages and watched him work.

"Why didn't you quit?" I asked. "There are so many good jobs open now."

Sid stopped mopping and glared at me. "Don't you think I wanted to?" Sid's voice shook with emotion. "I could get a job at a factory and pay Mr. Metz what my momma owed him in a month. But no—he said I had to work it off for $10 a week instead. Until her debt was paid." Sid gripped the mop handle so tightly I could almost hear the wood crack. "God, I hated that man!"

"Sid," I said, "you might want to think twice about saying you hated Mr. Metz…"

"Why? Because I might get arrested for murder? Since my fingerprints were all over that butcher knife?" A broad grin split his face. "Ma'am, I got the best alibi in the world. I told that cop and he already checked it out."

"The best alibi in the world?" I wondered.

"Rich white men!" Sid laughed out loud. "I was moonlighting at Mr. Lee Nelson's house on Dupont Circle Thursday night. Fetching drinks and emptying ashtrays for him and his poker buddies. I was there until four o'clock in the morning."

"I'm glad to hear that."

"Mr. Metz's book is missing too," Sid said. "Did you know?"

"The ledger," I said. "The one that lists the people who owed him money."

"That's right. Whoever inherits this dump won't be able to collect nothing from nobody."

* * * *

"I would like to know why this is any of your business." Pete Cousins stabbed a squeegee into the pail of water at his feet. I'd found the filling station owner cleaning his station's front windows. "Why should I answer your questions about Elmer Metz?"

"Because I was the last person who saw him alive, except for the murderer, that's why. Because I bought a pound of sugar from the man and I'm a government girl and don't want my name in the papers," I said. "I don't want to lose my job."

"Oh." He dipped his squeegee into the bucket and drew it over the expanse of glass with long, sweeping strokes. "Well then, I suppose I can tell you what I told the police. Yes, I did go into the market last night, to have it out with him."

"Have what out?"

"For years now, I been giving him free gas, oil changes, antifreeze, because he issued my family credit for a few groceries during the bad times. I got sick of it. I paid him twice over. But he had the gall to take out the ledger and show me what I owed him and there was nothing credited to my account. Said the free gas was just interest, that I still owed him the balance."

He flung the squeegee on the ground and shoved his hands in his pockets. "And no, I didn't go back later and kill him," he said. "The police took my fingerprints and they'll find out it wasn't me because I never touched that butcher knife. But I'll tell you something I didn't tell the police. If you mention it to anyone, I swear I'll call you a liar."

"What?"

"I took the ledger. Wrestled it right away from his greedy self. Burned it up in that incinerator over there." He pointed to a metal barrel, singed with black, on the edge of his property. "So no one can say all the folks who paid off their debts in kind still owe any money."

I shook my head, wishing he hadn't done that. I'd hoped to find a clue to Metz's killer in that ledger.

"What's the matter?" he asked. "Everything okay?"

"Sure," I said, collecting myself.

I was good at keeping secrets. That's why I'd risen in the Office of Strategic Services from clerk to Research Assistant. But I didn't see how

I could stay silent about this. A man had been murdered. And I suspected who'd done it.

* * * *

Sunday morning early I knocked on the back door of the café. Mrs. Jones opened it a crack.

"Yes, Mrs. Pearlie? What is it? I'm checking stock right now and it's not a good time for a visit."

"We need to talk," I said, "about Metz's murder."

She shrugged and opened the door. The café's kitchen was spotless. She pulled me up a stool, and I joined her at a wooden table deeply scored by years of chopping meat and vegetables.

"My husband and son are at the fish market this morning," she said. "Tom is going to quit his job and help me run the café."

"That's nice." I ran my hands across the deep scars on the table. "After all these years in this kitchen you must wield a butcher's knife pretty well. As well as any man."

"Sure can," she said, grinning and flexing her biceps like a boxer.

"You know, of all the people I talked to about Mr. Metz, you were the only person who said anything kind about him."

She shrugged. "He wasn't what you would call likeable. But my son and I would have wound up in a hobo camp if it weren't for the store credit he gave me."

"For which you fed him for free every day. Paid him in kind."

"It was the least I could do."

"There's more than one way for a woman to pay a man in kind."

She clapped her hands over her mouth to muffle her shocked cry. When she could speak her voice broke.

"How did you know?" she asked.

"It was a guess, really. I thought of how much Metz's murderer must have despised him, and the filling station guy mentioned paying him 'in kind', and I realized a woman had more than one way to pay a debt."

"Twice a week I left my bed at night and went to him on that awful cot in his storeroom," she said. "He didn't care that I hated him. After the war started, when the café started making good money, he wouldn't let me pay him back. I had to keep…screwing him."

I flinched at the nasty word, but she'd had to do a nasty thing. I felt terribly sorry for her.

"I was desperate. Thursday night I confronted Metz with a check in my hand, and told him it was over. He laughed at me. Said he'd tell Tom everything if I didn't keep sleeping with him. How could I do that? Tom would notice if I left our bed."

I reached for her hands and held them. She let me grip them for a second, then pulled back, a defiant look on her face. "I killed him, okay? I'm telling you because I can see from your face that you won't turn me in. The police don't suspect me. They haven't even taken my fingerprints."

She was right. I wouldn't tell on her for killing such a louse. What good would hanging her for murder do? She had a husband and a son who needed her.

"Metz was trimming pork chops," she continued. "The knife was right there on the butcher's block, just like this one." She nodded toward her own knife. "I couldn't stop myself. So many people hated Metz, I did the world a favor."

Then we heard a man clear his throat. We both looked towards the door.

Officer Bennett stood there with his small black leather case in his hand. "I'm sorry to interrupt, and so early in the morning. But Mrs. Jones, we're collecting the fingerprints of all Mr. Metz's acquaintances, and I'm afraid I neglected to take yours earlier. Is now a good time?"

ABOUT THE AUTHOR

Sarah Shaber is the author of the Louise Pearlie World War II mysteries published by Severn House. The third in the series, *Louise's Dilemma*, came out in November 2013, and the fourth, *Louise's Blunder*, is due in the Fall of 2014. Shaber is also the author of an earlier series, the Professor Simon Shaw mysteries, and editor of *Tar Heel Dead*, a collection of mystery short stories by North Carolina authors. Friend her at facebook.com/sarahrshaber. If you must tweet, her handle is @SShaber.

THE PLACE WHERE LOVE BEGINS

by Calvin Hall

Octavius Mead slumped into a chair in R.J.'s office. "I think Valerie's seeing someone," he said. His sadness made him look small and beaten in the Kenneth Cole suit he wore. He handed R.J. a copy of his wife's schedule. "I want you to follow her. I don't trust anyone else."

R.J. didn't normally investigate his friends' wives, but Octavius Mead was like a son to him. It didn't seem that long ago that he mentored him through college and became a father figure after the death of Octavius' father, R.J.'s college classmate and fraternity brother. He hated to see the younger man in such pain. Plus, except for bail bonds, business had been slow. He was surprised, though; the couple had seemed solid. Mead obviously cherished his wife, and Valerie didn't seem the type to run around, even though her looks—smooth brown complexion, large soulful eyes and bright smile—attracted plenty of male attention. She was a teacher, a church member, a community volunteer. Not your typical cheater, he thought, though really, who is?

So for days, he sat in a late-model GMC truck that he borrowed from a friend who owned a car lot for people with bad credit, trying to look inconspicuous as he shadowed Valerie. He followed her to the community college where she taught a course in business writing. To the hairdresser, the supermarket, a framing store, and Walmart. All routine, until the afternoon she left the house with a bright red suitcase and matching garment bag. She'd told her husband she was going to a conference in Greensboro, but she drove to a hotel near Blue Ridge University where she met a man just outside the front door. Valerie opened her arms to greet him with a long hug, embracing him as if she'd been waiting for the moment forever.

He was in his late 30s, Valerie's age, well-dressed in a black blazer, pastel blue polo and khakis, but not especially attractive otherwise. His appearance made a strong contrast to Mead, who took good care of himself even as he approached early middle age, and R.J. wondered what

Valerie could possibly see in this man. R.J. parked at a distant edge of the parking lot and recorded the moment with a military-grade surveillance camera. He was fond of his camera; he'd purchased it at a flea market from a pipe-smoking man wearing a tee shirt that said, "Welcome to the South! Now leave your daughters and go home!" You had to know to ask for the cameras or he'd try to sell you throwing-stars and hunting knives.

R.J. followed the pair for three days and two nights, making notes and taking photographs. He was bored yet soul-sick, beginning to hate Valerie for cheating on Mead. He began to hate his friend for asking him to confirm it. And he started to hate himself for not staying out of the whole sorry affair. But he kept taking pictures until the man drove away alone and Valerie returned to her home.

The next day, R.J. printed out the photographs, put them in an envelope, and called Octavius Mead to his office.

"My friend, I'm sorry," R.J. said as he handed Mead the envelope.

One by one, Mead studied the photographs: Valerie and her companion holding hands as they strolled around a lake in Pioneer City, kissing outside a concert at the amphitheater, smiling at each other as they entered a Thai restaurant. In the wee hours of each night, they returned to the sanctuary of the hotel.

"She lied to me." He fell into a chair as if someone had dropped an anvil into his lap, his face as pale as a black man's could get. "She said she was going to a conference but she hooked up with this clown."

"I'm sorry," R.J. said as sympathetically as he could. "I really am."

"It's not your fault. It's all mine, I guess."

"Who is he?"

"His name is Hugh Harrison. A friend of hers from college. Never met him in person though. I've only seen him in pictures. He sends cards, calls her occasionally."

"She talks to him and tells you?" R.J. thought that was unusual. Cheaters usually keep their lovers a secret.

"He wants advice. Wants to just say hello."

"You were OK with that?"

Mead looked at R.J. "I didn't like it. But she insisted that he was just a friend, there was nothing romantic between them. He was married. I tried to explain my point but she got defensive. Said she should be allowed to have friends." He rubbed his wedding band with his thumb as if it was burning his finger. "When I suspected she was cheating, I thought it would be someone from around here."

"If you need me, I'm still available." R.J. didn't know what else to say.

"Thanks," Mead said, frowning. "But what can I do? It's over."

"Before you do anything, get counseling. Find out what the problems are," R.J. said. Usually he kept himself detached from his clients' business, even ones he knew personally. But Mead was his friend and he felt obligated to try to help.

"I *know* what the damn problems are!" Mead slammed his palm on the desk. "She's been sleeping with someone else. I've been loyal to a goddamn fault. I've put up with her absences for church-this and charity-that, her committee meeting nights, her book club dinners. Supported her when she went back to school." He paused, as if being forced into a confession. "I know…I know I'm not the best husband. She says I can be a little moody, a little petty even. But I thought she accepted that as part of who I was. God…" His voice trailed off and he puffed out a sigh. "Dammit," he muttered.

"Talk to her," R.J. said, "And both of you should go see somebody. A counselor. A preacher."

"You're right," Mead said, still rubbing his ring with his thumb, albeit more slowly now, as if trying to discern its every detail. "I should see somebody about this." He stuffed the pictures back into the envelope and rolled it into a cylinder. "I know this was not something you wanted to do, but I appreciate your help, R.J. It's made me see things more clearly." He held out his hand. His face was pale but calm.

R.J. took his hand, held it a bit longer than necessary. "You're welcome. You sure you're all right?"

Mead nodded. "I'll be okay. Really. Don't worry." He appeared to brighten a little. "Now, how do I make out the check?"

"Pioneer City Bail Bonds & Investigations."

As Mead walked out of his office, R.J. felt unsettled. Something about Valerie and her lover bothered him, but he couldn't put his finger on it. And Mead—what was he going to do? Because Mead was his friend, he decided their situation deserved closer scrutiny.

* * * *

R.J. spent the next day in court testifying as a witness in a domestic violence case. He asked his partner, Xavier Martin, to find out as much as he could about Hugh Harrison, the man he'd seen with Valerie. Xavier, a former small-college football star with a degree in criminal justice, spent most of his time supervising the bail bond side of the business. But he enjoyed taking the occasional break from the bond world to help his partner.

When R.J. returned to the office at the end of the day, Xavier, holding a memo pad, was waiting for him. "How'd it go in court?"

"Same as always," R.J. said. "The system one, the people zero. You got information for me?"

"The dude's thirty-two, lives in Chicago. Works as a technical writer. He's single, has a five-year-old daughter from a previous relationship. He was in town for a seminar a few days before he was with Valerie Mead."

"Is that all?"

"Yeah. Except for the fact that, like you, I don't understand what she sees in him either."

R.J. smiled. "The heart wants what it wants—for whatever reason. Anything else?"

"Yeah. Seems our boy Harrison was a source of conflict between her and her husband three years ago. After one argument, Mead moved out of the house for six weeks."

"That's not public record."

"Word-of-mouth record. I know someone who knows someone who attends the same church as her. People talk. Even good Christian ones."

"Did you check on Octavius?"

"He didn't go to work today," Xavier said. "Went to a pawn shop on the west side of town. He didn't take anything in or bring anything out that I could see."

"Odd."

"I watched him go in and come out. Hands were empty both times."

"Then what?"

"To that Kmart near the mall. He spent twenty minutes there. Then he checked into a motel, the Daisy Inn on Glenn Chapel Road."

"Looks like you'll get paid this week after all. Damn."

Xavier laughed. "Why are you still interested in his case? I thought it was finished."

"It's personal, I guess," R.J. said. "His father and I knew each other a long time. Plus, I was a mentor to him after his father died. And I just feel bad for him. I've been there."

"But you're a big believer in that 'forgive and forget' stuff," he said. "If it was me, and I found out for sure my wife was with somebody else, I'd have to hurt somebody. Bad."

"I think everybody feels that way when it slips away from you," R.J. said. He thought about the time when, after eight years of marriage, his wife told him that they no longer had a future together. It felt like somebody had taken a bat to his face. "But you put it behind you. You think about consequences and don't act on impulse. You find someone and talk it out."

"Think Mead needs to talk to someone?" Xavier said.

"Yes. But I don't know if he will."

* * * *

For seventy-three dollars a night, the Daisy Inn offered a continental breakfast, free Wi-Fi, and cable movies. The receptionist, a five-foot tall woman with a Filipino accent, told R.J. that Octavius Mead was in Room 120.

"You should have called and asked him before sending a stranger to his room. I might have been a killer," R.J. said.

"But you look trustworthy," she said.

"So did Ted Bundy."

"Who?"

"Never mind." He found Room 120 and knocked. Knocked again.

It took Mead a long time to open the door. He frowned. "What do you want?"

"Were you asleep?" R.J. asked. He pushed the door open and moved past Mead into the room.

"No. I was…just…trying to nap, watching TV."

R.J. touched the television. Cold. "No, you weren't."

"I wasn't expecting anyone. Not out here. How did you know… Never mind. That's what you do, right? Find people for a living. What do you want?"

"A good businessman takes care of his customers even after the sale is done," R.J. said. "Are you all right?"

"I'm fine. Like I said, I was taking a nap."

R.J. figured that if Mead had been napping, he must've been lying on the floor. Neither of the two beds looked as if they had been disturbed since morning cleanup. But the room had a desk, and the chair had been moved. He took a seat on it, to let Mead know he wasn't going to leave any time soon. "How long you been here?"

Mead slumped onto one of the beds. "Couple of days. We had a fight. I told her I knew where she'd been. Who she'd been with. That someone saw her and I had proof."

"Did she ask to see it?"

"She didn't deny it and that told me all I wanted to know. She wanted to talk, but I was too disgusted with her. I left and came here." Mead rubbed his thumb across his ring finger, making a motion as if he was rotating his ring around the finger. But it was gone. Only a pale circle of lighter skin indicated where it had been.

"What happened to your wedding band?" R.J. asked.

"Lost it."

"In the vicinity of a pawn shop?"

"Look, I paid you," Mead said bitterly. "I don't need you anymore. What else do you want?"

"Same thing I wanted when I took you on as a client—to help."

"When I need your help, I know where to go. Right now, I just need some sleep." He leaned back on the bed and closed his eyes. "So I'd appreciate it if you'd leave."

R.J. tugged open the desk drawer. A Bible, a phone book. And a Colt .38-caliber pistol. "Where are the bullets?"

"Huh?"

"The ones you bought at Kmart. You were sitting here loading this gun, heard me knock, and put the bullets in your pocket. That's why it took you so long to answer the door. The TV hasn't been on in the last hour, if at all."

An uncomfortable silence occupied the room. Mead rolled onto his side but didn't answer.

R.J. stood and put his hand on his friend's shoulder. "Like you said, I find people—and figure them out for a living," he said. "I don't know what you planned to do with this gun. And I don't want to know. But I'm going to hold onto it for now." He walked to the door.

"Wait," Mead said. "We need to talk."

"I'm not the one you need to talk to."

* * * *

Valerie Mead's face expressed surprise, not welcome, when she opened her front door. Looking at her, dressed casually in a paisley top and jeans revealing her figure, R.J. became more determined to make sure that she and Octavius stayed together.

"May I come in?" R.J. asked.

Valerie stood aside and allowed him to enter. He had visited the house for dinners on a few occasions before and always felt comfortable here. The living room was decorated in warm earth tones. The dining room and its contemporary furnishings opened out to a patio leading to a large back yard. A red suitcase and a stuffed garment bag sat by the nearby staircase. "Octavius isn't here, Roger, and I'm in a rush." She spoke in soft tones that failed to mask her annoyance at the interruption.

"Going out of town?"

"For a few days, yes."

"Chicago?"

"Actually, I'm going to my mother's, if it's any of your business," she said, replacing annoyance with a cold anger. "But I must say that I don't care how close you are to him or his family. I do not appreciate my husband asking you to spy on me—or my friends."

"Seems to me he had good reason." R.J. handed her an envelope containing copies of the pictures he had taken of her with Hugh Harrison.

Valerie flipped through them quickly, then looked up at R.J. "You had a busy week. Is that why you're here?"

She reminded R.J. of his ex-wife—the same careful speech, the same controlled manner protecting a passionate center. "I just want to help," he said. "You're like family to me—both of you. And I don't want to see you break up."

"It's too late for that," she said.

"It's never too late to make something work."

"Roger, there's a place where love ends. Octavius and I are at that place. How can we make it work if we can't talk? He yells, accuses, twists my words. Always has." She handed R.J. the envelope. "Yes, you have pictures, but despite what you see there, we didn't sleep together at that hotel. I had my own room."

"Then why…"

"Why meet him? Why lie about it? Because I wanted to talk to him. I wanted to spend time with someone who understood my feelings without analyzing them, without attacking them. There was no need for anything sexual between us."

"Why didn't you tell Octavius?"

"I wanted to. I tried. But it's been a long time since I've been able to tell him what I need without getting a lecture. He doesn't listen. I think you've known him long enough to know that."

"Maybe," R.J. said, not wanting to concede the correctness of her assessment. "But the man I just left over an hour ago is ready to listen. Go to him."

Valerie seemed to consider what he said, but if his words had any effect, he didn't see it. She opened the door. "I'll think about it, Roger. But I really believe nothing can be done. There's too much negativity involved. Water under bridge and all that."

"He's at the Daisy Inn on Glenn Chapel Road," R.J. said, ignoring her protest. "I stopped him from doing something stupid and selfish. Go to him."

Valerie was unmoved. "Goodbye, Roger."

R.J. left the house and went to his truck. After about twenty minutes, Valerie came out with her packed bags, got into her Acura coupe, and drove away. But not in the direction that would take her by the Daisy Inn.

* * * *

When R.J. returned to the Daisy Inn, he didn't see Mead's car. He parked in a secluded spot and waited in the cool spring night air. Fifteen minutes later, Mead came back. Using a pair of night-vision binoculars, R.J. saw that Mead carried a six-pack and a bag of food from a bottom-feeder fast-food chain. Tired of watching the room—and certain Mead would be fine physically, if not emotionally—he prepared to leave. He had an early meeting with a lawyer in the morning.

Just then, Valerie's car entered the motel parking lot. She parked, went to the reception desk, and then to Room 120.

R.J. waited another hour, reminding himself to check whether the man who sold throwing stars, high-tech cameras, and night-vision binoculars also sold listening equipment. Around midnight, someone turned off the lights in Room 120, but neither Mead nor Valerie came out.

He yawned and drove off, thinking about what Valerie said about love ending at a place, wondering if they had found a place where love could begin again.

ABOUT THE AUTHOR

Calvin L. Hall is an associate professor in the Department of Communication at Appalachian State University in Boone, where he teaches journalism and serves as assistant chair. His creative work has been published in the journals *The Rectangle*, *Writer to Writer* and *A Thousand Faces*. He is the author of the book *African American Journalists: Autobiography as Memoir and Manifesto* published by The Scarecrow Press. Born and raised in Asheville, he earned a doctorate in mass communication from UNC-Chapel Hill's School of Journalism and Mass Communication. He also holds bachelor's and master's degrees in English from N.C. State University.

RILEY AND THE SAND DEMON

by Jamie Catcher

I never meant to hurt him. How could I when he was all I ever wanted? But I had, surely as if I'd pulled the trigger. Greer, my Greer, the one who lay sweet kisses to my collarbone just the night before.

Sideways rain pelts my face as bile inches up my throat. I press his wound harder and sink into the wet sand, desperate to stop the red seeping across his shirt. "Greer. Hang on. You're gonna be fine. They're almost here, and then you'll be in the best of hands."

His cool fingers fist my pant leg. "I already am."

I make a low choking sound, desperate for composure. I would gladly take his wound. Greer knows I'm lying about the being fine part, I can see it in his eyes. He coughs and the sticky blood under my fingers renews.

How could I have done this? You're supposed to listen to your handler—not get him killed!

"Please, Greer. Watch the hurricane blow in with me." I duck my head to his chest, tensing as a hotel lounge chair blows toward us. I cover Greer to protect him and the metal makes a *thud* on my shoulder as it passes by, taking a hunk of my hair with it. I am so wracked with guilt, I don't care about the pain, or anything else about the hurricane ravaging the Outer Banks. Janus, a Cat Four storm, threatens massive destruction in the next twelve hours.

His fingers grasp my leg as he blinks. "It's a sand demon, Riles. See its face in the sky? Keep an eye on it for me. Can't trust those sand demons."

I know this story, though I am not a believer in Greer's sand demon. He'd once seen a water spout spawned by a hurricane, and being gutsy Greer, he watched it come right up the beach to him, whipping sand everywhere before it collapsed. He swore it had a face, bewitching him to the spot.

As if to answer my disbelief, the awning over the hotel's outdoor restaurant spirals off. Well, maybe Janus and I do feel the same emotion. Rage.

I press harder on his wound, and hope it's sirens I hear coming from the west above the roar of the wind, the pounding surf. That would mean the trauma hospital got the call and was braving it through the storm to us, thank God. The Level 1 trauma center, the one you wanted to answer the call, officer down. *A GSW.*

Guh.

"Don't you dare die because the screw-up girl screwed up again. You're the only one who believes in me."

His face scrunches, and I can't tell if it's agreement or dispute.

Last night at check-in, he'd stood all gorgeous and dark Italian in his leather jacket, his mood even darker as he ordered me to back away from Vic. *You've gone too deep. I don't think you remember who you are, Riles.* He smoothed my hair from one eye and winced at the bruise I thought I'd so carefully hid as I hid everything else. *That's beyond,* he'd stuttered, something akin to outrage flickering in his grey eyes. He fingered the St. Christopher hanging around my neck, and for a tiny slice of a moment, I witnessed broody Greer, both rugged and tender with me.

I had fallen slow and deep for him long ago, but I hid that nonsense. Until last night, when he kissed me for the first time, and I knew I'd never hidden anything from him.

Afterwards, back in my dark room over Vic's garage, I took that kiss with me for strength. Only hours later, Vic would call me to meet him at our usual beachside bar, but something—a tense note in his voice, a new harshness—made me wary my cover was blown. I feared it every day, but this time I texted Greer to back me up, just in case. Little did I know I was summoning him to this…to his death. Oh, I pray not.

Greer tightens his grip on my wet leg as sirens scream onto the beach. They're here! I am so relieved to see the red square box, the flashing lights, and the navy jumpsuit-clad trio that pop out and come our way. Quickly, before they arrive, I feel in his pocket for his keys and cell phone and then ease his gun out of his hand.

"They're here. You're gonna be okay." I kiss his forehead goodbye. Greer doesn't move, his dark olive lids closed. "I promise, I *will* make this up to you," I half sob, half whisper in his ear. The paramedics swoop in and I back away, watching the rescue scene play out through gusts of wind and slashing rain. Before I know it, they are gone. Red taillights dim, sirens fade, and I'm left alone on the beach, soaking wet, my body weaving as gusts of wind from Janus's outer bands pummel me. One word is in my mind.

Vic.

I will bring him in or die trying. I swear it to the howling winds and spinning debris, to Greer's red blood sticky on my fingertips. Vic has been the town's most bastardly criminal for three years running, a criminal who traffics young girls for fun and profit, and runs drugs to buy fancy yachts and motorcycles. A criminal who killed the last undercover cop we sent inside his operation, yet always slimes his way out of charges.

Until me. I'm his handy dandy mechanic. I wear oil smears and smack wrenches around, using every bit of ace knowledge I have from my days in my father's garage. Vic trusts me, his concern for his precious machines spurring him to give poor-little-homeless-mechanic-girl a room above his garage. Now, Vic swears he *loves* me, as if someone that sick and twisted was capable of it. As I grew closer and closer to him, it was only a matter of time before I could provide the evidence we needed to arrest him, but no longer. Almost an hour ago, Vic shot Greer and watched me react in horror and tears. He'd left me alive, surprise-surprise, but he won't next time. No one crosses Vic.

I nod. I'll take the chance. I am a superb liar. What lie could I spin to explain my reaction? Long lost brother? Cousin? First, I need to regroup and find Vic to explain. The fact he didn't shoot me tells me I still have a chance.

My next thought is of Greer's car, and I run for the parking garage, anger powering every step. Part of me wants to follow the ambulance's path through the knocked-out stoplights to the hospital, but my desire to nail Vic wins out, though the decision hurts.

In desperate need to regroup before I go back into character, I end up at Greer's house. His driveway sits partially underwater, hibiscus blooms and sand scattered over the seashell-speckled concrete. I am homeless, my belongings sparse, but in the dark room above Vic's garage I pictured this ocean bungalow as *home*. Greer had inherited it and kept it in perfect shape, including the wood panels now covering the windows in case a hurricane turns this way—which Janus has.

A *mew* greets me. I feed Greer's cat, too sorrowful to look the grey tabby in the eyes. I shower for what feels like hours, but still feel dirty. I crawl into bed, soothed by Greer's smell, and find the sleep that eluded me the last twenty-four hours. I wake with a purring cat on my chest, surprised that my captain is not pounding on the door for answers, and then I remember Janus. The captain has widespread disaster to contend with.

Wait. I sit up. Vic would never hunker down—he would use the distraction of the storm to the fullest. He's been expecting a huge shipment, planning the drop for next week, but as nervous as he's been about it, I bet my left arm he's moved it up to coincide with the storm. He'd know the police would be tied up with emergencies and rescues. I bounce up.

With a parting pat to Greer's cat, I leave his Glock at his bedside, rummage in his gun safe for something easier to conceal. When I head to the warehouse, I'm armed only with a compact Sig Sauer P232 in a tiny Fobus holster, more determined than I've ever been in my misguided life. *Seven shots. I have only seven shots.*

Do this for Greer.

Janus is battering the palmettos to shreds as I pull into the lot behind the warehouse and see Vic's cars are parked outside. And so are the trucks. My heart pounds, and I catch my breath, jittery. I need to confirm the situation before I can call it in—if there's anyone around to call it in to.

I'm soaked by the time I reach the side door, but the noise of the storm has hidden my approach, and that's all that matters. Without Greer to tape and wire me up, I have no choice but to push *record* on Greer's phone and hope for the best.

Voices. My fingertips grow ice cold. Vic, with the musculature of a Greek god, has this menacing stance and these soul-reading eyes that control any room he steps into. Add a gravelly voice with snake-charming warmth and you somehow feel powerless in his presence. His people would do anything for him, and I need to remember I am no longer one of them.

I see Vic's tattooed and bald head over the cargo barrels ahead, and I dodge behind one, listening to his rant. Two voices. *Two*? Vic would never be that careless to bring only one guy along. Panic bubbles. Maybe this wasn't the drop.

"I don't need to justify why I didn't take care of her," Vic was saying.

"Because O'Rosie the Riveter is easy on the eyes?" Laughter.

"Yes, there's that. But this is an opportunity. She's so lost, I bet she comes back to us, not them. I can turn her. Do you know how useful it will be to have a mole in the police department?"

I bite my lip, tasting blood. No. It wasn't true. It wasn't! But here I stood, just like he said. I'd returned to him, not them.

"Scene looked like Romeo and Juliet."

"Yeah, but with Romeo dead, Juliet will turn desperate."

The damning memory replays. The wet and windy beach, the soft light of a stormy dawn. Vic slapping me, then kissing me, then slapping me again. Greer charging from the side of the hotel's beach deck, straight into Vic's bullet. The blood. The sand. The swirling dark grey hurricane bands. Janus wasn't the sand demon wooing Greer into danger on the beach. I was. I tighten my grip on the Sig.

Laughter again. I begin to shake, As the winds strip a panel off the warehouse roof, the screaming metal silences Vic's taunt. Rain pours in, footsteps scatter. Vic yells orders. I hear whimpers, cries, girls' voices and banging coming from a metal shipping container. This wasn't just a drug drop! I push buttons on Greer's phone, a desperate text, misspelled and disjointed. I send it to every cop on Greer's contact list, praying somebody will respond, despite this storm.

Vic and his goons are hurrying. I run straight into the middle of the chaos, and take out goon number one before he can fire the gun he's leveling at me. I see Vic's muscled arms stacking cocaine bricks, then a flash of silver appears. A knife. Vic always was a knife man. He said killing someone with a knife was more personal, and then he would laugh in that deep, rolling laugh, the one that both soothed and disturbed your psyche.

Vic smiles when he registers it's me, surprise and relief mingled in his expression, yet he comes at me with the knife through the sheets of rain. I grab a block of his precious cocaine and throw it at his face before dodging behind a barrel. Hearing his steps, I roll to the other side of the barrel and pop up. Vic is not to my right where I expect him to be—he is at my left, slowly waving the knife as he snarls, "Pretty boy dead? He shouldn't have snuck up on us lovebirds."

Bastard. "How many girls do you have in those moving metal coffins?" I ask, hearing their fists pounding the sides, dozens upon dozens of hands, and I want to forget Vic so I can free them. "You promised fancy waitressing jobs abroad? See the world? Earn good money? You make me sick. They're daughters. Sisters."

Vic gives a roll of laughter. "They're whores. But you—I'll give you all the money you could ever want. No more poor little cop girl. The high life is yours. Clothes. Jewelry. My bed."

My fate would be no different from the girls in those containers. "So you can kill me like the last undercover."

"She fought a good fight."

Please let the recorder have caught that. I shudder. Too late, I hear footsteps. Vic's men step from the shadows, and a warm and wet arm circles my throat from behind. I lunge to escape, but it crushes on my windpipe. Hands rip the gun from my grasp, and though I buck against my captor, he lifts me off my feet and swings me through the air, shaking me.

Vic isn't laughing. The wind and rain are pouring into the warehouse, soaking the bricks of coke strewn across his table. He looks up at the angry sky and bellows to his men. "Throw her in a barrel and clamp it shut, then get over here and help me get this high dollar stuff out. Girls later."

Death by suffocation inside a barrel is not my choice of a way to go. I kick, spit, and bite, and they laugh. My elbows bang the rim of the barrel, and I hear and feel the bones of my left arm crunch. As the metal lid bangs down on my head with a clanging echo, I cry out, pushing and bucking against it, but the lid doesn't budge.

My breaths shorten, and I can't calm down. I am trapped, in the dark, in a foul metal barrel. I'm soaked with sweat, the air stale and already thinning. I try to kick, to flail, but there is no room to move. Pain paralyzes my left arm, so I use the right to push up on the lid. If I do not lift this lid, I will suffocate!

A crash sounds against the building. Metal gives a slow, scream from above, and Vic begins yelling. Something slams against my barrel, toppling it and I begin to roll, a nauseating sensation until an abrupt impact pops off the barrel's lid and cool air fills my lungs. Greer's sand demon has saved me!

I crawl out into a ruined warehouse. Vic and his goons have vanished. The girls are screaming. So many voices. I snap up a fallen gun and start to shoot off the lock on the metal container door, but sense movement, a bloodied Vic pounding toward me, knife raised. My breath catches, and I run, dodging waving sheets of twisted metal, toppled barrels, and strewn beams, the full force of Janus battering me with wind and rain.

I lead Vic outside, straight toward the familiar unmarked police cars. My captain is there, snapping orders from behind his car door, and in seconds, Vic is surrounded by a dozen of officers bristling with guns, shouting at him to surrender his weapon. No stranger to police authority, Vic drops the knife and raises his arms in surrender. Quickly encircled and cuffed, he scans the faces, and pins me with his stare. I return the glare. *Enjoy death row, Vic.* Relief floods me as the reality of his capture sinks in, and I remember the girls. "There's girls! Inside a shipping container. Free them!" Officers scatter.

My captain looks me over, his eyes fixed on my dangling left arm. "Thought we lost you, Riley. Good work."

I shake my head. No. I hurt the man I thought of as home. "Greer?" I ask, dreading the answer.

My captain shakes his head, and I try to read his expression—exasperation, sorrow, or finality? "When we got your texts, Greer left the hospital AMA to come with us. Would you straighten him out before he bleeds to death?" He moves to the side and I see a lone figure sitting in the passenger seat of his car.

Greer. Alive. He holds half-hidden bandages under his leather jacket and nudges toward the door as I approach.

My pain, regret, and rage leave me. Greer is looking at me with warm, full eyes. I do not think I can manage a single word, but I smile.

Greer, with his stubbly jaw and his dark hair rumpled to the side, smiles back, and I know that for the first time in months, I am safe. I sigh, thankful. The hurricane blows a gust that rocks the car, a sandy palmetto frond hitting the glass. With a wince, Greer laughs and points to the grey bands of hurricane clouds. I see two dark eyes topped with waggling brows in that swirl, and a very definite face. I am now a believer.

Greer's sand demon.

ABOUT THE AUTHOR

Jamie Catcher writes from her home in Aiken, South Carolina. She has a B.S. in English and a background in pediatric registered nursing. Her short stories have appeared in regional publications, and she is currently seeking publication of her novel, *SYN 11*, a psychological thriller and love story. She believes in fairies and coffee, and writes because it's the only thing that keeps the persuasive characters in her head quiet. Contact her at jamiecatcherbooks@gmail.com and follow her on Twitter @jamiecatcherbks.

BAD HAIR DAY

by Meg Leader

Hanging out with the dead is not your ordinary lifestyle choice, but, then again, in my case it's not exactly a choice. For as long as I can remember, I've been able to see folks no one else could see. I was seven years old before I realized that my BFF, little Clara Marie, wasn't among the living-and-breathing set. Until I figured that out, I thought she wouldn't invite me to play at her house because my family was from the trailer park side of town instead of the five-columned ego-mansion district. Just goes to show how easy it is to assume prejudice where none exists.

It took me a lot of years and a lot of experimenting before I figured out a way to make my predilection for the departed into a viable career option. So now I'm the country's only spectral detective. See, dead folks—at least the ones who hang around and don't pass into the light—they *notice* stuff. They wander around watching us living screw up our lives. They offer suggestions, snide commentary, and more than a few I-told-you-so's from the sidelines. Of course, they don't exactly make good witnesses in court because it's hard to get them to place a palm on a Bible and swear to tell the truth when their hands pass right through the book. Not to mention that the judge, jury, and attorneys involved can't see or hear them. Still, they do pay attention to what goes on, and many of them enjoy hanging out at crime scenes.

Especially murder crime scenes.

My big brother Charlie is a homicide detective. While Greensboro, North Carolina. isn't exactly overrun with your high-profile murder cases, we do have our share of bad guys, jealous husbands, and disgruntled employees. When the case is tough, Charlie, who knows very well what I can do, brings me in as a "consultant" for the case. Consultant—doesn't that sound just way cool? I get a laminated badge and everything. Sometimes they even pay me.

So anyways, an hour ago Charlie called me to a murder scene, the foyer of one of the old-line Irving Park mansions. The corpse is an expensive-looking young woman wearing only the bottom half of the tiniest pink thong bikini I've ever seen—a mere triangle and a few strings—and a butt-length cover-up, open wide to reveal an impressive set of implants. Despite her casual lack of attire, she's carefully groomed except for one thing—her hair. I suppose her blonde and copper highlights and lowlights and multi-strand weaves cost her a bundle of money. Unfortunately, a violent bash on her head has ruined the effect of all that pampering.

Charlie hovers at my elbow, impatient.

"Who is she?" I ask.

"Juliette Irving. Third wife of Gomez Irving. The developer," he says. I recognize the name. Irving's full of civic pride, spending his time—and the public's money—improving the scenery by planting shopping centers and housing developments all over the landscape.

Off to one side, the late Mrs. Irving's tantrum is worthy of a paparazzi-crazed rock star. No one else can hear her, of course, but she's shrieking louder than a hyperactive three-year-old squalling for a candy bar. It hurts my ears. I edge away from the corpse, but no one notices. All the cops are too busy elbowing each other to get a better view of the lady's attributes. I move down the main hallway toward the quieter back of the house to escape the confusion. To my surprise Juliette follows me.

"Did you see what he did to my hair? I paid a fortune for that. Look at it. It's awful!" Juliette Irving is fixated on her ruined hairdo, all right. That trumps getting murdered.

The rich really are different.

At least she's calmed enough to lower her voice. Turning my back to the cluster of cops hovering over her body, I quietly ask, "Do you know who murdered you, Mrs. Irving?"

"How could I know? Haven't you seen the back of my head? The *back*? You think I have eyes in the back of my head?" She glares at me, hands on hips, her cover-up spread wide so it covers up nothing. I try to imagine going through eternity wearing only a pink thong bikini bottom. Actually, I try *not* to imagine that.

"If you could tell me what happened…?"

It's the wrong question to ask. "Tell you what happened? Just look what was done to my hair! The color's a disaster. And the cut…! Any idiot can see it. Are you an idiot?" Her glare spikes from outrage to flat-out fury. Not waiting for me to defend my IQ, she stalks toward her corpse—and flies into more hysterics over what the murderer has done to her hair.

Unfortunately for Charlie, not to mention my rep with the Greensboro PD, Juliette Irving doesn't know who bashed her on the back of the head with the bust of Beethoven. Shame about that. I've seen a lot of Beethoven busts—when I'm not revealing murderers, I study composition at the excellent School of Music at UNC Greensboro here in town—and this bust seems one of the finer examples, once you get past the matted, copper-highlighted hair and bloody gore splattered down one side.

"Well?" Charles has the patience of a famished vampire mosquito as he edges up beside me. "Who did this to her?" he whispers out of the side of his mouth in his best Bogart style.

I shrug, not wanting to admit I haven't the faintest idea. "Any fingerprints?"

"Several sets on the bust. We're collecting elimination prints. Maid, housekeeper, husband. The victim too, of course. Too early to tell, but one set seems oddly placed for casual touches. We'll know soon if it's an unsub."

Unsub. Love that cop talk. Unknown subject of course. I haven't spent my life watching *CSI* and *Law and Order* for nothing. "Let me know if you get a match, okay?"

Charlie nods. With a slight inclination of my head, I indicate I'm heading outside. I'm hoping there's a DP—that's my own personal cop-on-a-case jargon for Deceased Person—hovering around out there who'll have something useful to tell me.

Leaving the dear departed Juliette to continue her tantrum, I step outside and away from the front door, with Charlie following. The news vans are all over this, of course, but they're kept a couple houses away by the yellow tape and a few officers who are standing so stiffly it's like they're practicing to become one of those royal guards who never crack a smile. I ignore the reporters peppering me with questions and cut around the side of the house to the back yard. Happily, this well-established mansion in Greensboro's old-money district has lush landscaping, so once I duck behind a huge magnolia I'm out of sight. As soon as we have privacy, Charlie asks again, "So?"

"Don't know." I'm admiring the gorgeous swimming pool and stone-paved patio, not paying a lot of attention to him.

"What do you mean you don't know?"

"I mean I don't know. What am I? Wikipedia? Stay here." Without listening to any further bluster, I stride over to the other side of the pool, where I see a DP loitering. Charlie knows better than to follow me when I'm on the scent. "Hi," I greet the DP.

"You can see me?" This DP is a young kid, maybe eighteen, nineteen. He has the hollow-eyed skin-and-bone look of a long-time drug user. No need to wonder what caused his demise. He's the poster boy of a druggie gone dead.

"Sure. What's your name?"

"Blinky." It's a nickname of course, and suitable since he has a constant, exaggerated blink that's impossible to miss.

"Nice to meet you, Blinky. You hang out here much?"

He shrugs. "Yeah. It's nice."

I nod. "Nice scenery." From my admittedly brief view of Juliette Irving, her scenery would be extremely nice. And from her lack of tan lines, my guess is that the bottom half of that bikini was strictly reserved for more formal occasions than poolside lounging.

He giggles. "Yeah. Woulda liked to done something about that. Too late now."

"Yeah. Death's a bitch, isn't it?"

Though Blinky looks startled at that profound philosophical observation, he doesn't comment. "So how come you can see me? Nobody else does."

My turn to shrug. "It's what I do." Things are friendly, so I figure it's okay to ask him about what he knows. "Where were you when all the excitement happened? See anything?"

"Naw. I was back here, like always."

I eye him. "How come you're not comforting the newly departed Mrs. Irving?"

He shuffles his feet. "That lady is *loud*. Never heard such screeching. Just pissed off over her hair getting mussed."

"Getting bonked over the head will do that to a hairstyle. Were you pretty familiar with her?"

A sly look creeps over his face and he snickers. "I guess. I like to come over here and watch."

"Watch?"

"Her and her guy. They like—liked—to do it here, by the pool. Pretty good entertainment."

I think about that. "I don't suppose you mean her husband?"

"Dunno." He blinks, scratches his nose. "What's he look like?"

I dredge up a memory of Mr. Irving's photograph from the paper—he got some civic award for something or another last week that made a big splash in the local news. "About sixty, gray hair, goatee—"

Blinky laughed. "Naw. She was humpin' a younger guy. Maybe thirty, thirty-five. Black hair. Works out, I guess. Has muscles on him anyway."

Aha! My finely tuned detective instincts scream at me. I'm onto a hot trail here. "You ever hear her call him by name? Even a first name?"

He snickers. "You mean other than Muffbuster?"

I can't help the grin that escapes. "I mean like a real name."

He scratches his nose again. "Hard to understand her—she was distracted if you know what I mean. And loud. Hurt my ears to listen to her, so I kinda stopped paying attention. But I think she used to call him something like Gary? Larry?"

I run through the possibilities: Barry, Cary, Harry, Jerry, Perry... Blinky settles on being "pretty sure" it was Gary. Last name? Blinky hasn't a clue. I figure he wasn't bothering much with the male participant in the trysts when he had the luscious Juliette in front of him wearing nothing more concealing than a slick of sunscreen.

I ask a few more questions, then thank Blinky—it's always good to be polite to DPs since you never know when you'll become one yourself. Then I head back over to Charlie. He's impatient, waiting for me to pull a solution out of the sky. That's what he expects—a miracle cure, like penicillin. Unfortunately, I never was good at science.

"Guess what?" I ask. "Mrs. Irving had a lover. Gary somebody. And their last tryst was...guess when...earlier today."

Nothing warms the shiny badges of a homicide detective's heart more than the prospect of adding a hot suspect to his list of possible perps. Charlie's practically quivering as he runs through scenarios. "So...the husband, comes home, finds wifey doing the rumpty-humpty with her boy toy. Boy toy escapes, husband gets mad, wifey gets bonked."

"But Charlie—"

He doesn't wait for me to point out the flaws in that. "Or it could be the other way around. Boy toy is here, has an argument with wifey, they get mad, he bonks her with the bust, then high-tails it out of town."

"But Charlie—"

He's so obviously pleased to have narrowed down the suspects that he doesn't wait for me to point out one gigantic hole in both his theories. Before I can say more, he trots away toward the front of the house, hoping he'll be the first to reveal the lover angle.

Don't get me wrong. Charlie's a good cop and a good detective. Statistics are on his side. Most murdered women are done in by their husbands, lovers, or exes. But he has forgotten one key thing in his eagerness.

Juliette doesn't know who killed her. If it had been either husband or lover, I'd think even the hair-obsessed Juliette would have recognized *something* about her killer. Then again, maybe it's worth trying to talk to her again. If she's stopped being traumatized over her tresses, maybe she can tell me something more specific about her attacker.

I go back to the front of the mansion. Charlie has pulled a couple cops off to one side. His body language shows the same shivery eagerness of his favorite pointer when she catches scent of a bird. The criminalists are packing up and the medical examiner is preparing to wheel Juliette's corpse to the van to take her to the morgue. Meantime, the DP version of Juliette is still haranguing everyone in sight about her hair. Sheesh. You'd think she'd be done with that topic.

I quietly walk up to her. "Mrs. Irving? Juliette? Could I ask you a question?"

"You again! How come you're talking to me, anyway? None of these other cretin-cops will."

Hmmm. "Cretin"—that's not the kind of word your average trophy wife will use. My assessment of Juliette Irving elevates. "No, ma'am. I'm the only one who can see or hear you."

She still looks mad enough to haunt me for eternity, but with a little more talk I calm her down and convince her to answer a few questions.

"I was just seeing a friend out—" she pauses to look at me to see if I am buying her euphemism.

"You mean your lover? Gary?"

"How do you know about him? Did that scumbag husband of mine tell you?"

"No, ma'am. As far as I know, Mr. Irving doesn't know about your... friend." True enough. I haven't had the pleasure of meeting her husband yet, so I have no reason to believe he knows about her activities. I always try to be truthful with DPs. They're easier to deal with if they trust me. She looks skeptical, but I guide her back to the main question. It's like herding a rabid rabbit. "So you were seeing Gary out—can you tell me his last name?"

She hesitates, but after I point out that under the circumstances, she's not likely to get served with divorce papers, she admits he's Gary Frankenship. I can't keep back a whistle. The Reverend Frankenship is the minister of the very popular Apocalyptic Mission Church. The church membership has surged since Frankenship took over, even in this area where competition for tithe money is fierce and there are more churches per acre than coffee shops. Gradually, I get her to tell me what happened.

She and her lover Gary are indulging in a tryst back by the pool. She's given the servants the afternoon off. Today, however, her joy-jumping with the Reverend Gary isn't going all that well. She's too upset about the butchery done to her hair. That part starts another rant about her plans to sue the hairdresser and spread the word all over town that he's an incompetent hack. She even told the ungrateful little snip exactly that yesterday when he refused to give her a refund.

Again, I have to steer her back on the main track. What happened earlier *today*?

After a bit more bluster, she explains that she tells Gary her husband might be catching on about her extracurricular activities. He's threatening to cut off her allowance, maybe even kick her out. That's okay with her. She wants to get a divorce and marry Gary. She has a yen to be a minister's wife…she could help him "minister" to the congregation. I gather by then, she's ministering pretty good to Gary. She starts to tell me some of her special dick-tricks to persuade men to do what she wants, until I pull her back onto the subject.

"And what did Gary say to that idea?" I ask.

Her face crumples. "He yelled at me! Said he can't afford to marry me, has no intention of marrying me, and wouldn't marry a scarlet Jezebel ever. That's when I bit his dick."

Ouch. That had to *hurt*.

I ask her how Gary reacted to that.

"He was pretty mad," she admits. "There was a little, uh, name-calling."

"Nothing more physical?" Maybe lover-boy got mad and bonked her.

"Nah. Gary wouldn't lay a hand on a woman." She slants a sly glance my way. "Not in anger, anyway."

"Uh-huh. So what happened next?"

"I pulled on my bikini and my jacket and showed him out."

Just as I thought. Juliette isn't used to wearing much of anything around that pool. No wonder Blinky likes to hang out here. One thing makes me curious, though. "Why bother with dressing up just to show him out?"

She shrugs. "I like to be a bit more formal when I go to the front door. This is the South, you know."

Right. Formal. Wide open jacket revealing every inch of her boobs, and a bottom that covers nothing of her butt.

"Besides," she adds with another sly glance, "I wanted Gary to see exactly what he was passing up. He's a very, uh, *visual*, kind of guy. And he loves the look of my butt in that pink thong. It's his favorite. So I did a few butt-twitches on the way to the front door. Just as a reminder, you know?"

"But he did leave?"

That sly smirk switches to a bad-tempered frown. "Yes," she says sourly. "I slammed the door behind him."

"I see." So I can push the not-so-holy Gary to the bottom of my suspect list. "What happened next?"

Now she looks puzzled. "I had just turned away, walking toward the stairs, when I heard the door open again. I thought it was Gary coming back, so I made sure the jacket gave him a good look at my butt. He really is an ass man, you know. He just loves—"

"And was it Gary?" I interrupt. This is definitely too much information. And I'm *never* going to attend Apocalyptic Mission Church.

"Well, I was starting to turn and then…that's it. My head felt like it exploded. It's all I remember."

And thus a new DP is made.

I ponder all she has told me as I drive away from the mansion. Charlie's two theories could both fit. Lover leaves the house in a rage, changes his mind, walks back inside, grabs Ludwig and just like that—his problem lover isn't a problem anymore. Or, husband is home early enough to see virtually naked wife showing another man out the front door. He's enraged, opens the door, grabs the bust, and again Juliette is the newest member of the DP community.

Somehow, though, neither of those scenarios is quite right. I don't see the super-controlled Mr. Irving as the type to indulge in rage. As for the Reverend Gary, well, he too seems unlikely to resort to an assault with a deadly Beethoven. I think the husband would be more likely to coldly hire a hit, and Reverend Gary more likely to arrange an accident, like getting her drunk and drowning her in the pool, something like that. The Beethoven bust thing—it just doesn't seem like either one's style.

I'll have to talk to Charlie soon, but first I want to follow one other clue I winkled out of Juliette's story.

An hour later, by begging and pleading, I get an appointment with Juliette's stylist. Henri most likely grew up in the *Montagnes d'Arête Bleues* region, based on the traces of hillbilly that creep into his fake French accent. I want a new hairstyle, I tell him. My shoulder-length light brown hair needs a makeover, and I want only the best, no matter what the cost. I explain that I spotted Juliette Irving's gorgeous new hairstyle last night at Underground, Greensboro's most exclusive eatery, and I immediately recognized the work of an artiste. I'm so impressed that I can confidently place my hair in his talented hands. He has carte blanche to do whatever he thinks best.

After a suitable period of lamenting the talentless hacks who (as he claims) have all but destroyed my hair, Henri agrees to take on my "*dee-fi-ceel*" case. While he's sectioning and dabbing my hair, he starts a rant about Juliette. After discreetly discovering that I'm not a personal friend of hers, just an admirer of her hair, he goes into a long diatribe about how "eempos-*see*-blay" customers can be and how they have no *appreciation* of his skills.

While we're waiting for the chemicals to do their thing, I'm installed in a comfortable chair in a quiet corner of the salon and handed a glass of chardonnay. Too bad I don't much like chards—too oaky for my taste. But it gives me a chance to observe everyone in the salon. I'm interested in how they all interact. Henri is a sensitive soul in many ways. He seems deeply hurt by the altercation he had with Juliette. I'm just thinking about this when I realize a DP has settled beside me. A quick glance around shows me no one is in hearing distance if I speak softly.

"Hi," I say. The DP is a middle-aged woman with tears running down her cheeks. "Is anything wrong?"

She pointed in the general direction of the salon where Henri and his staff were bustling around with clients. "*That's* wrong."

"I don't know what you mean."

"I had my hair done here a few months ago. Can't you tell?"

I study her more carefully. She does look freshly coifed. But there's something off about the style…no, the color. It's much too orange for this lady's delicate fair skin. "It's a nice style…" A lie. I should never lie to a DP.

"No, it's not." She turns her head so I can see the area just behind her left ear. Sure enough, there's another bashed-in spot that reminds me a lot of Juliette's bonked head.

"What happened?"

"I shouldn't have complained," she says. "I could have just gone to another stylist somewhere else and it could have been fixed. Now…it'll never be fixed. And I ruined my daughter's wedding day!"

A little coaxing and a few more half-coherent sobs, and I start to remember her story. Mrs. Chichioni had come here to get her hair done for the ceremony. The style was OK, but the color was too orange, not at all the golden blonde she had requested. She'd complained and refused to pay Henri. Later that evening…she's in the DP set with nary a clue as to how she got there. The cops, if I remember rightly, thought the son-in-law might have done it. Or her husband. But no evidence supports either theory. Last I heard, the case still lingers in the "Unsolved" folder and shows every sign of staying there. Now Mrs. Chichioni wails to me that her daughter's wedding day memories are forever destroyed by the tragedy.

"Will it help if I see to it that no one else ever has the same problem?" I ask her.

She's sobbing now, but she nods into her handkerchief. As Henri's assistant comes over to lead me back to his station, I give my poor DP an encouraging smile and nod as I walk away.

My appointment continues as Henri works his magic on my hair. He's jovial until a stylist nearby drops a bottle of their exclusive, over-priced conditioner on the floor. He erupts into an expletive-filled tirade, grabs a hair dryer, and throws it at her. She jumps, I'm shaken, but no one else reacts. They must be used to his tantrums.

Three hours and a maxed-out credit card later, I'm ready to go. My hair has a funky asymmetrical, slightly punk bob and a mixture of about fifteen colors ranging from ash blonde to coppery red. I'm not convinced that it's very "me," but I make sure I tell Henri he's a true artist. Don't want him getting mad at me. No sir, I don't.

* * * *

Time to find Charlie.

Charlie is back at the station. He's got Reverend Gary and Mr. Irving in different interrogation rooms, letting them sit there to contemplate their sins. "What's up? You do something weird to your hair?"

Something weird, he says. Men are insensitive asses.

"Which one do you think did it?" I nod toward the interrogation rooms as I perch on the hard chair opposite his desk.

"My money's on the good reverend. It's always those holy types."

I prop my elbow on his desk and rest my chin in my palm. "You want to know what I think?"

Charlie immediately perks up. "Whatcha got? C'mon. Give."

"You've got the wrong guys. The perp is—" Just to torment him, I insert a dramatic pause while I listen to the *Final Jeopardy* countdown music in my head: la-la-la-la, la-la-la…

"You want me to arrest you for obstruction of an investigation? *Who is it?*"

"Okay, okay. I think it's Juliette's hairdresser, Henri. She made very public threats to sue him and ruin his business. I'll bet if you check, those unsub prints on our buddy Beethoven will turn out to be his. If you talk to Henri's staff, I'm sure you'll find that he was missing from his shop at the time of Juliette's murder. And they'll tell you all about his temper. It's ferocious. You might also check where he was when Mrs. Chichioni was murdered—you remember her?"

He nods. "You mean—?"

"Yep. Turns out Mrs. C. had her own run-in with Henri the morning before she was bonked."

"Thanks, Sis. I'll take a look at that case file," he says. "But maybe you should do something about your hair."

I smile sweetly as I get up to leave. "The cost of Henri's services will be included in my invoice. And I'll expect a bonus for wrapping up the Chichioni case too."

I ignore Charlie's sputters as I saunter out the door. I spot my reflection in the window. I'm getting used to my funky new look. My hair looks great. Money well spent as far as I'm concerned, especially because it's the PD's money. But having a bad hair day—now, that can lead to all kinds of consequences. Like just a little murder.

ABOUT THE AUTHOR

Meg Leader's first published fiction was in the romance genre, so her stories range from the romantic to the mysterious. Nearly all of her stories have a thread of the paranormal running through them. Her characters are a little funky, a little off-center, and their perspectives on the world might make you laugh—or cry. Most of all, the stories set out to provide a wonderful reading experience that entertains, amuses, and touches the heart. You can contact Meg at her websites, megleader.com and mhleader.com, email her at megleader@megleader.com, or follow her on Facebook at MegLeaderWriter.

A ONE-CAT WOMAN

by Antoinette Brown

Holy Hannah. Mom hadn't said anything about all *these* cats. Five carriers, lined up in her mother's living room. Cori knelt to examine their hissing occupants: a tuxedo, a yellow mom with three matching kittens, an agitated tabby, and an enormous white longhair. The fifth carrier contained a tiny kitten, no more than a few weeks old, fluffy and gray with white feet and ears. At the sight of her, they each cowered and hissed. Ferals. Where did they come from? And where was Blue, her mother's Abyssinian show cat?

"Blue! Kitty, kitty?" She heard a mournful cry from the kitchen. There he was, perched on top of the refrigerator. Cori shook treats onto the counter. The cat would come down on his own time.

Cori Stanton was on cat-sitting duty this week, caring for Blue while her mother judged a cat show in Wisconsin. Mom hadn't said anything about feral cats. Cori searched the house. The front and back doors were locked. No sign of forced entry but the security system was unarmed. Not like Mom to forget.

Cori pulled her phone from her jeans pocket and left her mother a voice mail. *Five cages of feral cats in your living room? Call me.*

Blue's cry brought Cori back to the kitchen. No wonder the cat was complaining. His food bowl was empty. She scooped him up and examined him. No sign of fleas or scratches. She decided to take him home tonight. She would examine him more carefully, and bring him with her to the Piney Woods Animal Hospital tomorrow if necessary. With the Mid-Atlantic Abyssinian and Somali Cat Show two weeks away, Blue needed to look his best.

In search of Blue's carrier, Cori opened the door to the garage, switched on the light, and was startled to see at least thirty carriers stacked on top of one other. What on earth? Flat out bizarre. She pushed through the piles looking for Blue's distinctive silver one.

"Hey, watch it."

Cori jumped. "Who's there?"

A stout older woman dressed in a peasant skirt and a faded t-shirt, clutching a flowered tote bag, stepped from behind the carriers. "I'm Hollis Hogarth. Joan said I could use her garage while she's away." Hollis had cropped gray hair, bushy eyebrows, and a face full of furrows and ridges sharp as mountains. "The bird people have been rounding up cats and euthanizing them. I'm trying to save as many strays as I can."

Cori put the pieces together. "So those are your cats in the living room?"

"Not exactly. After my kids put me in an institution they took my two cats—Siamese—to the shelter. These guys are from a colony I feed."

Cori sat down on a big bag of kitty litter. This might take a while. Had the woman escaped? "Where do you live?"

"Bayview. But they won't let me have my cats."

Bayview was an exclusive senior residence, not a memory care unit and definitely not an 'institution.' "So you brought them here."

"I had to. There was nowhere else. If I take strays to the shelter they'll be put down."

"But the shelter doesn't euthanize. It's trap, neuter, and release."

"Not if Elise is successful with her petition."

Cori had no idea what petition Hollis was talking about. But she did know her mother would not be pleased to come home to a house full of caged feral cats. "May I please have Mom's house key back?"

Hollis took a step back, her eyes darting around the garage. "Why?"

"I'm sure Mom doesn't want a lot of cats in her house. As it is, I'll have to spray for fleas before she gets home."

"No." Hollis grimaced, tightening her grip on the flowered tote.

"I don't want to have to change the locks. And you can't leave those cats here."

Hollis sighed and dug through her tote until she found the key. She shoved it at Cori. "Guess I have to take them back to the Wayfarer's Motel. They've been living behind dumpsters."

"I love cats too, so maybe I can help you with them," Cori said. She gave Hollis her phone number, and they loaded the cat carriers, both occupied and empty, into Hollis's SUV.

Glory be, Cori thought, that problem was solved, at least momentarily. She put Blue into his carrier and headed home. It had been a long day in her grooming studio, and she was ready to warm leftovers in the microwave and watch *Castle* reruns. But the minute she flopped into a chair, her phone rang.

"After I let my cats out of their carriers, they ate something poisonous!" Hollis sounded hysterical. "Someone's poisoned them and they're dying!"

"That's horrible! Where are you?"

"Wayfarer's Motel. In back, by the dumpster."

"Stay where you are. And don't touch anything."

"I can't stay. Got to follow 'em."

Follow them? Hollis hung up before Cori could ask what she meant. Punching numbers on her cell phone to alert Animal Control, Cori drove to the motel.

The scene was appalling. Cori recoiled at the sight of three dead cats, dried saliva and foam around their mouths. Nearby, in the waves of heat rising from the scorching asphalt, flies buzzed around two open cans of cat food. She glimpsed movement under an azalea bush—the gray kitten with white boots, crawling toward the cans and wobbling with each step. Cori's heart lurched. She needed Animal Control right away. And where was Hollis?

She snapped photos with her phone as the Animal Control truck approached. She waved it down. "Over here!"

Jim Hawkins swung out of the truck. He was short, stocky, bald, and the kindest man Cori had ever known. "What have we got here?" he asked.

Cori pointed to the dumpster. "Three dead cats. Hollis Hogarth called in the report, says they were poisoned. She feeds this colony. I told her to wait for me, but she took off."

"Aw geez," Jim said, pulling on thick rubber gloves. "This is terrible. Could be poison, but I wouldn't rule out feline distemper." He slid the dead cats into a plastic garbage bag. "And none of these cats has a clipped ear that would indicate it's a trap, neuter, release colony, so they won't have had a rabies vaccination."

"Hollis was afraid that if she took the cats to the shelter they'd be killed."

"Does she think it's better to die of rabies or a feline virus? Allow the females to produce more strays?" Jim tied up the plastic bag and placed it into the back of the truck, along with a second bag containing the open cat food cans and drinking bowls.

"There's a kitten over there." Cori pointed to the azaleas. "It looks pretty frail."

As Jim approached the gray kitten, it hissed weakly. He took it gently by the back of its neck. "I'll take this guy and the others to the vet school and let you know what they find."

Cori had to track down Hollis. If rabies had caused any of these deaths, and if Hollis had been exposed to the disease from a scratch or bite, she'd have to start the shots right away. Cori looked up Bayview on her phone. "Hollis, why didn't you wait at the motel?"

"Had to follow the trail. Come over. I'll show you what I found."

Cori sighed loudly. This woman's mysterious act was wearing thin. "After I take a shower and feed Blue, I'll be there."

* * * *

At nine p.m., Cori knocked on Hollis's door.

"Took you long enough," said Hollis. Her nightgown was pink flannel printed with—what else—cats.

"What do you have?"

"A license plate number." Hollis waved a cat food label. "A black car pulled out of the parking lot real fast as I called you for help. I tried to follow but lost it after a few blocks."

Cori sank into the nearest armchair, closed her eyes, and wished she was in bed with the new Margaret Maron novel and a glass of merlot.

"Your mom would want you to help me."

"Hollis, we don't know yet if the cats were poisoned. It might be rabies, in which case you're in danger."

"It was poison. I know it. The crazy bird people. Had to be them. The ones who pushed for the ban on feeding strays."

Cori dug paper and a pen out of her purse. "We'll make a list of suspects. Number one, if it's poison: bird lovers. Anyone specific?"

"Elise Weatherbee."

"Weatherbee. Is she related to the new vet in town?"

"Yeah, his mom. Elise started a petition for a trap-and-euthanize policy."

"Why the petition? Who stands to gain by a euthanize policy?"

"Just the birders," Hollis said.

If there's a motive for poisoning cats there, I'm not seeing it, Cori thought. "So who else should be on the suspect list?"

"The Wayfarer Motel. They're always threatening to call the cops on me."

"I imagine they don't appreciate the stink of male cats spraying all over everything. Or the noisy cat fights in the middle of the night."

Hollis opened her mouth, probably to defend the cats, so Cori continued. "Two: Wayfarer Motel. Anyone else?"

"No."

"What about your kids?"

"Fiona and Matt?" Hollis frowned and crossed her arms over her chest.

"You're spending all your money on cat food and vet bills, and violating the stray cat feeding ban."

"My kids would never hurt my cats."

"Didn't you tell me they took away your Siamese before they moved you to Bayview?"

Hollis clamped her mouth shut, her lips nearly invisible.

"Number three: Fiona and Matt," said Cori. "Who else?" Silence. "What about the other cat feeders?"

"No, we stick together," Hollis said.

"Don't most of them feed TNR colonies? Round up the strays, neuter and vaccinate them? Makes it harder for them when the cats from your colony reproduce, sending new feral cats to their colonies, spreading disease. Who has most of the TNR colonies?"

"Marsha Block."

"Number four: Marsha Block."

Hollis hunched down into her recliner and turned her face to the wall. Cori placed the list on Hollis's lap and headed toward the door. "I'll leave this list with you. If the test results come back positive for rabies, I'll let you know right away so you can get started on the shots. And you might want to share that license plate number with Animal Control."

* * * *

The next morning, the phone awakened Cori from a nightmare of cats giving birth to hundreds of kittens, piling up in front of her windows and doors, trapping her inside. It faded quickly as she checked her phone screen. "Mom. What a relief to hear your voice."

"How's Blue?"

"He's fine." Cori told her mother about Hollis, the cats in her house, and the poisonings.

"How awful. Any idea who might be the poisoner?"

"I was hoping you might have a suggestion."

"Half the Garden Club hates the feral cats, but my friends aren't animal killers. You'll help Hollis, won't you?"

"I'll do what I can."

Cori hung up and looked at the clock. Six-thirty. Mom always was an early riser, and especially before judging a cat show, like today. Judges at Cat Fanciers Association shows were expected to look sharp.

Too late to go back to sleep, Cori decided. She showered, dressed, fed Blue, and made coffee. She was in the yard filling the bird bath when her phone rang.

"Mornin', Cori." It was Jim. "The lab called. Definitely poison. Antifreeze. And I got a report about more dead cats out by the Kmart. I'm on my way there."

Cori's heart sank. Feral cat colonies were hated by some, she knew, but poisoning was a horrible way to deal with them. She thought about the list of names Hollis had given her. The Wayfarer Motel or Hollis's children wouldn't be poisoning cats at Kmart. That left Elise Weatherbee as the sole remaining suspect. Cori packed her lunch, topped off Blue's water bowl and was headed for her car when her phone rang. Hollis.

"Marsha's colony's been poisoned."

"I heard. Jim just called. Was hers a TNR colony?"

"Yes," Hollis said. "That eliminates the other feeders. They may disagree with me, but they wouldn't turn on each other."

"So you still think it's a birder? Elise?"

"Yep, and I'm looking for the black car I saw at the motel."

The parking lot of the Pine Tree Animal Hospital and Spa was full when Cori pulled in at eight. Every chair in the waiting room was occupied. C.J., Pine Tree's manager, looked frazzled. Cat hair covered her black jeans and green Pine Tree polo shirt. "Any chance you can help out for a few minutes this morning? We have a dozen clients waiting."

Cori checked her schedule; she had twenty minutes until her first grooming appointment. "Sure, I can help." She replenished bandages and antiseptics in the examining rooms, disinfected equipment, and entered a few credit card payments. On her way to the supply room, she ran into the petite Vera Bertoli holding a kitten. Cori knew her from the cat show circuit—she bred and showed Devon Rex cats. As always, she looked perfect—her blonde hair expensively disarrayed, her teal St. John accessorized with her signature pearl necklace and earrings.

"Adorable kitten you've got there," Cori said, admiring its elfin face and oversized ears.

"One of Kirlee's offspring. He was such a wonderful tom." Vera reached for a handkerchief in her coat pocket. "Picked up a virus. Dr. Weatherbee couldn't save him."

"I'm so sorry. Is that why the little guy is here? To test for a virus?"

"No, I want his ears checked for mites. Dr. Weatherbee's my usual vet, but he cut back his morning hours now that his tech is busy with euthanasia and incineration."

"So he has the town's contract now?"

"Yeah," said Vera. "Guess he had the low bid."

Could there a connection between the contract and the poisonings? Cori wondered. More dead cats meant more incinerations, which meant more income for Dr. Weatherbee. That might explain Elise Weatherbee's petition, maybe the poisonings.

Cori looked at her watch. Cats were waiting for her. She had a Persian, a Maine Coon, and two British Longhairs on her schedule today. Combing, baths, tangles, and nails made up her standard treatment, then each owner would ask for something special: volume, texture, curls, shine. Cat owners were picky but she worked hard to satisfy them.

At six, Cori stopped by the waiting room to see if C.J. still needed help, but it was finally empty. She checked her phone, saw a text. A few minutes earlier, Hollis had spotted the black car in the Walmart parking lot.

Cori called Hollis. "You're sure it's the same car you saw at the motel?"

"Yeah. And it has a CFA sticker on the back. Do you know what that means?"

"Cat Fanciers Association. Jim Hawkins needs more than that for a warrant," Cori said.

"I don't."

"What do you mean?"

"I'll follow the black car, see where it goes, and maybe catch some-one in the act."

"That could be dangerous."

"I know what I'm doing. Trust me."

Cori couldn't trust her, a loose cannon, no doubt about it. Should she let Animal Control know what Hollis was doing? Should she call Matt and Fiona? Hollis wasn't doing anything illegal, was she?

Five minutes later, Hollis called again. "The black car is slowing down. It's stopping. I'm at the vacant lot next to 177 Thornton!"

Cori made a decision. She couldn't let Hollis confront the poisoner alone. Cori didn't know Elise Weatherbee, but a cat poisoner could be hostile, even violent.

"Stay in your car, Hollis. I'll be there quick as I can."

"Just hurry!"

Cori made a U-turn and soon reached the vacant lot, a weedy patch with overgrown shrubs and scraggly trees. Good hiding places for a feral cat colony. There was the black car, unoccupied. She parked behind it and slowly pushed her way through the bushes toward the cats eating out of bowls and cans. Suddenly a hand gripped her sleeve and pulled her under the branches of a large magnolia tree.

Cori stifled a yelp.

"I've been waiting for you," Hollis whispered. "There she is, pour-ing antifreeze into a water bowl. Over there, by the fence."

Cori couldn't see past the tree's low branches. "Call Jim Hawkins," she said, and waited impatiently while Hollis dialed Animal Control. But she couldn't wait for Jim, she had to stop the poisoner. "Stay down," she said to Hollis. "I'm going closer." She crept forward until she saw the figure crouched by the water bowls.

It wasn't Elise Weatherbee. Cori recognized the blonde woman in a beautiful teal suit and pearls. "Hello, Vera. Taking care of Hollis's colony today?"

Vera Bertoli twisted around, a jug of antifreeze in her hands. "Don't come any closer."

"Put it down. Animal Control is on the way."

"Why do you care about these horrible strays?"

"Are they so bad?" Cori inched closer. She needed to wrench the poisonous jug away from Vera.

"They're filthy and disgusting." Vera tipped the jug, splashing antifreeze into bowls. "They carry disease, like the virus that took my Kirlee from me."

Cori had to stop her. As she charged toward Vera to grab the jug, Vera threw the jug at Cori and ran toward her car.

She was getting away.

"Stop!" Cori shouted, and ran after her, closing the gap between them. With a leap she tackled Vera and they fell to the ground. Vera twisted, jabbed Cori with her elbows and smacked her in the nose. For a tiny woman, Vera packed a punch.

"Help me, Hollis," Cori gasped, pinning down Vera's shoulders. As the woman screamed obscenities, Hollis fell onto Vera's legs and held them tight, trying to avoid her flailing arms. Panting, Cori and Hollis held her on the ground until Jim arrived.

* * * *

The next day, Cori visited Hollis at her Bayview apartment and was dismayed to see Hollis's face. "Oh no! Did Vera give you that black eye?"

"Yeah. My cat fight," Hollis chuckled. "You look like you recovered."

"I have a few bruises," Cori said. "We fought a good fight, for a good cause. No animal deserves to die like that."

"I'm glad Jim came when he did."

"And antifreeze doesn't cause burns. Although it did stain my favorite jeans."

"Your mother will be sorry she missed the drama," Hollis said.

Cori nodded. No doubt last night's events would be broadcast throughout town. "What about you, Hollis? Another colony?"

"Bayview has a no-pets policy."

"Don't be so sure." Cori stepped into the hallway and returned holding the tiny gray kitten with white boots.

"Oh wow! For me?" Hollis's smile deepened the furrows in her cheeks.

"If you promise to take care of him, the manager said this guy can be Bayview's resident cat,"

Hollis cuddled the kitten, now purring loudly, against her cheek. "He's precious. Thank you, Cori. For everything."

"Happy to help." Cori let herself out, pleased by Hollis's obvious delight.

Tomorrow she had to return Blue to her mother's house. Funny how she'd grown accustomed to him, his rusty muffler purr, his warm solid body wedged behind her knees as she slept. He'd been more entertaining than TV reruns, a better companion than a mystery novel. She looked at her watch, an hour before her afternoon appointments. Enough time to stop by the cat refuge and administer head rubs to the kittens. One little fellow in particular, a green-eyed tabby with extra toes, always jumped into her lap and wouldn't budge.

Maybe Cori was a one-cat woman too.

ABOUT THE AUTHOR

Antoinette Brown loves writing and reading mysteries, especially cozies. She lives in Apex, North Carolina with two rescue Chihuahuas.

FOREVER MINE

by Polly Iyer

After my detective delivered the folder, I sat for a solid hour with it clutched in my sweaty hand, my heart beating like a furious metronome. I broke the seal and flipped through the photographs. My stomach revolted with each image. I'd suspected, but this was one time I didn't want to be right. My son David and his stepmother—my *loving* wife. Embracing, kissing…loving. The ache between my shoulder blades felt as if the lovers plunged a knife deep, with a twist for good measure.

I braced myself and turned on the recorder. The audio was faint, but I made out the muffled sounds of sex amid whispered words of passion. In hushed tones, they swore each other to secrecy to avoid destroying her career and his inheritance.

My lunch churned to acid.

Stashing the folder and recorder in my desk drawer, I leaned back in my chair and focused on my trophy wall. Two Emmys, seven Golden Globes, and five Oscars in three disciplines: directing, producing, and writing. Dozens of laminated awards, statues, and tributes shared shelf space with framed photographs depicting the highlights of my life, many featuring Magdalene in all her exquisite beauty.

Magdalene the ingénue. Magdalene accepting one of her two Oscars for Best Actress. Her captivating smile as she pressed her hands in the cement on the Walk of Fame. In that photo, in the background, David.

David.

My son from my first marriage. My own personal Judas. I gave him everything, and he repaid me by stealing my wife.

I studied our wedding photo, and my icy heart stuttered. I created Magdalene. Me, Ben Steiner. I took Maggie Healy, a young model with a little talent, and taught her how to be a star. How to—

"Reminiscing?"

I spun at the sound of her silky voice, praying the treachery I'd discovered didn't flash across my face. "Magdalene, I didn't hear you come in."

She floated toward me in a way uniquely hers, reminiscent of Loretta Young, breezing through the door at the beginning of her TV show, decades before. Lovely and feminine.

"I'm on my way out," she said. "I met with Henry to discuss your script. *Mata Hari* will be a great movie. Another Oscar nomination for both of us, I'm sure. I wish you were directing rather than Henry. He'll only be second best."

"I'll be home soon," I said. "I'll pick up a bottle of Cristal. We'll toast the new movie."

"Oh, darling, I have an appointment with Dr. Andari, then dinner with Celeste. I thought you had a film preservation meeting tonight. I can break dinner. Let me call her."

"No, no. Don't change your plans. My meeting was canceled. We'll celebrate tomorrow night if you have nothing planned. And as far as Dr. Andari—I don't know why you want to mess with your perfect face. You're beautiful as you are."

"You're sweet, darling, but the camera doesn't lie. I saw the screen shots today. Those tiny lines are glaring. Besides, I'm not ready to play the mother of that young actress you just signed."

I eyed the actress's contract on my desk. "Savannah Charles isn't that young—early thirties—but she looks younger."

"My point exactly. I'm forty-four and prefer looking younger as well. The doctor promised not to overdo the nips and tucks."

"Andari," I said. "Where's he from?"

"The Middle East, I think. He's attractive and cultured. The poor man is going through an ugly divorce. Fortunately, no children are involved. I doubt he'll be alone for long. Actresses are his clientele. One will latch onto him to assure lifetime cosmetic surgery."

Magdalene leaned down and kissed me.

"After the surgery, you'll love me even more."

I rose, put my hands on her waist, and looked into her dark blue eyes. "I couldn't possibly love you more, Mags."

Her arched brows rose. "Mags? You haven't called me that in years. Must be from looking at my old pictures, when I was young and flawless."

"To me, you still are."

"That's the positive side of marrying an older man. I'll always be young in your eyes."

"And I'll always be old."

"Nonsense. You're as sexy today as the day I married you twenty-three years ago."

She threw her arms around my neck and kissed me with a passion she hadn't expressed in a while—probably since the start of her affair with David. Thinking back, I could almost pinpoint the day. In spite of knowing about her infidelity, my body responded to her lush sensuality. I drew her closer. She didn't pull away as my erection pressed on her thighs.

"Oh, darling," she murmured. "Are you sure you don't want me to cancel my plans?"

"No. You meet with your doctor and dine with Celeste. We have years ahead of us." I almost gagged on the words. *Did we even have days ahead of us?* I couldn't lose her. I wouldn't. "Lose" wasn't in my vocabulary.

"If you're sure. I'll be home around ten. See you then. Love you." She pecked me on the cheek and left, her scent lingering in the air, the eponymous scent I'd arranged with the biggest cosmetic company in the world. Magdalene, subtitled The Scent of Beauty. I shuddered at the trace of fragrance I'd approved and now found sickeningly sweet.

I collapsed into my desk chair, overwhelmed by such a range of emotions I couldn't decide which one took precedence. Denial. Grief. No. What plagued me most was anger at their betrayal.

I was not a man who let others control his fate. But this time was different. The two people closest to me in all the world had broken my heart. I sat for a long time, thinking, remembering, reassessing my future.

I reread the contract I signed only last week. Things had changed. I would revise the wording. But first I needed to make a call.

* * * *

I'd just hung up the phone when David charged through my door. Other than my secretary, he and Magdalene were the only people allowed to enter my office unannounced.

David is everything I'm not in the looks department. Tall where I'm short, buff where I'm paunchy. At the moment, I cursed the fact that he took after his mother, another beauty, taken from life too soon.

"Magdalene will be magnificent as Mata Hari, Dad."

"As she is in every role. I'm worried though. She's insisting on cosmetic surgery. Maybe you can change her mind. This is the first time she won't take my advice."

"If she won't listen to you, what makes you think I can change her mind?"

I wanted to strangle the traitorous bastard. I swallowed hard to regain my composure. "You're friends, and she knows I have a blind eye where she's concerned."

"Whatever you say, but in all honesty, her age lines *are* showing on the big screen. I'm sure whatever her surgeon does will be subtle. No sense waiting until she obviously needs a facelift."

* * * *

The following night at dinner, I opened a chilled bottle of Cristal to accompany our baked sole and tried to talk Magdalene out of the surgery. The harder I made my case, the more determined she became to go through with the facelift.

"Why spoil perfection?" I asked, giving the argument my last best shot.

"A little nip and tuck will make me *more* perfect, darling," she said, sipping the champagne.

"I see you've made up your mind."

"I have."

Magdalene told me her surgery was scheduled for Friday morning. "Dr. Andari cleared his schedule after I explained filming on *Mata Hari* will start soon, and I need to be picture-perfect from the first take."

"How nice of him."

"He's a lovely man. I want you to meet him."

"I will. I'll cancel whatever I have scheduled."

"You're a dear."

After Carmela cleared the dishes, Magdalene leaned across the table, her champagne flute held precariously in one hand, and said in her sultriest voice, "Wasn't there something we were supposed to continue from yesterday?"

I couldn't believe my ears. We'd never stopped having sex, even if I required a little blue pill sometimes. I felt she obliged me to keep the old man happy. Considering what I now knew, I'd been right. I was her puppet. Here I sat, one of the most powerful men in Hollywood, and my wife had an invisible string tied around my balls. Schmuck. More humiliating, I gratefully accepted the scenario.

I got up, removed the champagne glass from her hand, and led her upstairs to her bedroom. I wouldn't need a pill tonight. I was hard as a rock with the thought that Magdalene initiated the lovemaking. I blocked out the photos of her and David screwing in the motel room. This was a screenplay, and I would play the part.

I'd never been egotistical enough to believe Magdalene married me for love. No matter what wealthy, powerful men looked like, we had our pick of beautiful women. Carlo Ponti spoke those exact words to me years ago when talking about Sophia. In the bedroom, Magdalene stripped off her clothes, allowing me the pleasure of gazing at her voluptuous body as she unbuttoned my shirt. I suppose she wanted to take the lead tonight. That was fine with me.

She peeled off the rest of my clothes and led me to the bed as if I were a stray puppy. Propping a pillow behind my head, she leaned down and kissed me—an openmouthed, tongue-exploring kiss that electrified every nerve in my body. Then she proceeded to pleasure me in a way she hadn't in years. I chose not to intellectualize why she was doing it now—honest passion, sexual gratification…guilt. I didn't care. Instead, I lay there, enjoying every moment of her performance until I achieved her objective. When my heart stopped pounding, I returned the favor, much to her delight.

I didn't know how great an actress Magdalene was until this moment. Tonight was the best night I'd experienced with my gorgeous wife in a long time. I was putty in her hands.

* * * *

Friday morning came too soon. I shook hands with Dr. Rafiq Andari, a clone of Omar Sharif from his *Doctor Zhivago* days, and he explained the surgery.

"I'll keep your wife overnight." He had a slight accent I couldn't identify. "The rest will speed her healing, and I'll be here to check on her. She can go home tomorrow after we change the dressing. I suggest she relax for a few weeks, but"—he turned to Magdalene—"you'll be ready for filming on the required date." He crossed his heart. "Promise."

I stayed with Magdalene in her private room. We talked about the film and its inevitable success, until a nurse gave her a sedative. When Magdalene grew drowsy, they wheeled her bed to the surgical unit.

Another nurse directed me to a luxurious private waiting room and a soft leather sofa. She brought me a glass of pinot noir and the latest *Variety*.

I tried to read, but my thoughts strayed. To Magdalene and David. To their duplicity. I drank the wine, paced the floor, waited.

When they brought her back to her room, she was groggy. I held her hand until she slept.

* * * *

The next morning, Magdalene was awake, anxious to leave the clinic. The bandages were driving her crazy. A different doctor came into the room.

"Where's Dr. Andari?" I asked.

"Honestly? We don't know. He's never been late before, and we can't reach him."

"I want him," Magdalene said. "Call him. Get him here. Dr. Andari wouldn't desert me."

"Many times," the doctor said, "he leaves the bandage removal to one of his associates. The surgery is the most important part."

Magdalene huffed and puffed, obviously furious.

"Don't excite yourself," I said. "You'll pull your stitches."

After a moment, she calmed down. "You're right, but I can't believe he's not here this morning."

"Now let's see Dr. Andari's fine work." The young doctor began to gently remove the bandages. As he pulled away the last strip of gauze, I saw a look of shock come over his face, and he turned as pale as his crisp, white tunic. He didn't speak.

I moved to face Magdalene and sucked in a quick, deep breath. The right side of her face sagged.

She must have noticed our reaction. "What?" When the word came out, she touched her lips, then tapped her cheek. Her eyes—eye—opened wide. "Give me a goddamn mirror. Now."

"This—this s-sometimes happens," the doctor said. "Usually the face returns to normal in a matter of weeks, maybe months."

"Usually? Months?" Magdalene's voice sounded like a feline cater-waul, high-pitched and shrill. She grabbed the mirror. "Oh. My. God. I'm a freak. Ben, do something."

For an instant I was too shocked to speak. My beautiful Magdalene. I turned to the doctor, regaining my voice. "Find Andari. Tell him to fix this or I'll take everything he owns. His house, his clinic, his nuts. Everything."

Sweat beaded the doctor's face. "I understand." He rushed from the room, no doubt relieved to get away from such a disaster.

Magdalene couldn't take her eyes from the mirror. Tears ran down her mismatched cheeks. Drool dribbled from the right corner of her mouth. "God, Ben. Look at me. I'm a horror show. I'll never make another movie."

I wanted to say she was still beautiful to me, but I thought the moment inappropriate. "Give yourself time, Mags. If you don't return to normal, I'll find the best doctor in the world. Someone will be able to fix this. I promise."

"Andari promised. He crossed his heart I'd be perfect." She stole another glance in the mirror and burst into wracking sobs.

I put my arms around her and she leaned against me, her right side hidden against my chest. I stroked her silky hair. I wondered if Andari knew crossing his heart meant telling the truth.

"I want to die. Kill me, Ben. Put me out of my misery."

I stared straight in her swollen, lopsided face. "I will always think you're beautiful." Though my heart broke for her, I meant every word.

* * * *

David showed up at the house. Magdalene refused to see him, but he pushed by me and scaled the stairs to the second floor. I hurried after him, afraid of what would happen. He barged into her dark room where she'd brooded in bed for days, refusing food.

"Magdalene, are you all right?" he asked. He turned on the bedside light.

"No," she cried, covering her face with the sheet. "Get out. Get out!"

All pretense tumbled when he said, "Darling, it's me, David."

"I know who it is. Get. Out."

"Let me see."

Unable to move, I stood to the side like a totem and watched them. A short, pudgy totem. Neither paid me any mind or realized what he'd just said. *Darling.* Magdalene used the word all the time, but David didn't. Until a few seconds ago.

Then David tugged the sheet away from her face.

She groaned and propped herself on her elbows. "Happy now?"

He gasped and stepped back as if she'd contracted a contagious disease. "My God," was all he said as he fled the bedroom.

Magdalene released a guttural cry unlike any sound I'd ever heard. A sharp pain pierced my gut. How could he do that? He'd made love to her. For a moment I chastised myself as a failed father. Had I raised him to be not only deceitful but a coward?

I hurried to her side and pulled her into a deep embrace, calming her sobs. "The callous little shit," I said. She looked up.

Darling.

I could see her brain at work, debating whether I knew about her affair. I was all she had now. She couldn't lose me.

"I—I'd never have expected his reaction," she said. "Never. Please, Ben, I know he's your son and you love him, but don't allow him to enter my room again."

A dark corner of my brain celebrated. "You can be sure I won't, *darling.*" She looked at me quizzically but again let the moment pass.

* * * *

The next month was as miserable as I'd been since my first wife died. Magdalene was inconsolable. She wouldn't see anyone. She cursed Andari and cried. I consoled. We made love, delicately, caressing. The affection helped her recover. She knew I still loved her.

The swelling went down, but nerve damage remained. She couldn't feel the right side of her face, and every doctor we visited said nothing could be done. Magdalene stayed in her darkened room, allowing only me and Carmela to enter.

* * * *

David barged into my office at the studio, fire in his eyes. We hadn't spoken since the day in Magdalene's bedroom. He tossed a memo onto my desk. "You've replaced me as assistant director? How could you?"

"Quite easily. I don't want you on the set as assistant asswipe. You've hung onto my coattails long enough. I could forgive anything but your affair with Magdalene."

His body went rigid, and he sputtered, "You…you know? She t-told you?"

"No, she didn't, but you just did. Thank you for confirming my suspicions."

"She—she came onto me, Dad. I'm only human. She's—she *was* beautiful and desirable. I—"

"Get out of my office, David," I said in a calm voice. "Find a job. I'll give you a recommendation, but we're finished. That you would have an affair with my wife, a woman you knew I loved more than life itself, makes you the lowest of the low. Time for you to go your own way."

"But—"

"Goodbye. I'm glad your mother isn't around to see what an untrustworthy, devious prick you turned out to be." He looked at me as if I stabbed him in the heart, which I probably had, but no more than he'd stabbed me. "Get out."

He stormed out of the office.

I swallowed the lump in my throat and carried on with my business.

* * * *

Dr. Andari had pulled a disappearing act the day after Magdalene's surgery. He wiped out his and the clinic's accounts. The authorities had tracked him to an overseas flight to Abu Dhabi, then he vanished into thin air. His ex-wife's private detectives and mine came up empty-handed. Magdalene wanted revenge. I couldn't blame her. I had no idea where he went…until he called.

"Ben."

"Rafiq. Where are you?"

"I'd rather not say, but there is no extradition treaty with the United States. I'm in a beautiful place. Blue waters, good food, compliant women." He paused for a long moment. "How is she?"

"Distraught but adjusting."

"Such a beauty, but like my wife, a superficial, self-absorbed adulteress."

"You received everything on time?"

"The transfer went through to my Swiss account. Thank you."

"No, Rafiq. Thank you." I hung up, feeling content. The limo waited to take me home.

"Dinner in Mrs. Steiner's sitting room, Carmela," I said when I arrived.

"Yes, Mr. Steiner. Drinks first?"

"Open a bottle of Cristal, and make the caviar plate she likes."

"Of course."

I climbed the stairs and entered the sitting room that adjoined Magdalene's bedroom. The one we now shared. The suite had been remodeled to her wishes.

No mirrors.

She sat at the computer, writing her memoir. The world believed Magdalene retired from films. Rumors persisted that she'd been ill, but no one really knew.

"Darling," she drawled. "How's the film going? How's Savannah Charles in the part?"

I admired her for being able to speak of the film, of the young star I signed for the part of Mata Hari right *before* Magdalene's surgery. "Not as good as you would have been, but she's coming along. She ages well in the role."

"Maybe I was too old to play the young Mata Hari. Aging an actress is easier than making her look younger."

I shed my jacket and tie. "Carmela's bringing up a bottle of Cristal and some caviar. Then we'll have a quiet dinner and watch a movie."

"Sounds wonderful."

"How's the writing going?"

"I'm enjoying the challenge. I even have an idea for a screenplay. Maybe we can work on the treatment together."

"Of course." I rubbed her shoulders. "You look beautiful tonight."

"Oh, stop. You know that's not true."

"I told you once you'd always be beautiful to me."

She stood, planted her wet, half-drooping lips on mine, and kissed me hard. A tear slipped from her good eye. "Thank you, darling."

"You're mine," I said, taking her hand. "Forever."

ABOUT THE AUTHOR

Most writers mention the dozens of stories they've written from the time they first held a pencil. Not Polly Iyer. She drew pictures. That led to art school and a degree in art. She spent the next few decades working in art-related fields in Rome, Italy, Boston, and Atlanta, finally settling in the beautiful Piedmont region of South Carolina. Then one day, an idea got her to the computer. That was thirteen years ago, and she been parked there writing ever since. She's written six mystery/suspense/romance novels under her own name and three romances under a pen name. There's usually an artistic element incorporated in her novels. The characters who fill her pages and her mind have been, respectively, an ex-con artisan and a female author in *Murder Déjà Vu*; a psychic performer in *Mind Games* and *Goddess of the Moon*; a docent at the Metropolitan Museum of Art in *Hooked*—oh, and she's also an ex-call girl; a blind psychologist and a deaf cop in *InSight*; and another author in *Threads*.

She'll swipe one reviewer's comment as a log line to describe her books: "Iyer's specialty is making heroes out of broken people." She challenges her characters to overcome insurmountable odds, and of course they do. Maybe she'll do that herself one day when she makes the bestsellers' list. She's on the web at PollyIyer.com

BIG GIRLS NOW

by Judith Stanton

"Inge, Inge!" Tatum McRae cries.

Yesterday her parents flew down to their estate in the Virgin Islands in their private plane. Today, Tatum's nanny called in sick. I'm the back-up expert riding instructor at McRae Equestrian Center in Southern Pines but today Tatum needs me.

"Look," she says. "I cut my hand."

She crimps her mouth against a cry of pain and shows me her wound, a nasty gouge between her left forefinger and thumb. Blood trickles across her palm and down her skinny wrist. I inspect her wound with care and admiration.

"Oooh, good work!" I say.

She gives a brave, proud grin. There are no girly-girls at the McRae Center, paradise for horse lovers of all ages. We're tough.

"What happened, honey?" I take her good hand and lead her into the tack room at the Center. It's furnished, like every utility room in the barns and apartments and house, with a Pony-Club-approved first-aid kit. With horses, scary bad things can happen any day—a kick, a fall, a broken ankle, a concussion. Paralysis. Death. I take the kit from the cabinet beside the stainless steel utility sink.

"Why didn't Nigel fix it?" My husband's the celebrated trainer at the Center, a premier training facility for three-day eventers in Southern Pines, North Carolina. I get the students he doesn't want, the young and the inept, though I'm a better teacher. He's just got more wins. And balls.

I wipe off drying blood with a Betadine solution the color of iced tea. Sweet tea, they call it here.

"He said—show you—you know—how to fix it."

She hiccups between words, curbing tears.

"Of course I can fix it, sweet pea. But what happened?" I gently press a square antiseptic gauze pad on the wound.

"I was grooming Molly for our lesson." Molly is Tatum's first big pony, a fancy Connemara, show name, Macaroon. "Nigel says my bridle's dirty—time I learn to clean it by myself."

Bloody bully, lording it over the boss's daughter while her parents Chip and Sloan celebrate their anniversary in luxury.

"You're getting better, honey bunny."

I was born in Sweden, learned English in the cradle, British English, so my last two years in the United States I have struggled to learn to talk like I belonged. I loved the day I learned that *honey bunny* and *pumpkin* are endearments. *Sweet pea* is my favorite.

Tatum sniffles, obviously embarrassed. "Take your bridle apart, he says. Clean it good before you put it back together." Another sniffle, but she goes on. "I do it for Molly. Time I learn. Big girl now."

I admire her struggle to be clear, stay strong.

"You *are* a big girl," I say soothingly, thinking. Good thing Tatum *isn't* a big girl, or Nigel, my horny husband—*a hound dog,* as Sloan McRae once slipped and called her husband Chip—would have his hands all over hers, showing her exactly how to clean that bridle and put it back together, end straps snugly secured in their tight keepers. Or at lessons when she gets a little older he'd run his hands up the inside of her thigh to show her exactly where and how flat it should be against the saddle. It's legal, lots of trainers do it. Position in the saddle is a hard concept to grasp. I always suspected Nigel, skanky bastard, went too far but couldn't prove it.

No more. The hair in the little Zip-Loc bag scrunched in my breeches' pocket is my best evidence ever.

He's got something going on with someone, a brunette whose hair is shoulder length, not my hair, not our kids' hair either. They inherited my Swedish blond locks to their roots. (How I got from Sweden to England to here is another story, but he was older, dazzling with his success, and I was poor and desperate. "Horses" says it all.)

I take the gauze away and hold up Tatum's hand. "See, bunny, better already." I make a butterfly bandage and fit it over the delicate webbing. "Could happen to the best of us."

"Even you?"

"Especially me. You want to skip our four o'clock?"

Lesson, that is. Because she's way too young for Nigel to bother with. Only after my students show talent—or hit puberty—does he graduate them to his exacting, ever-loving care.

I mean, that's how I see it. Two years is about his limit before some helicopter mom starts to suspect exactly what his wandering hands are doing. Then our latest stable "lets him go" and so me too, and so our kids, Scott, sixteen and keen to leave, and Jennifer, twelve, talented, and oblivious to anything but her next ride on a horse or pony we couldn't afford any other way. If Nigel wasn't such a brilliant coach and trainer— and handsome charmer with a British accent—he'd be in jail for taking indecent liberties with a minor. I'd be tainted by his crime, unemployable in other barns, a Wal-Mart checker, raising two kids in a trailer park.

Tatum studies her new bandage, chin quivering with disappointment. "But I can't hold the reins, or saddle Molly."

"I'll take care of Molly, and you can wear gloves. No, better, let's do gymnastics, no reins."

"You think Molly'll like that?" Her sad green eyes go round with hope.

"She gets bored standing around. She'll love it, honey bunch."

* * * *

Molly doesn't love it. Today Tatum's little babysitter of a mare is, well, marish. Thin-skinned to the touch of a hand, a comb, a brush, her tack. Skittery in the flux of horses, grooms, and riders around the barn, and fidgety in lulls.

Maybe she's in season to be bred and estrus is hitting her hard this go-round, like horsy PMS. It never hit her like this before. She sidles across the yard, shies at a familiar brown lab lolling under the pines, whinnies desperately to stablemates in distant paddocks.

Worse, the arena's full. We have to wait.

Nigel's finishing lessons with two of the three brunettes on my suspect list. My little Zip-Loc bag is burning in my hip pocket.

The long single strand of hair I retrieved from the teeth of the zipper of his riding breeches is a rich dark brown, somewhere between the walnut and nutmeg Lady Clairol demi-permanent dye Tatum's mother secretly uses to hide a sprinkling of gray hairs, too proud to trust her hairdresser not to tell.

I measured it so I'll know exactly who I'm looking for—a woman whose hair is at least ten and three-quarter inches long.

From across the arena, Nigel sees me with Tatum and Molly, and touches a finger to the brim of his baseball cap, labeled Land-Rover Burghley Three-Day. He finished in the top five that year, the year we married, Scottie on the way.

Nigel's friendly gesture is part of his public image, happily married man, devoted father.

I nod back, then zero in on his two current students, both advanced. He's aiming to qualify them for the Pan Am Games next year. They're jumping four-foot, three-inch high stadium jumps so both are wearing helmets, not good for my investigation.

Beside me Molly paws. "We'll be fine," I reassure Tatum. "Soon as they leave we'll warm up."

Tatum casts her eyes down. "Will you start her?"

Not my mare's not right, not I'm scared to do this.

Just help, this once.

"Of course, pumpkin."

The brunettes dismount, loosen their horses' girths, then take off their helmets, and I'm stumped. Kelsey, twenty-something, known to party hard, has the exact right color hair but it's cropped short. That's odd as most girls keep their hair long enough to knot it into a bun for dressage tests. She couldn't have been Nigel's fling a couple of days ago.

Stunningly beautiful, Charlotte stands beside her gorgeous Irish sport horse gelding, Da Vinci, Vinnie, formerly owned and ridden by a New Zealand Olympian. Serious money. Her father invented a sprocket for a gizmo that makes rocket launchers work and owns the company that makes it.

Vinnie can jump the moon and make it look easy as a foot-high cavaletti.

Charlotte strokes his forehead, blows in his nose, and he exhales a horsy sigh.

I'd be jealous, but I love a woman who loves her horse and...*and*... This close I see her long brown hair is fine and frizzy.

Cross off suspect number two.

"Inge." It's Tatum. "Molly's weird."

The mare's still not herself, flicking her tail, gnawing her Happy Bit. She'll be okay, I tell myself. Even the best horses have bad days.

"I'll hop on," I say. "Trot circles. Serpentines. She'll settle down." Maybe I will too.

* * * *

After a jarring trot around the arena, I dismount.

"Bring the longe line and the cavesson," I tell Tatum. "Maybe Molly's lame. Something I can't feel. Let's take a look, see what we can see."

Tatum's back in minutes. I take off Molly's bridle, put on the longing cavesson, and send Molly trotting out on a twenty-meter circle around us in the middle.

"Doesn't look lame to me," Tatum says. For a child, she has an amazing eye.

I don't see lameness either.

I see a mare snorting and tossing her dainty head, switching her luxuriously long thick tail, and kicking out. Whatever's on her mind, it would be dangerous, even cruel, to put a child on her back.

"Honey, let's hand-walk her, then put her up. I'll call the vet to check her in the morning."

Tatum has hit the limits of her brave girl act, and her lower lip pokes out.

I go for best news cheer. "You can have a lesson on Archer, okay?" Her mother's retired foxhunter, thirty years old, salt of the earth.

For an instant, Tatum looks disappointed, then smiles. "Mama loves Archer. I do too."

"He'll give you a solid workout, and he needs the exercise."

And she'll be safe on him. On a day when nothing feels safe for me.

* * * *

Archer comes through for Tatum, and she's elated to ride a big horse. A groom helps Tatum cool Archer down and put him in his stall. Nigel's still with students, but I have one more brunette bitch to rule out. Downstairs I look for Giada, a boarder, Nigel's best student. Her family's Italian—I keep thinking Corleone—but it's Galifa-something—and their money comes from God knows what. Drugs, imported prosciutto, rare aged balsamic vinegar? Giada's the most experienced rider in the barn after Nigel and me. She competes all over Europe, even Dubai, and probably sleeps with sheiks for kicks. Her dark brown hair is a good ten inches long.

I hope I nail her. I turn on the bright fluorescents. The boarders' horses who don't get night turnout are snuffling their hay. I can't find Giada, then there she is in the shadows of Heidi's dimly lit stall.

"Inge, thank God," she says earnestly.

"What's the matter?" I ask, concerned in spite of my suspicions.

"Heidi's beside herself. Nothing wrong I can find—pulse, heart rate, gut sounds, all normal, but she's not herself."

Neither is Giada, unflappable when jumping solid obstacles bigger than my used Honda FIT, now twisting diamond rings around her fingers.

"How can I help?"

"The vet's on her way," she says. "I'd appreciate another pair of eyes."

She steps out of the stall into the brightly lit aisle. Her long straight dark brown hair has rich auburn highlights that are no match for the hair I found caught in the zipper of my husband's breeches.

* * * *

The vet, a tiny, pretty, young, clinically competent *redhead*—I can't stop ruling women out—finds nothing wrong with Heidi other than a little irritation from a minor bout of diarrhea. Horses get diarrhea when grass greens in the spring, if we change their feed too fast, or often under stress. The pretty young vet recommends petroleum jelly to soothe the irritation and a couple of days of psyllium for the runs.

She's off my suspect list but first-call on my cell.

As she drives off to her next farm call, I realize I should have asked her to take a look at Molly.

* * * *

Relieved on Giada's account and Heidi's, I round up Tatum, change her bandage in the tack room, lead her upstairs to our apartment and tuck afghans around her on our couch, grinding my teeth on her behalf. I'm sure her mom, her nurse, the maid—everybody—will be back tomorrow. Someday, she'll understand she was abandoned, but not by me.

Tonight with the TV on low, she falls fast asleep, and I sign off on Jen's homework and Scott's. They go to their rooms to sleep or text their friends or…whatever they do when I'm not looking.

Two or three nights a week Nigel works under lights, coaching students with day jobs who drive in, some from a couple of hours away. So I have time alone. I help myself to a small bowl of my favorite splurge, double chocolate Extreme Moose Tracks, sure the calcium will help me sleep, and go to bed. Falling asleep's not easy after such a day—Tatum's injury, Molly's freak out, Giada's surprising confidence in me, the telltale hair.

My husband has a lover and I can't find out who she is.

But Jen and Scott and Tatum, Molly too, matter far more to me so I check off everything I did all day for each, all good, and drift off.

* * * *

I wake and reach for Nigel. I miss his lean hot body. I loved him once, thought he loved me. My body still wants sex, but I can't turn off my brain. Is he comparing me to her? Did he learn this new move from her, or is he just that creative?

And tonight, this night, he's not home, where he faithfully is by midnight. I check my watch. It's almost one. I panic. He spends his life with horses, all accidents waiting to happen.

Where is he tonight? I throw on dirty jeans, a ratty hoody, sneakers, grab a flashlight. He could have been kicked. He could be dead.

I ratchet down our apartment's narrow stairs to the ground floor—the boarders' stalls—then walk up and down the clean swept aisle as quietly as I can. Horses whuffle for feed they must know they won't get and I know they don't need. No Nigel.

I spin out into a moon-drenched night to check the broodmares' barn. The ones who foaled are in paddocks with their babies, the big mares' outlines and their matching foals safe in the silver light. In the barn, the three remaining pregnant girls whicker for more food. Sorry, darlings.

Nigel is nowhere to be seen, nor should he be. The broodmares have their own groom and manager, a horse midwife, British ex-pat with long gray hair, great gal.

I'm hating Nigel now for putting me through this, but have to keep on looking. He wouldn't be out at some local bar. He's dead, I know he's dead, horses are so dangerous. A sinking fear I never ever had before grips me. The third barn houses Molly, Archer, Sloan's other foxhunters, and the McRaes' sales and competition horses.

I never go there at this hour and feel like a trespasser.

No sound but boy frogs croaking for their lovers and male crickets scraping their wings to attract a mate. I creep along the dark wide aisle, peering into shadows, all senses on alert.

Then I hear grunts and groans, unh, and unh, and unh, a rhythm I know all too well from years of being fucked by him, and know I've found him with her. I'm shaking now with anger, flashes hot and cold, heart pounding, mouth dry, the works. I creep closer to the sound of his voice, disgusted.

He's fucking her in some horse's stall, door closed, like he always shuts our bedroom's.

"Hold still, bitch," he growls, then smacks her hard, once, twice, again. She squeals, not a woman's squeal but a horse's squeal, resentful but scared.

Not a horse, a pony.

Molly. I fly to her stall, shock and revulsion pumping through me, the full moon's light showing more than I can bear to see, Tatum's darling pony mare, her head hitched up tight to the stall's iron bars that ought to keep her safe. Tonight they look like prison bars, and my husband, my children's father, stands on a red plastic two-step mounting block behind the little mare, his eyes riveted on her alone, fly open, cock out, her tail switching, her *chestnut* tail—a rich mix, I know, of black and brunette hairs from short to long.

He doesn't notice me. I gag and choke and suck for breath, shaking suddenly all over, a hard chill in mid-summer. I hear the slap of a whip, and Molly squeals again, pain now in her high whinny.

Then I see the slipknot of her leadline tying her to the bars.

With both hands, I grab its knotted end and jerk to set her free.

She lurches back, knocking Nigel off the mounting block into the back stall wall. He howls in pain but leaps to his feet and grabs the silver-handled dressage whip I gave him years ago. Then his eyes meet mine.

He knows I know, after years of secrecy and shadows, exactly what he is. Worms of disgust and hatred crawl through me.

"Don't stand there, you stupid bitch," he barks, not one scintilla of doubt or shame. "Open the goddam door."

I would, I should, I think, even now, but Molly bolts across the stall. He grabs her leadline—must have sustained a stinger to his shoulder—and slashes her face with that damn whip.

Panicked, she ricochets around the stall, slamming him against the side wall, his head cracking the hard oak boards. He crumples into the crisp pine shavings, whip clutched in his hand. Cursing, weaving, he draws himself up and strikes once more at her sensitive velvet muzzle. With a squeal of terror, she rears and paws and strikes his head.

He slides limply down the wall.

Help, he cries weakly, then in Swedish, weaker still, *Hjälp mig, Inge. Hjälp mig.*

I find I cannot raise my knotted fists to open that stall door.

Molly senses the danger has passed and slowly settles, and once more all I hear is frogs and crickets.

* * * *

I don't pass out. I'm not a girly girl. But I stagger outside retching, revulsion coursing through me. A quarter, half an hour—I don't know how long—I come back and shine my light on Nigel's broken body. He's staring blankly nowhere, his chest stalled on his final breath. His fly is open, and his limp member sports a wrinkled condom, odd hygiene for a pervert. Molly huddles in her farthest corner, head sunk to the bedding, tail switching at the welts on her hindquarters.

I want to ice them, comfort her, but I leave the scene exactly as it is.

Ropes don't show fingerprints and mares can't be charged with murder.

I'll let the morning groom find Nigel's body and call the sheriff.

When she comes to question me, I'll say I told Nigel Molly was acting strange and could he please check on her before he comes to bed?

* * * *

I will always know I could have saved him. How I'll live with what I did—murder by proxy, me now more corrupt than him—I have no idea.

And how to explain to Tatum that Nigel died in Molly's stall?

With horses, I'll remind her, anything can happen. It's why we have all those safety rules, sweet pea—the buddy system, never wrap a lead-line around your hand, and never close yourself in a horse's stall, no matter how much faith you have in it.

We can teach Molly to trust again, carrots and baby steps, hand-walking her, easy lazy sessions on the longe line, I'll say. She'll tell us when she's ready to be ridden again. Tatum will cry, but I'll tell her we'll be fine. We're all big girls now.

ABOUT THE AUTHOR

Author of seven novels, a RITA finalist, poet and scholar, Judith Stanton first imagined equestrian triumphs on her granddaddy's per-snickety black Shetland pony and balky donkey, her daddy's mule, even the milk cows. At nine, riding bareback with only a halter, she taught her pinto Blaze to jump hay bales. During a career as a scholar, professor, technical writer and fiction editor, she kept fit riding three-day eventers. Her first contemporary suspense, *A Stallion to Die For* (2012) has top reviews on Amazon. In 2014, her two Regency romances—*The Mad Marquis* and *The Kissing Gate*—are being reissued by Amazon Publishing Montlake. And *Under a Prairie Moon*, a western historical romance, is being published by Cat Crossing Press. Judith lives on a farm in the country near Chapel Hill, North Carolina, where she and her husband tend to their elderly equine friends and a steady stream of rescued cats.

Made in the USA
Lexington, KY
22 April 2014